ONE RIGHT THING

ONE RIGHT THING

A MARTY SINGER MYSTERY

MATTHEW IDEN

THOMAS & MERCER

Text copyright © 2013 Matthew Iden

Published by Thomas & Mercer, Seattle
www.apub.com

Amazon, the Amazon logo, and Thomas & Mercer are trademarks of Amazon.com, Inc., or its affiliates.

ISBN-13: 9781477829431
ISBN-10: 1477829431

Printed in the United States of America

For Renee, who continues to make the whole thing possible.
For my family.
For my friends.

CHAPTER ONE

The billboard was colossal and would've gotten my attention, if only for a brief second, no matter what had been on it. The verdant hills and bucolic horse farms lining southern Virginia's Route 29 are cute enough for a postcard, but they go on and on and on in a mind-numbing mosaic of pastoral beauty. Anything that breaks up the monotony will catch the eye, and a sign fifty feet wide and twenty feet high, in the middle of nowhere—a nowhere called Cain's Crossing, according to the last road sign I'd passed—qualified.

But it was what I saw on the sign that caused me to glance back once, twice, and swear out loud. Unable to look away, my head swiveled, following the billboard as I passed. The semi next to me let me know that I'd drifted into his lane by laying on his air horn and I twitched the wheel to the right to keep from getting flattened, my heart in my throat. We zipped down the road at seventy, though my mind was churning faster than that. A mile passed in a blur before I found a good place for a U-turn. I raced back to the billboard, crossed at one of those turnarounds that says "Authorized Vehicles Only," and pulled off the highway at the base of the enormous metal pillar. I hunched forward in the driver's seat, my chin almost resting on the steering wheel, in order to see the whole sign.

A white man—slim, forty-something, with messy blond hair and a beard going gray—gazed out over the highway. Deep crow's-feet around dark brown eyes made him appear older than I knew he was and the beard was patchy in places, like he'd trimmed it in the dark. His mouth was open and his eyebrows slightly raised in mild surprise, as though the photo had been snapped just as he'd turned around. Next to the picture was some text. It said:

J.D. HOPE WAS MURDERED ON MAY 6TH. DO YOU KNOW WHY?

Underneath it was a phone number. Nothing else. Without taking my eyes off the sign, I pawed open my glove compartment and fumbled for my notebook and a pen. I jotted down the number, then scribbled "J.D. HOPE" beneath it and underlined the name twice. I stared at it, barely aware of the traffic hurtling past me, buffeting my car, rocking it from side to side.

I peered at the face on the billboard again. Given time, I would've recognized him, I think, but he hadn't worn a beard when I'd known him and the lines around his eyes hadn't been so deep that they gave him a permanent squint. Aggressively white teeth that I knew had to be dentures or prosthetics peeked out from the open mouth. I thought about the last time I'd seen him and a jumble of emotions welled up from some hidden place I thought I'd tucked away.

I pulled out my phone and stared at it.

Options, choices, decisions. I was a retired homicide cop with time on my hands. No job to return to, no pressing deadlines. Connections, maybe, but no real family obligations tugging me home. The journey to the heartland of south-central Virginia to visit a friend was one of the few pleasure trips I'd taken in the last year, but I was on my way back, not down; I was tired and ready to be home. I could, in good conscience, put the car in drive, point it toward Arlington, and forget

I'd ever seen the billboard. I didn't owe J.D. Hope or the people who cared for him a thing. Theoretically.

I glanced at the sign a third time. J.D. Hope continued to look back at me with the same expression of mild surprise. Perhaps at the fact that he'd been murdered. The car rocked again from a passing truck. I sat there for maybe another five minutes until, in a daze, like my fingers were working on their own, I turned on my phone and punched in the number. I raised the phone to my ear, but looked up at the billboard while it rang, as though I were calling J.D. himself. But it was a woman's voice that answered.

"Mrs. Hope?" I asked.

"No, this is Mary Beth Able," she said. "I am—I . . . was J.D.'s sister. Are you calling about the sign?"

I took a deep breath and said, "Yes, ma'am. My name is Marty Singer. Twenty years ago, I arrested your brother for murder."

I.

Marine smells curl off the Anacostia in the black morning, fighting the diesel fumes that have been rolling over the Jersey walls on 295 all night and the coal stink rising from the train yard at the end of the block. There's a church on the corner, a playground on the next street, the gray top of RFK Stadium in the distance. Slick, pebbled streets shine with night rain. A traffic light turns green-amber-red in succession, throwing a long wash of color on the street every twenty-three seconds. It's joined by blues and reds flashing in place. A single car slows down, pauses, speeds on.

A body slumps on the sidewalk. Five shots, small caliber. Shoulder, abdomen, left buttock, calf. He turned, tried to run. Made it thirty feet, fell down holding on to one leg of a blue mailbox. The last shot was in the back of the head. Four more bullets have embedded themselves in cars and walls around the neighborhood. A forensics guy is placing small yellow tents on the ground to mark the casings, like invitations to a party. I'm bothered by the count. Nine's not enough. Gangbangers don't aim, they pull the trigger until the magazine runs dry. I hear distant knocking as beat cops rap on doors, ask questions.

"Darnell Anthony Moore," Stan Lowry says. White hair, lined face. He looks at the body like it's his first. Sad, sick, a little angry. He takes out

a tube of lip balm and applies it carefully to the logical place. "How old you think he is?"

"Twenty-six?" I ask.

"Twenty-five."

"Second one tonight."

"No," Stan says and puts the cap on the balm, tucks it into a breast pocket. "The other one was five hours ago. Makes it yesterday."

"Better for our average," I say. "Spread it out."

Stan grunts. I probably said it just like that last week. Humor so thin, you can see through it.

"Anything special about this one?" I ask.

"Neighbor says he was sleeping with the local crack warlord's girl. Or one of them, at least. Guy's mother says he was with her all night. No way he could've killed this boy."

"So . . . no," I say. "Nothing special."

Stan sighs. "I am tired of this shit. Nothing we do makes a dent. This kid is like every other sorry fuck that got capped this year. And last year, and will be next year. Doesn't matter."

"We're not here to stop them all," I say, sick of the argument before it starts. It comes up every other time with Stan. "Just this one."

He opens his mouth to reply, to give me one of his stock retorts, when we hear a wail start down the street. The pitch is so high that, for a heartbeat, I think it's an alarm. Then the half-formed words come through the screams.

"Oh, shit," Stan says. "Oh, no."

And we take off at a jog to find the tenth bullet.

CHAPTER TWO

Armed with directions to the Hope house, I turned the nose of the car off the highway and in the general direction of a white church steeple poking up over the trees, though I wasn't ready to head straight there. I'd already been driving for hours and the car was running on empty. Not to mention I needed a little mental adjustment time to think about what I was doing. As I headed down the exit ramp, I saw a faceless strip of asphalt with a no-name gas station squatting a hundred yards away. It would do. I eased off the road, pulled up to the number three pump, and got out.

I stood there for a second, transitioning from my car's air-conditioned interior to the outside world, a transition that nearly sucked the air from my lungs. It was late summer in rural Virginia and, as morning marched on toward noon, the heat lay like a thick blanket over everything, slowing the day until it was reduced to the sound of grass dying and my car's engine ticking as it cooled. Only the occasional hum of truck or car tires on Route 29 broke the monotony, a brief reminder that the world was moving on, rushing north and south, leaving Cain's Crossing behind.

I popped the cover, unscrewed the cap, and chose my grade of fuel. Like everyone else in the world, I had nothing to do while I pumped the gas, so I looked around. There wasn't much to see. A big, chunky blond-haired kid leaned against the driver's door of a battered Ford Bronco, maroon where it wasn't covered with mangy spots of patching compound. The kid's head was cocked downward at a ninety-degree angle while he tinkered with a cell phone. Cutoff jean shorts and a powder-blue T-shirt with the sleeves rolled to the shoulder displayed thick arms and legs, hairless and pink. The truck sat squarely in front of the entrance to the combo station office and convenience store. Shadows moved and twisted behind the thick glass.

When there was no familiar clicking as I pulled the trigger on the gas nozzle, I double-checked the front of the pump. A handwritten notice on a yellow Post-it note said I had to pay inside if I wanted gas. I put the nozzle back and headed for the office. As I passed him to go inside, the kid on the phone didn't so much as glance up. Or blink, maybe.

I shivered a little at a second transition, this time into sixty-five-degree air-conditioning. Behind the counter was an old man with a sunburnt face creased in unlikely places, down the muscles of his jaw rather than from his cheekbones. He wore a long-sleeved plaid flannel shirt and those moss-green work pants old men prefer, held in place by a thin black belt. One sleeve was empty and the fabric was pinned neatly to the breast of the shirt with a shiny steel safety pin. He swayed in place with small movements, like he was on the deck of a sailboat.

He was watching the only other person in the place, a rail-thin twenty-something in jeans and a dirty Black Sabbath T-shirt standing in front of a drink machine. He had a tiresome number of tattoos running up his forearms and peeking out from under the T-shirt. A lank brown curtain of hair hung past his face as he concentrated on filling an enormous plastic cup, moving it under each of the three nozzles in turn. One-two-three, one-two-three. As I watched, he raised the cup and drained a third of it before putting it back and filling it again. The machine's mascot, a sad basset hound with a tasseled ski cap, looked down mournfully as the kid tried to empty the machine single-handedly.

"You got to pay for that," the old man called. "We can't afford to fill your belly all day."

"Fuck you, Henry," the kid said without turning around. The corners of his mouth were electric blue from the dye in one of the drinks. He punched the button on the Radical Raspberry and a stream of something oozed from the tap into the cup.

The old man's eyes turned to me. "Help you?"

"Number three, please," I said.

"How much?"

"Let's start with forty, see where that takes us," I said and put two twenties on the counter.

He nodded, swept up the bills, and flipped a switch on a control panel off to one side. I went outside and began filling my car. The husky kid was done texting or checking the weather or whatever it was people did on their phones these days and stood with his thumbs hooked in his pockets, watching me. I filled the tank like I do every time, so I'm not sure what there was to see. But if that's what passed for entertainment in Cain's Crossing, I wasn't going to deny him.

I finished gassing the car, then used the windshield squeegee to scrape a million bugs off the windshield and front bumper of my car. I caved after a minute. It was going to take more than rainwater and a ten-year-old sponge on a stick to get them off. I chucked the squeegee into its bucket and headed back to the office for my change and a drink.

As I passed him, the husky kid suddenly said, "Hey, you a cop?"

I stopped and looked at him. "Why, you need one?"

He blinked, surprised. "Nah. Just asking."

"Okay," I said and went into the office.

The old man was still swaying in place, watching the punk drain the slushie machine. His gaze switched over to me as I walked up to the counter.

"Thirty-six eighty-three," he said.

"Okay."

He rang up the sale and counted my change by putting the bills and the coins on the counter one at a time. It was a dangerous gamble between staying upright and getting the money from the register.

"This a family-run station?" I asked as I scooped the change off the counter.

"Yep," he said. "Son bought it. Got killed driving over to Nashville about a year ago. He was hoping to give us an income ever since I lost my arm driving tractor. Don't think he had this in mind."

"How's business?"

His eyes flicked over to the kid at the slushie machine. "We get by."

I stared at him for a second, feeling something sharp and angry click into place, then walked over to the kid. He ignored me, going for his third or fifth or twelfth refill. He was focused, I'll give him that. All his powers of concentration had been brought to bear on whether he should go for the Tantalizing Tangerine, Whacky Watermelon, or—the old standby—Radical Raspberry. I could've been a potato chip stand for all the notice he paid me.

I tapped him on the shoulder. His head swung around, his hair following the motion. His face was blank and the eyes void, as though he'd been put together this morning in a robot factory. They'd just forgotten to add brains and a personality to this particular model.

I gestured to his cup. "You gotta pay for that."

"Huh?"

"The stuff in this machine isn't yours. It's not a bottomless cup of coffee. You have to pay for what you've drunk."

"I don't have to pay for shit," he said, showing some animation. A change in air pressure told me the front door had swung open.

I jerked my thumb toward the counter. "This guy is trying to make ends meet working at a gas station a half mile from the ass end of nowhere. Every ounce of that crap you drink without paying for it is hurting his bottom line, which is hurting him."

"Fuck is it to you?"

"I am the Shadow. The fear of retribution in men's minds. I am justice."

He frowned. "What?"

"Just pay the man at the counter, please. You don't have enough mind to generate the fear of retribution."

"*Fuck* you." He was facing me square, so I saw it when his gaze flicked over my shoulder.

"I appreciate the offer, but no thanks. Just pay the man, please."

His lip curled and then he threw the drink at me.

It was as predictable, really, as his buddy—who was such a mouth-breather that I heard him from ten feet away—grabbing me in a bear hug from behind. I'm not psychic, but most guys who grab you in a bear hug lean back. So, after dodging the slushie and letting the big kid pin my arms, I reared back, going with it, and planted my size-twelve foot square in the skinny kid's sternum between Ozzy on mic and Tony Iommi on guitar.

His eyes popped wide and his head—followed by that hair—snapped forward, then back in a graceful, almost artistic, whiplash. The momentum of my kick sent him staggering back into a giant display of pretzels and beef jerky. Both hit the floor with a crash.

The fat kid swung me back and forth with those ham-sized arms, but I was a half foot taller. I held on to his arms like we were dancing, moving with the ineffectual thrashing. Except with each swing to the left, I stomped down, aiming for his instep. I missed once, then twice. But on the third try I came down on the top of his foot with the sharp edge of my heel. I felt something give and he hollered in my ear like he'd been shot. The hug disappeared and I shoved him back to get some distance.

"You pussy," he yelled, reaching for his foot. His face was red and twisted in agony.

Bending over and holding your boot with both hands isn't a recommended hand-to-hand-combat stance. But it worked out just fine for me.

I didn't want to hit him with my hand. The movies and TV shows never show broken knuckles and swollen fingers. And I didn't have a brick, which is what I wanted to hit him with. But I had alternatives. I shuffled forward, twisted from the waist, and whipped the point of my elbow into the squinched-up flesh just above his cheek. The skin split over the bone and the kid kissed the floor.

The crinkling of chip bags and rattle of wire mesh told me that the skinny kid hadn't been done in by my kick to the chest. I turned in time to see him pull a butterfly knife—the weapon of choice for punks and bravos the world over—from his back pocket. This particular punk, however, wasn't quite as intimidating as he might've been, since he was clutching his chest with his off hand, telling me his breastbone must feel like it had been cracked in half.

"Pay the man and you won't have to regret this," I said. I was panting and not nearly as strong as I once was, but I wouldn't be the one going to the hospital today if I could keep the odds down to one-on-one. "I'm serious. Slap a couple of fives on the counter and I'll even help drag your buddy outside."

The kid called me a bad word instead and moved in with the knife, using tight slashes and quick stabs to keep me from grabbing his arm. He was smarter or more experienced than I gave him credit for. Amateurs go for the big swing and find themselves with their wrist touching their shirt collar from the back or an elbow suddenly folding the wrong way. So, healthy, he might've been a problem. Not to mention he was half my age and I wasn't in what you might call the best shape of my life. But holding one hand to his chest put him off balance and that's all I needed.

His tight swing became an exaggerated slash. I sidestepped, he missed, then his eyes bugged out for a second time as I doubled up my fore and middle fingers and jammed them into his throat, right at the divot where the collarbone dips to make the sternum. That divot made a handy guide for my fingers as they punched inward, hitting his larynx with a metric ton of force concentrated in an area the size of a quarter. The kid dropped the knife and clutched his throat with both hands, the universal response when one fears one is choking to death.

While he doubled over and made gagging noises, I picked up the knife and slid it into the gap between two drink coolers. Two twists and the blade snapped off. I tossed the handle behind the coolers, then walked over to the kid. I rolled him, unresisting, onto his belly and swatted him on the back a few times.

"You'll be fine," I said. "The choking is only temporary. There's going to be some bruising and you'll be drinking dinner for a while. In fact, a slushie would probably be just the thing. Hang in there."

I frisked him, finding the keys to the Bronco and an impressive wad of bills for a rather unskilled thug causing trouble in the middle of nowhere. I peeled three fives off the roll, tossed the rest on the ground, and handed the money to the old man behind the counter, who took it without blinking.

"You always have this much trouble around here?" I asked. I was a little dizzy and my hands shook, so I took a deep, steady breath and shoved my hands in my pockets. It wouldn't be very heroic to pass out in front of the old codger. "I didn't expect to rumble the second I pulled into Cain's Crossing."

The old man chewed on something before shrugging. "Brower boys making a mess of things lately. Paying kids like these two to rough people up. But jerks with too much money are still jerks."

"Browers a local gang or something?"

"Yep."

"They need better recruiting." I pointed my chin toward the two bodies on the ground. "This bother you? Me stepping in like that?"

"Nope."

"You got security tapes running?" I asked.

"Yep."

"They erasable?"

"They are now," he said.

I glanced toward the two tough guys. The fat kid was unconscious, bleeding onto the linoleum floor. "You might want to call an ambulance. I don't think I did any permanent damage, but at least it would get them out of your hair."

The old eyes slid over to the skinny kid, who was still bucking and wheezing. "I'll try, mister. I don't move as fast as I used to."

CHAPTER THREE

I stopped in front of a white-sided Queen Anne–style home on the corner of Beal and Market. It was a sprawling pile, with wraparound porch, octagonal tower, and meticulously carved gingerbread under the eaves. The knobs, pilasters, dentils, and other features that I'm sure an architect would have a word for were painted a slate blue with salmon trim, giving the whole thing a slightly silly, fairy-tale cast. A massive oak tree, planted before Sherman marched on Atlanta, shaded most of the front lawn and a portion of the house. Coupled with a slight breeze that rustled leaves and swayed flags, it almost made the August heat bearable. Mums, dahlias, and marigolds, kept in neat beds at the foot of the wraparound porch, were holding up bravely against the temperature; I wondered how they did it. Sunlight pierced the oak's broad leaves, dappling the herringbone brick walk leading to the house. A glass wind chime tinkled half a block away.

To one side of the house was a carriage-style garage with two stalls. Both doors were raised. The gleaming chrome grille of a mint '71 Coupe de Ville grinned at me from one of the stalls. A man in denim coveralls and a dirty T-shirt swept out the other. As I watched, he leaned the broom against the wall and disappeared into the dim recesses of the garage. He reappeared carrying something in both arms. I blinked when I saw the "something" was the better part of an engine block. He crab-walked the two or three hundred pounds clear of the garage and placed it on the driveway pavement carefully and without apparent effort. As I followed the path to the front door, I had the impression the man sensed I was there, but he turned and disappeared between the house and the garage without once looking at me, leaving the engine block looking abandoned and lonely in the driveway.

The door opened as I scuffed up the steps of the porch. Peering around the door, as if using it as a shield, was a lady in her mid- to late thirties. From what I could see, she had honey-blonde hair to her shoulders and brown eyes. Artfully applied makeup made the most of a face that was round and a little heavy.

When she didn't say anything, I figured the opening gambit was up to me.

"Ma'am." If I'd had a hat, I might've tipped it. "I'm Marty Singer. I called earlier."

She continued to say nothing. I waited. The sour look on her face seemed to belie the much-vaunted tales of Southern hospitality. I took a step back and craned my neck to check on the house number.

"You've got the right place," she said. "I just don't know if I'm interested in letting you in."

"Mary Beth, I presume?"

"Yes."

I tilted my head. "If you didn't want me to come, why'd you give me your address?"

"I don't know. It seems like a mistake now."

I held her eyes for a moment. "Look, Mary Beth, I understand why you might hate my guts, but that billboard out on 29 must be costing you a bundle. And since you bothered to give me your address, I'm guessing no one else has knocked down your door. Seems like it might be a good idea to at least talk to me about J.D. for ten minutes. If you don't want my help after that, I'll go away."

The sour look didn't go anywhere, but she backed away, opening the door wide enough to let me in, and no more. I entered into a foyer, cool and smelling of polishes and oils, aging wood and stone, the scent of age that hovers somewhere between comforting and decrepit. I let my eyes follow the walls up to the ceiling and back down. Dark hardwoods dominated, giving it a ponderous, old-world feel. A mahogany sideboard, ornate silver mirror, and umbrella stand fit the setting like a glove. The ceiling faded into darkness above me. It was like a museum.

I turned my attention to Mary Beth. Now that she was out from behind the door, I could see she was about five seven, with a figure that was more lithe than her face would've suggested. She wore a snuggish dress with a large floral pattern on it that stopped just above her knees. The neckline was conservative, though a strand of pearls added a dash of style. She looked ready for cocktails or afternoon theater.

She said nothing about my inspection, only saying, "Mother is waiting in the sunroom."

She closed the door and led the way, her dress making a whisking sound as she walked. I followed, admiring both the hips that made the whisking sound as well as the finely appointed parlor we passed through.

The sunroom was a greenhouse of floor-to-ceiling glass panes. Small windows of stained glass decorated the middle break where the walls stopped and an angled ceiling began. The place was filled with flowers: hydrangeas, orchids, and a dozen others I couldn't name. The air sat humid from the heat trapped by the windows and the scent of rosewater perfume. A prickling sensation along my hairline and upper lip warned me I was going to be sticky and uncomfortable in this part of the house. I fought an urge to sprint back to the gloomy, cool corners of the foyer. Or even the summer heat of the front lawn, where at least there was a breeze.

Sitting at a glass-and-wrought-iron bistro table, staring out one of the windows, was an old woman in a full-length lavender dress. Her hair, the color of tarnished silver, was wound on her head in a complicated fashion. Both hands, bumped and gnarled with veins, rested in her lap. She pinned me with a disdainful expression as we came into the room.

"Mother, this is Mr. Singer," Mary Beth said.

"So I guessed," the old woman said. Her voice was stronger than I'd expected.

"Mr. Singer, this is my mother, Dorothea Hope."

"My pleasure," I said, though I wondered.

Mary Beth took up a position behind and to the left of her mother, leaving me feeling distinctly outnumbered. "Mr. Singer saw the billboard."

Dorothea sighed extravagantly, like something you'd see on an old soap opera. "That damned thing. Why are you even paying for it, Mary Beth? If this is who it brings in, of all people."

"We're not getting anywhere with the police, Mother, and I can't stay here forever. We need to make some kind of headway before I leave. We need an answer."

"Perhaps if you'd chosen to live in Cain's Crossing, we could get one."

Mary Beth colored. "That has nothing to do with this."

"Well, we're not going to get any satisfaction from this man."

I cleared my throat. *This man would like to say something.*

Dorothea arched her eyebrow. "Yes?"

"I wanted to say that I'm sorry to hear about J.D."

"Really? I would've thought you would've been overjoyed at the news."

"I never wanted anyone I arrested to die a violent death, Mrs. Hope," I said, stretching things a bit. "J.D. served his time and had every right to a normal, fulfilling life. If he stayed clean, of course."

"And if he hadn't, he deserved what he got?" Mary Beth asked, color high on her cheeks.

"*Deserved* is a strong word," I said. "*Expected* would be more in the ballpark."

"So you *expected* him to be killed, is that it?"

I took a deep breath. "Look, maybe J.D. was president of the Kiwanis Club and got the key to the city. Or maybe he picked up where he left off in DC and got right back into trouble in his hometown. I don't know and I don't care. I saw the billboard and called the number."

"Why are you here, Mr. Singer?" Dorothea asked.

"I just told you."

"No, you said *what* you did, not *why*. Why would the man who put my son in jail for the twenty best years of his life want to lift a finger to help solve his murder?"

"One action doesn't preclude the other."

"Theoretically, perhaps not," she said. "But theory, in my experience, has very little to do with life. I ask you again. Why do you want to help find J.D.'s murderer?"

Her eyes, tucked deep in folds of skin, glittered shrewdly. I felt very close to telling the truth then, but something inside of me wrenched the possibility away, and I settled for a half-truth, instead. "When I arrested him, J.D. was mixed up in all the wrong things. But he was unlucky and, I think, honestly trying to reform himself."

"You don't think he was guilty?"

"He was," I said. "But the way in which he arrived there was unfortunate."

"I'm sure most convicts feel that way."

"They do," I agreed. "But after he got put away, J.D. seemed to recognize that he had a choice. Had always had it. He realized he'd screwed up badly enough to get put in jail, but that it didn't mean he had to *keep* screwing up. The realization came a little late, maybe, but he seemed to understand he could be something better, right then."

"The crook with a heart of gold," she sneered, "and the noble reformer. Did he look up to you, then, Mr. Singer?"

"I'm sure he hated my guts," I said. "But I think he probably deserved better from the system. And life."

That gave her pause, but only for a split second. "So, you're here to make amends?"

The wrenching feeling returned, twice as strong. I fought to keep my face impassive. "I saw your sign, I made a snap decision, I called. Maybe I'm terminally curious. Maybe I just want to see justice served. I don't know that you want my help or even if I *can* help. Hell, at this point, I don't even know if I *want* to help. But, if it makes a difference, I'm here."

She sat back in her chair, still staring at me with a frosty gaze. We were quiet for a moment. Water dripped somewhere nearby, a plant recently watered or condensation gathering into drops and falling. I heard the sound of a door opening deep within the house and a moment later the man I'd seen working in the garage appeared from behind a plant. He was mixed race, with latte-colored skin and short, wiry black hair. A lack of wrinkles and facial hair kept me from pinning down his age. Thirty? Sixty? The features of his face were at odds with the rest of him—a fine, almost feminine pointed nose and small eyes, but massive shoulders and arms corded with muscle. His hands were scarred and chalky from work. The smell of motor oil and sweat rolled off him.

The man didn't look at me, staring instead at Dorothea. The matron smiled slightly and said, "Are you all done with the garage, Ferris?"

"Yes, ma'am," he said. His voice was mellow, but not deep.

"Would you mind terribly if I asked you to trim that crab apple tree in the back? I'm afraid it's going to fall on the potter's table one of these days."

"No, ma'am," Ferris said. His eyes flicked to me, then he turned and left the way he'd come.

"A man of few words," I said after he'd gone. "And large muscles."

"Ferris has been helping Mother for years," Mary Beth said sharply. "She pays him a very good wage for keeping the house."

"I'm sure," I said, though I wasn't.

"My daughter is afraid you'll think we're some kind of Confederate holdout, pining for the days of Dixie," Dorothea sniffed. "Ferris isn't a slave, Mary Beth."

"I don't want Mr. Singer to get the wrong idea," Mary Beth said.

"I don't give a damn what Mr. Singer thinks and neither should you."

"Look," I said. "This isn't getting us anywhere. I understand, you hate my guts for putting J.D. in jail. But your son was murdered, Mrs. Hope. And I'd like to help you find his killer. I'm good at that kind of thing. It's what I used to do for a living, after all."

"What if we don't want your help?"

"I'll do it myself. I owe him, or his memory at least, something."

"Goodness. You really do want to make amends, don't you?"

"I don't care what you call it," I said, my patience finally starting to unravel. "Are you going to tell me what happened or not?"

Dorothea's eyes narrowed. "No."

I blinked. "No?"

"Mother," Mary Beth said, protesting.

The old woman plowed on, ignoring her daughter. "I'm not in the business of handing out forgiveness to those who have harmed me or my family, Mr. Singer. If you want redemption, you'll have to find it yourself."

"You're passing on the only help you're likely to get?"

"If yours is the only aid that comes to us, we don't want it."

Mary Beth looked like she wanted to interrupt, as though she might've accepted my help after a certain amount of bloodletting and browbeating, but in the end she stayed silent, and I soon found myself back out on the herringbone walk with the slight breeze and the tinkling wind chime, bemused, and certainly none the wiser about J.D. Hope's death.

CHAPTER FOUR

I'd planned on anger. Insults. Snide comments. I hadn't planned on being refused.

It left me with a decision to make. I could hit the road and be back to my slice of suburban heaven by suppertime. Or I could stick around and satisfy my curiosity. It might not even take much. Poke my nose in a few places, make a couple of calls. Maybe even gather the tattered rags of my charm to assail Mary Beth and Dorothea's mountain of frigid disapproval again. The idea made me almost giddy with pleasure.

I pretended to weigh the two options but, in the end, there wasn't much to decide. I'd lied to Mary Beth about turning around and leaving. There were things I hadn't told the two women that meant I had to look into J.D.'s murder. Their approval or help or even just a little bit of information would've been a nice-to-have, but my sticking around didn't have anything to do with what they wanted. Or, hell, what I wanted.

I drove back toward the spire-like white church steeple, figuring it marked the historical area of Cain's Crossing, hunting for a place to stay. I could've headed back out of town, trying to find a cheap, cookie-cutter hotel, but the stiff courtesies and plastic culture of chain hotels squatting just off highway exits made me feel like my life was being sucked away. Expense was a minor issue. I'd stayed with friends on my pleasure trip and, combined with my pension and natural penny-pinching ways, I could afford to spring for modestly priced digs for a short time. I didn't need the Ritz. A bed-and-breakfast or a fading, family-run hotel with a little bit of character would work just fine.

The Mosby's Arms was close enough. It was a three-story brick square with a Georgian front sitting proudly at the corner of Main and Market. It was a building with history and personality, an edifice with a chipped, dignified exterior. The windows badly needed painting and the shrubs and flower beds out front were overgrown in some places, brown and dead in others, but the front stoop was marble and the windows were triple-sashed and stately. Regal yet humbled by age. It was a look I could identify with, though I tried not to take the analogy too far, since in most towns and cities in America the Mosby would've been demolished by now to make room for a sparkly new bank, drugstore, or car wash.

Check-in was an antiquated process. Cash only and a sign-in book like you read about in an Edith Wharton novel. The manager was an elderly white woman wearing a paisley dress and her hair in a bun. She handed me an honest-to-god brass key and told me that the diner next door was the best in town and probably all I could get after seven o'clock.

"Any place to get a drink?" I asked on a whim.

"There's a family restaurant down the highway that serves beer I think," she said, uncertainly. "But this is a dry county so you won't be able to get anything on Sundays."

"Good to know if I want to paint the town," I said. "Maybe I'll go there later."

"We don't really countenance drinking at the Mosby," she said, trying to sound firm.

"I'll probably just use the room for sleeping," I said, then smiled. "Though I do like to dance sometimes, when I'm alone."

Her face took on a horrified expression. I grabbed my day bag and hurried up the steps before she could return my money and demand I leave.

Room 302 was musty, but fit my requirements of character with its twelve-foot ceilings, dusty chandelier, and ruby glass lamps. The room was hot. An old window AC unit rattled alarmingly for a minute after I switched it on, quieting down once the coolant hit the pipes. A good-sized TV sat in a corner. Surprisingly, it was connected to a cable box, so there were some concessions to the modern age. I turned the comforter down on the bed, kicked off my shoes, and called home.

Amanda answered after three rings. "Arlington Area Morgue. You plug 'em, we plant 'em."

"You answer the phone that way all the time?" I asked.

"It's a cell, Marty," she said. "I can see it's you when you call, remember?"

Right. "How's Pierre?"

"He's fine."

"When you say it that way it means you're giving him too many treats," I said.

"He's just so cute," she said. "He looks at me this one way, I just have to give him a couple."

"A couple what?" I asked, a warning note in my voice.

"Handfuls."

"Oh, God," I said. "Amanda, he's playing you."

"I know. But you'll be back soon and can go back to starving him."

I stretched and stifled a yawn. "About that. I may not be home as soon as I thought."

"What's up?"

I gave her the scoop. Amanda was smart and a good kid. I'd helped her out of a tight spot the previous year. Or, should I say, she helped me. I'd just been handed some pretty shitty news about my health; she'd just discovered that her mother's killer was back in DC and planning to stalk her. Since he was somebody I'd failed to put away when I'd had the chance, I'd agreed to help her—reluctant, initially, to get involved since I thought I had enough problems of my own—but it turned out to be the best thing I could've done for myself. Life didn't end until your heart stopped beating, I learned, and acting any other way was a waste of time.

"You know, I don't have a long career in law enforcement, like you do . . ." she said when I was done.

"Uh-huh."

"But even I can deduce the family doesn't want you there. Why are you sticking around?"

That twist in the gut again. Not as strong. I could tell Amanda, but later. No reason to ruin the nice conversation we had going. "I don't know. Maybe it's the perverted injustice of it. Guy goes to jail, does his time, comes back to his hometown to make a new beginning, and gets aced."

"Maybe that new beginning is what got him killed," Amanda said. "Maybe he had it coming."

"You sound like a cop."

"I run with the wrong crowd," she said, and I could hear the grin in her voice. "What makes this guy so special? There must be dozens of crooks you arrested over the years that don't get this kind of treatment."

Twist. "He just kind of stood out, I guess. And what was I supposed to do, just fly past the billboard without at least calling?"

"Uh-huh." She could tell something wasn't quite square, but didn't have the lingo—or respected me too much—to drill any deeper. "So, what will you do?"

"I'll nose around, ask some questions. I don't even know how J.D. died yet or the state of the investigation. I can make sure the local cops are doing their job," I said. "The fact that Mary Beth is advertising on Route 29 leads me to believe that J.D.'s case hasn't been handled to the family's satisfaction. I can give the ladies some tips on their rights, where they can push, where they can't."

"If they'll talk to you again."

"I think I can work on the daughter. She's not as much of a bit—I mean, she seemed more willing to talk. Plus, I have unflappable charm. And virtue is on my side. I think."

She laughed. "You worried about what you'll find out?"

"If the cops are sandbagging this, then I can try and set it right. If they're not and just stuck, maybe I can help out."

"Marty Singer, Knight of the Round Table," Amanda said, not unkindly.

"Yeah, yeah. J.D. probably turned out to be a total slimeball that got exactly what was coming to him."

"What if that's the case?"

"Then I tell Mary Beth and her mother that they're on their own and I come home with a clear conscience."

"But fewer friends in Cain's Crossing, Virginia," she said.

"There's that," I admitted. "Good thing I don't plan on coming back."

We chatted some more about the money she wasn't making as a recent graduate from George Washington University, the work she was doing at a local women's shelter, and just how dumb even philanthropic bureaucracies could be. The local news in town was as sordid as ever. The DC city council was in a vote-buying scandal, all the sports teams were on record-setting losing streaks, and people were running from air-conditioned homes to air-conditioned cars to air-conditioned offices to escape the heat and humidity that was DC in late summer.

"How are you feeling?" she asked.

"I'm good," I said, truthfully. I knew better than to lie. "I mean, you saw me when I got out of the hospital. I had trouble making it from the bedroom to the bathroom. But I feel almost normal now. Nothing like last year. I can eat solid food and it actually stays in my stomach!"

"But you're not going to overdo it on this little . . . what would you call it?"

"Inquiry?"

"You're not going to overdo this inquiry, right?" she said. "A couple questions here, a few phone calls there, and then you're coming home?"

I smiled. "Yes, mom. Shouldn't take me but a day or two or three and then I'll be heading north to add to the traffic on the Beltway."

We said our good-byes and hung up. I rolled off the bed and stretched, groaning as vertebrae that had been scrunched together popped, then went into the bathroom. I splashed some water on my face and took my shirt off.

Life had taken its toll. I'd had time to recover from everything that had been thrown at me, but my ribs still stuck out—I'd lost thirty pounds the previous year that I hadn't found yet—and a wicked, web-shaped scar decorated my shoulder from where I'd taken a slug not long ago. A network of other permanent scratches and gouges and burns traced over my chest and back. My face was thinner than I pictured it and there was gray in hair that had always been black. I wouldn't win any Over Fifty beauty contests, but I caught myself smiling like a butcher's dog anyway.

I was alive.

It was a simple, straightforward fact and one I'd taken for granted for fifty-three years, right up until my diagnosis of colorectal cancer almost a year ago. After a quick retirement, life looked like it was on an inevitable downward spiral. No family, no career, and a disease that had taken over any future I might have. But helping Amanda had given me something back. I don't know what you call it. A spark, a wake-up call, a reason to live. And I'd used that to fight back, figuratively and literally. Even when chemo hadn't really done the trick, I'd taken a deep breath and plowed ahead. If getting shot hadn't done me in, I was damned if my own body was going to finish the job.

Chemo had been a dominant force for months until my oncologist had decided it was time to give the knockout blow and go for surgery. I'd undergone what my hospital bill called a partial colectomy two months ago. They'd taken almost a foot of my lower intestine in an effort to stop the disease in its tracks and, to the delight of both my oncologist and myself, it seemed to have worked. Thirty years of being a cop and a year of dealing with cancer had made me leery of believing anything one hundred percent, but after a short hospital stay and some convalescing at home with Amanda clucking over me like a mother hen, I'd been up, about, and cancer-free in just a few weeks. This trip south to see some friends had been the first real test.

I ran a hand over my lower stomach. Two small scars, each an inch long and on opposite sides of my stomach, marked where the surgeon had gone in, eliminated all the bad parts, and sewn me back up. I had trouble believing it. And part of me wanted to ask, *Why didn't we just do this from the start? Couldn't we have just skipped the nausea and weight loss, the anxiety and insomnia?* But it hadn't been that easy and I knew it. I'd told myself once before that cancer wasn't a bump in the road, it *was* the road, and life was what you made of it as you moved along.

CHAPTER FIVE

The Cain's Crossing Police Department was a tidy, two-story brick-and-tan building with sharp corners, no-nonsense lettering, and thigh-high anti-car pillars spaced every five feet. I walked through two sets of bulletproof glass doors, between the metal detectors, and straight to the front desk, where I asked for the lead investigator in John Delaney Hope's murder. I gave my name and was told to wait by the pretty lady behind the glass. I wandered over to the sets of "Just Say No" and "Citizens' Watch" posters gummed to the wall with layers of Scotch tape. I entertained myself by wondering if the posters were cheaper or more expensive than paint, since they might as well be invisible for all the attention anybody paid them. A couple cops went in and out, tossing a wave to the duty officer, flicking their eyes over me as they passed through the door.

After fifteen minutes, I heard a door open. "Mr. Singer?"

I turned. A heavyset, forty-something cop with black hair cropped close enough to see the scalp was holding a glass door open, looking my way with eyebrows raised. I nodded and he waved me through, gesturing with a manila folder in his hand, then led us into a side room that turned out to be a conference room. Not a good sign. If he wasn't willing to take me back to his desk, then he didn't plan to give me any details or spend much time on me.

"Have a seat," he said, tossing the folder onto the table. He was stuffed into a maroon shirt a size too small that made the skin of his neck spill over the collar, threatening to cover a skinny black tie that was aggressively out of fashion. A giant belly swelled underneath both like a platform. I watched as he moved around it like it was a separate entity before dropping into a conference room chair with a grunt.

I stuck out my hand. "Marty Singer."

He looked at my hand, shook it reluctantly. "Detective Shane Warren."

"Nice to meet you, Detective."

"Yeah," Warren said, waving me to a seat. "What's the problem, Mr. Singer?"

"I'm looking into J.D. Hope's murder," I said.

"Yeah, Stacey out front told me," he said. "But 'looking' covers a lot of ground. What are you looking for?"

"I'm trying to clear up a few things about the killing," I said, choosing my words. "Get some facts straight."

"And what makes you qualified to do the looking?"

"Thirty years in the MPDC," I said, not trying to brag. It was true and he'd asked, so how else do you say it? "Homicide."

"This something official? We didn't get anything over the wire."

"No. I'm retired. This is purely on my own time."

His face settled, flattened, as if a thin layer of superglue had been applied. He raised a hand, palm up. *Care to explain?*

I leaned back in my chair. "It's complicated. I was Hope's arresting officer in the swoop that put him away. Later on, he got religion and promised to turn himself around."

"And, now that he got himself killed, you're here to set things right?" Warren asked. His tone of voice let me know what he thought of that.

"Not exactly," I said. "I'm not even sure what I'm doing. I was literally driving by your town when I saw this billboard—"

Warren slapped the top of the table, hard. "That goddamned billboard. Makes the whole town look like a bunch of yahoos. Like we didn't know there'd been a murder in town."

I paused for a second, giving him a chance to simmer down. "I got the sense from their taking out advertising about the case that the family feels your department hasn't shown, uh, due diligence," I said. "That perhaps J.D. wasn't very high on your list when it came to victims of crime."

"John Delaney Hope was a shitbird," Warren said. "That's as plain as I can put it. He was a waste of space from the day he was born. Sixteen priors when he left Cain's Crossing and that's before he moved to DC and he got in trouble with you folks. So, no. J.D. Hope's murder was not, and is not, a high priority for this department."

"I understand where you're coming from, but we both know that the easiest way to get the family off your back is to give them something. Shitbird or not, Hope's murder has to have caused some kind of stir down here. Feed the family a couple of tidbits and they'll probably drop it."

Warren was about to answer when the door swung open without a knock and a trim, fiftyish cop came into the room. His uniform was in perfect order: the commendations just so, the pants without a hint of a wrinkle, the shoes shined to a mirror gloss. His face was clean-shaven and lean, but the skin had a doughy look, which laugh lines and creases didn't help. His eyes caught mine, then switched to Warren.

"You got anything on that McCreary burning, Shane?" the man asked.

"Not yet, Chief," Warren said, his voice guarded. "Patty's been there since eight and hasn't called in yet."

"You'll let me know when she does?" he asked, then turned to me without waiting for an answer. He did a once-over. "You don't look like a felon."

I put on my party smile and stuck out my hand. It wouldn't hurt to get on the Cain's Crossing chief of police's good side. "Not yet, Chief. Marty Singer, formerly of DC Homicide."

The chief pumped my arm up and down. "Lloyd Palmer. What brings you to our little ol' burg, Marty?"

I explained in quick detail, trying to convey my mission without boring him. If his eyes glazed over and he left, I'd be stuck with the not-so-cooperative Detective Warren.

Once I'd finished, Palmer nodded, then gestured to Warren. "Well, you're in good hands with Shane, here. I'm sure he's told you that we've pretty much done everything we could, but we're a small town with a small budget and . . ."

". . . a small force with no time to dig into the murders of die-hard cons," I finished for him. "I understand, Chief, and, believe me, I sympathize. But as I was telling the detective here, the family would be happy with almost any news. You don't have to bring them the killer's head on a pole; they just want to know they're being heard."

I expected Palmer to grit his teeth or tell me to get the hell out of his town, but his face softened instead. He sighed. "Marty, believe me, if I could give Dorothea and Mary Beth some solace, I would. But when I say we're a small department on a limited budget, that's not just a line of bull. Off the record, our best leads on the case are that J.D. was killed by dealers or gangbangers from your neck of the woods. Not surprising, really, considering his history and the fact that, at the heart of it, J.D. was a real small fish swimming in a great big pond. It doesn't take much imagination to see him ticking off the wrong people and then thinking he could just scuttle back to his hometown to hide. Not to be melodramatic, but his past caught up with him."

"You think he was offed by someone from DC?" I asked.

Palmer nodded. "A deal gone wrong, a grudge from when he was on the inside, who knows? Whatever it was, J.D. thought no one could track him to Cain's Crossing. Now you see where the 'limited budget' thing comes in. I can't afford to send Shane to DC just to work the leads on this. Best we can do is send a couple of e-mails, try to get some interdepartmental cooperation, but I think you know better than we do what kind of priority a request from some backwater Virginia town would get from DC Homicide."

"I can guess," I said.

"Exactly. So, in the meantime, what do we tell the family? That our theory is some faceless hit man killed their son and brother? That we'd be lucky to even get a name? Or do we let the process roll along and see if, by some miracle, somebody in DC helps us? So far, I've gone with the second option. Unfortunately, that means no news for the Hope family, because I'm not going to give them something half-baked. Not to mention, I don't need them road-tripping to DC and plastering your hometown with billboards and handbills. Lord knows they've embarrassed all of us enough already."

"I understand. But you know, until recently, I was a respected member of that big-city police department you mentioned," I said. "Well, respected is pushing it. But I still know people. I could make a couple of calls, see what I could find. Try to cut through the red tape for you."

Warren studied the top of the table. Palmer grimaced and gave one of those cringing, single shrugs people do when they want to let you down easy. "I appreciate that, Marty. I really do. But I'd just as soon ask you to keep this to yourself. We've already got requests in to several departments. If you started calling in favors for us, it would seem like we were trying to cheat. To do an end run around the process. Can't really afford that right now. But I thank you for the suggestion."

I nodded, thoughtful. I'd never met a cop who wouldn't cheat if it helped him close the book on an investigation, but maybe they did things differently here.

Palmer continued. "And, I don't want to be a bad host, but I sure would appreciate it if you wouldn't nose around things yourself. I know you might be tempted. You've certainly got the pedigree for it. But we've got some problems of our own and it could really send the wrong message if an ex-cop were to start asking questions real similar to the ones we're going to be asking."

I said I understood, which wasn't really agreeing. Palmer slapped me on the back and left, a bundle of well-groomed energy. I turned back to Warren.

"Any chance you'd tell me what the lead is that convinced your chief that Hope's murder is an out-of-town snuff job?" I asked.

He gave me a look. "What part of 'don't poke your nose into this' did you not understand?"

"Never hurts to ask," I said.

"You don't know that," Warren said, a trifle grimly I thought, and showed me the door.

II.

Stale coffee, bright lights. Too early. A phone bleeps three desks over. The smell of paper and copier ink, sweet and burnt, is making me nauseous as I try to finish a report. Stan walks over, a little hitch-swing in his step. He stands there, sipping loudly from his mug.

I sigh and look up. "Land something?"

"You could say that," Stan says. He wipes a finger over his upper lip, trying to hide a smile.

He's a good cop, I remind myself. "You in a sharing mood?"

"You know Francis, over in Major Narcotics? Looks like he's had his eye on our crack king over in Fort Dupont for a while. Piece of trash named Maurice Watts. Wastes anybody who takes a shine to his girl or his car or his music."

"Like our friend Darnell?"

"He was number two. If you don't count the little girl."

"Out of?"

"Four. Ballistics links to all of them."

I frowned. "They been sitting on this?"

"No evidence, no witnesses. Not all of them were soldiers or street dealing for him, so it took a while to make the connection."

"Okay."

"One call came through. Seems they got themselves a bitch. Some white kid from the sticks, trying to make his bones."

"You're shitting me."

Stan wipes his lip again. "I shit you not. Looks like this loser delivers product, picks up the cash, shines the shoes, does whatever the boss tells him."

"And you think he's good for Darnell and the rest?"

A theater shrug. "Francis says the homies are falling-down laughing at this kid. They've got him running all over God's green earth, he's so damn eager to please. Not much of a stretch to see him capping whoever the boss tells him to."

"So, this hick goes from dropping off baggies to stone-cold killer?"

"It's a theory."

"A lousy one, Stan," I say. "Nobody saw a white kid in black Southeast shooting people? Four different times? Gimme a break."

"He shot that little girl."

"Someone shot her. And that's all we know."

His smile fades. "Hey, Marty. Don't shit on this, okay? I didn't say we're ready to pick him up. I said it's a theory."

"Okay, Stan," I say, turning back to my screen. "You let me know when you got something to back it up."

Stan stomps away and I forget about it.

CHAPTER SIX

Breakfast that morning had been a tepid cup of coffee, two eggs, cheddar grits, and toast at a diner named Lula Belle's. The seats were sticky and the wallpaper was a tan-and-brown affair with a Civil War motif of exploding cannons, charging Confederate infantry, and mustachioed men on horseback waving sabers. My paper place mat listed famous landmarks of central Virginia and informed me that the state bird was the cardinal, the state tree was the dogwood, and the state mammal was the Townsend's big-eared bat. The diner was next door to my hotel and my waitress was a woman I would swear was the sister to—or clone of—the desk clerk at the Mosby. I ordered breakfast, then leaned over to snag a newspaper from the table beside mine.

I leafed through it in five minutes, noting two things of interest—that a teeny-tiny town like Cain's Crossing had its own newspaper, the *Sentinel*, and that ninety percent of the articles were written by one man, Chick Reyes. I went through the paper a second time, wondering when the *Sentinel*'s star reporter found time to sleep. Reyes had three front-page stories, the crime wire, a feature on a new interstate spur going in, a garden section, a town council meeting, and the obits—all covered in one issue. Either his stories were complete inventions or the guy had an energy level I could only dream about.

The articles were well written and to the point, snappy, in perfect inverted-triangle pattern of the type they teach in journalism class. For a town as small as Cain's Crossing, there was a conspicuous lack of fluff. I would've expected half the columns to be on swimming pools opening or Mrs. Carter's grandfather found wandering around the town square in his boxers. But the articles had real subjects, presented the facts, disclosed an interview or two, and ended succinctly. Reyes could've been writing for the *Washington Post* or *New York Times*.

I'd just turned back to the first page to go through the paper a third time when I caught a glimpse of Ferris, Dorothea's helper, walking down the sidewalk. I scrambled out from behind the table to catch up with him. Oblivious to the heat, he was dressed in jeans and a waffled, long-sleeved undershirt that had a dark sweat stain discoloring the small of his back.

"Ferris," I called, chasing after him.

Ferris glanced over his shoulder. When he saw me, he hesitated, struggling between ignoring me and stopping. In the end, courtesy won. He stopped and turned to face me. "Yes?"

"Got time for a cup of coffee? I'd like to ask you a few questions."

He shook his head. "Running errands for Ms. Hope. Can't stop."

"Not even for a second?"

"Sorry." He turned to go.

I grabbed his arm. My hand, not small, didn't make it halfway around his bicep. Ferris turned to look at me, and I saw something interesting in his eyes. Not a threat, exactly, but not the expression of hired help I'd seen in the sunroom of the Hope house.

"You know Mrs. Hope and Mary Beth have asked me to look into J.D.'s murder," I said, letting go of his arm. "You don't care who killed J.D.?"

"I care," he said. "I grew up with him."

"You did?"

He sighed slightly, already tired of our conversation. "Never knew my dad. My mama cleaned house for the Hopes. She died when I was seven. Ms. Hope raised me like I was one of her own."

"So, J.D. was like a brother to you?"

"No."

"No?" I asked. "What do you mean?"

"J.D. wasn't so bad when he ran around here, busting into cars and getting into trouble. Ms. Hope didn't like it, but at least he was around. But it hurt her terrible when he went away and got himself thrown in jail. J.D. was my brother until then."

"And when he came back?"

Ferris just shook his head, turned, and walked away. I called his name again, but he didn't even break stride. I could've chased him, but for what? I needed his cooperation. If I were to get on his bad side, I would not only lose any hint from him about J.D., I'd never actually hear another word out of his mouth.

I went back inside and picked up the paper again. The family of the murder victim had told me to get lost, I'd had a fruitless meeting with the local police department, and Ferris had shucked my questions without missing a beat. When it came to solving J.D. Hope's murder, I had some background, but no real leads. What I needed was someone with real information who didn't have a personal interest in the case. Someone with contacts, hard facts, and maybe a theory or two about Hope's murder that didn't lead down a dead end. Someone who might have an interest in hearing what I turned up.

I got into my car to drive to the *Sentinel*, using a one-page tourist map I'd grabbed off the diner's counter, then realized that the newspaper office was a block and a half away. So I got back out of the car and walked to the corner of Maple and Pearl where the *Sentinel*, according to a sign in the front window, had taken residence in 1923. I was drenched with sweat from the short walk and sighed with pleasure when I hit an ice-cold wall of air-conditioning inside the front door.

The foyer was a real throwback, with maple-carved doors topped by transoms and pebbled-glass windows with hand-painted letters. A door on the left was open and through it I could hear the tapping of computer keys. As I made my way down the hall, pinching my shirt away from my body, a palm slapped hard on a desk, and someone yelled, "Shit!"

I poked my head in. A man was seated at an antiquated rolltop desk in front of a computer screen, his back turned to me. He was cursing under his breath and alternately looking down at the keyboard, then at the screen, as if the answer to his problem could be found somewhere in between. He had thick black hair and what I assumed was a gunslinger's mustache since I could see the tips extending past his face. The jeans and blue-and-white checkered shirt he wore could be made more formal by the corduroy blazer hanging from the back of the chair. While I watched, he yanked open a side drawer and pulled forth a small tin of what I figured were mints. He grabbed two, popped them in his mouth, and went back to focusing on the computer.

I tapped on the glass of the door with my keys. "You Chick?"

He jumped, startled, and I expected him to growl at me in his best J. Jonah Jameson voice. Instead, he spun around and jumped out of his chair, a smile on his face and his hand extended like a lance. "That's me. *Sentinel*'s owner, operator, and star reporter. Who am I shaking hands with?"

I introduced myself and asked him if he had time for some questions. "Though judging by the number of bylines you've got," I said, "I understand if you can't talk until after dinner."

Reyes grinned, which spread his mustache wide, displaying very white teeth. "It's not so bad. The trick is to write something early in the morning. Then, if you feel like slacking off, you've at least got something to build on. Learned that in the army."

He gestured to an old ladder-back chair next to the desk. I sat. Reyes took the seat in front of the computer. He clicked the monitor off, then turned to give me his full attention. "What can I do for you?"

"I'm interested in the murder of J.D. Hope," I said.

"Pulled in by the billboard?" he asked, grinning again.

"It caught my eye," I said. "But I, uh, knew J.D. in a former life and felt obligated to do more than just give the family my condolences."

"Knew him how?"

I considered. I might as well tell him. Reyes was going to find out anyhow, sooner or later. "I was his arresting officer years ago in DC. It sounds stupid, but I had a soft spot for the guy and was surprised when I saw he'd been killed."

"You thought Hope would die an old man?"

"Not necessarily. But let's just say your odds of making it to retirement age increase significantly once you stop running drugs for crack gangs in Southeast DC and move back to the boonies."

"Can't argue with that," Reyes said. He leaned back in his chair, grabbed a pencil off his desk, and started turning it in his hands. "The Cain's Crossing PD give you any help?"

"Sure," I said. "They told me J.D. Hope was a shitbird who got what was coming to him and that I should keep from meddling as long as I was in your fair town."

The grin popped on again, like a flashlight. "Lloyd runs a tight ship over there, doesn't he? I do all the crime reporting in this town—hell, I do *all* the reporting—and I can't get more than three sentences from the chief that actually mean anything. I'd be lucky to get a full statement if a meteor hit the mayor's house."

I frowned. "He didn't seem tight-lipped to me."

"No, no, no. Not tight-lipped. He talks a lot. But when you're an intrepid reporter like myself, you're hunting for meat on the bone, you know? Something you can tear off and turn into a real story. Lloyd says plenty, but when it comes to substance . . . well, let's just say that when I get back to the computer here and check my notes after interviewing him, most of the time I don't have shit. He's one cagey dude."

I squirmed in the chair. It was a perfect L shape and, while great for my posture, was about as comfortable as sitting on a waffle iron. "So you've had to cultivate other sources for times when the chief doesn't want to sink any ships?"

"I have," he said and sat there, grinning at me.

I sighed. "Quid pro quo?"

"An ex-cop that knows Latin. Amazing." Reyes got serious for a second. "You said it yourself: I've got most of the bylines in the paper. If I see a chance to get a shortcut on a story, I have to take it."

"Okay. I'm here totally unofficially. I couldn't be more unofficial. I'm not even a private investigator. I'm just a guy who's got more experience than most and has a penchant for getting to the bottom of things. I'd be happy to find even one little nugget of proof that J.D. got offed the way Chief Palmer says he did. If I had that, I'd drive right back over to the family and let them know their son and brother got what was coming to him."

"But?"

"The brush-off I got wasn't that severe, but it was total. And I don't like walking away from things empty-handed when I've made up my mind to get some answers. So, I'm checking this out on my own."

"And you don't have squat to work with?"

"That's about the size of it," I admitted.

"You figure you'll talk to the *Sentinel*'s ace reporter Chick Reyes and see what you can get out of him."

"Nothing so crass," I said. "I was going to see what I could get out of you in return for me sharing with you whatever I find."

"A mutual scratching of backs, huh?" he asked, grinning.

"Exactly. You tell me what you know, I use it to get some answers. If those answers add up to a Pulitzer for you, great. Just keep my name out of it. Simple."

"I'm supposed to invent some story for how an entirely new angle of the investigation just suddenly made an appearance?"

I shrugged. "You're the reporter. But that's only if there's something to find. I've got a feeling that there's not much more to see here than what Palmer is saying. Unless you've got something to tell me?"

Reyes tossed the pencil onto the desk, opened the drawer, and took two more mints from the tin. He offered me one, which I declined. "Ever try to quit smoking?"

I shook my head. "My dad smoked cigars. That was enough to keep me from starting."

"Lucky," he said and popped the mints. "So, J.D. Hope. Not the prodigal son. I wasn't here when he left for greener pastures and a jail term, but stories cropped up all the time. Like when I'd do background. I'd ask someone what the drug scene had been like or where they chopped cars or who boosted stereos and J.D.'s name would be at the top of the list. Fondly, you know. Shake their heads and say something like, 'that old so-and-so.'"

"And when he came back?"

"Different story," he said. "I tried interviewing him, got nowhere. Tried the old lady. Same thing. Everyone was curious, of course. Would Dorothea take him back in? Was all forgiven? But they kept their distance and pretty soon the town got bored and went back to talking about NASCAR."

"That doesn't explain why the cops think he got popped by a hitter from DC," I said. "Or, if he did, why he deserved it. The chief said Cain's Crossing had some gang trouble. Was he mixed up in that?"

"Not that I've heard, but I'm a known quantity, you might say," Reyes said. "It's not like I can pretend there are other reporters in town. Somebody tells me something, they know it'll be in tomorrow's paper."

"So you know someone who might know something, but they won't talk to you?"

"Yep."

"But they might talk to me?"

"Uh-huh."

I waited. He grinned. I sighed. "Quid pro quo?"

"Promise you'll tell me what you find?"

I pretended to lick my finger and cross my heart. Reyes grabbed the pencil off the desk, scribbled something on the back of an envelope he plucked from the trash, and handed it to me.

I glanced at it. "What's this?"

"That's the address of J.D. Hope's ex-wife."

CHAPTER SEVEN

The address Chick gave me was for a mobile-home park on the outside of town called Woodland Corner. There was no office, just a small gravel lot that combined visitor parking spots with a huge Dumpster. I parked my car and walked into the lot. The soft hum of window-mounted AC units filled the air, punctuated occasionally by a distant barking and a mother yelling for "Jack" at the top of her lungs.

The lot numbering in the trailer park wasn't even close to being complete or even coherent, and I wandered for fifteen minutes trying to find the number I'd jotted down. It gave me a new appreciation for mobile homes. The trailers were a mishmash of styles and construction, temporary homes turned into permanent abodes. Each was set back from the border with its neighbor by a car-length of grass. Toys and grills and tools took up the extra space. Clotheslines—some empty, some with long-forgotten tenants—webbed a few of the yards. Kids splashed and played in a stream that ran behind the property, trying to make the most of it on a sizzling-hot day. I had half a mind to join them.

Ginny Decker's residence was a Fleetwood that hadn't been moved in so long that a seven-foot sapling had grown through the triangular-shaped hitch on the front. The rotting of the wood deck that led to the door also testified to the long-term nature of the trailer's placement, though it wasn't a standout in the neighborhood. Of the sixty or so mobile homes that called the Woodland Corner trailer park home, it looked as though fifty had been wheeled into place decades earlier.

I eyed the cracked and bowed steps leading to the deck as I approached the Fleetwood, wondering if it was safe to step on them. They held my weight, though, and at the top, I thumbed an orange plastic doorbell. The bubble of plastic made a clicking noise but didn't ring, so I rapped on the door.

"'Round back," a voice yelled.

I retreated down the steps and went around the Fleetwood. Another raised deck tumbled from the rear of the trailer, sporting the same weathered, graying, and missing boards as the one in front. Six-foot-wide diamond-patterned wooden lattices, crudely cut away to make room for storage, hid the underbelly of the deck. A propane tank stood sentinel next to a couple of bald truck tires and a weed whacker, its orange cord snarled and lying in a pile next to it.

On the deck sitting in a plastic lawn chair was a woman with a Coors in one hand and a lit cigarette in the other. As I rounded the corner, she stood and leaned over the railing to take a gander at me. She was slim and well built, which was made obvious by cutoff denim shorts and a white V-neck T-shirt. Her hair was a frosted brown or black, making it hard to tell her age, but her face gave her away. Forty tough years were written in the creases of her skin and the hard, flat stare.

"Ginny Decker?" I asked.

She took a drag and stared at me boldly without speaking for a minute. When she did start to talk, it was with a hoarse voice made raw by too many cigarettes and midnight binges in bars. "Insurance or God?"

"Have you found Jesus, Ms. Decker?" I asked.

"Shit," she said, and straightened up. "I thought for sure you was insurance."

I held up a hand to apologize. "Sorry, couldn't resist. Name's Marty Singer. I'd like to ask you a few questions about J.D. Hope."

Her face became very still and I had the impression she wanted to turn around and run inside. She opted for wrapping her arms around herself instead, propping an elbow on her wrist to hold the cigarette. Too casual. "You a cop?"

"Retired," I said.

"What do you want? I told that redneck Warren everything I know."

"I'm not connected with the local police. Scout's honor. I just need five minutes of your time."

"What for?"

"I'm looking into J.D.'s murder."

She gave a little huff of a laugh, too high and too nervous to be real. "Retirement too slow for you?"

I shrugged. "From what I hear, J.D.'s case isn't being investigated as thoroughly as it could be because of his previous . . . proclivities. I knew J.D. years ago, heard about his murder, and thought I'd spend a few days down here to see if I could get to the bottom of it."

"What do you want from me?"

"Well," I said. "If you're the Ginny Decker who married the guy, I think you could tell me a hell of a lot more than anyone else around here. No one seems to know much of anything about the guy and it's getting frustrating."

She took another drag, watched me through the smoke as it drifted in front of her face. Her eyes flicked over my shoulder and back, as if expecting someone to sprout up behind me. Finally, she shook her head.

"Is that 'no' as in, *You're right, no one else knows anything*?" I asked. "Or 'no' as in you're not going to talk to me?"

"Like I'm not going to talk to you."

"Just like that?"

"That's right. Just like that."

"Anything I could say to change your mind?"

She shook her head. "You got an airplane ticket to California on you? And a million bucks, maybe?"

I patted my pockets. "Afraid not."

"Then, no, there's nothing you can say. There's a reason nobody wants to tell you anything about J.D., mister. Take a hint."

She straightened up, stubbed her cigarette out, and went inside the mobile home with a bang of the screen door. After a minute, I got the sense she wasn't going to come back out and I didn't want to feel any dumber than I already did, so I walked back to my car and drove away.

CHAPTER EIGHT

I headed back to town from Woodland Corner, chewing over Ginny Decker's reaction. It wasn't just fear. There'd been defiance . . . and something else. A calculation, maybe? Like she'd wanted to say something, weighed her options, and found I came up short. Which was too bad, since I'd been counting on her to shed some light on the situation. I could pound on her door and demand answers, but somehow I didn't feel like that option would get me very far, seeing as how I didn't have a jot of authority in this town. I'd have to wait her out or find something that would get her to talk.

A doughnut shop caught my eye and I found myself pulling into the parking lot before I'd even thought about it. Even when I was a cop, I wasn't a big doughnut guy—stereotypes be damned—but I did like coffee. With no Starbucks within sixty miles, a doughnut shop was my best option if I didn't want to get stuck with what they were serving at Lula Belle's diner. I parked between a black SUV and a gray Cadillac and went inside.

Midday, midweek there wasn't much going on. I was third in line behind a grandmother taking her time picking her dozen doughnuts one by one, and a young, tall, thin guy in a gray suit clutching a pen that he clicked spastically. It made a sound like a tiny machine gun going off and put my nerves on edge. The old woman muttered something in his direction as she paid and left. He moved to the counter, then turned and called to a booth on the side, "You guys want anything?"

I glanced over. The booth had three other men in it, all in their twenties or thirties, all dressed in gray or blue suits with cheap ties like the guy in front of me. One of the three answered, "Second cup is on you, Freddie. You know you can only expense the first one."

Freddie paid for a twenty-ounce refill and carefully tucked the receipt away in his wallet. I got my own twenty-ounce house blend, snapped the plastic lid into place, and walked back to my car, sparing a glance at the other vehicles in the lot. The plates on the SUV and Caddy were both Virginia, which didn't tell me anything, but there were other signs if you knew what to look for and were sharper than a butter knife.

I had my hand on the handle, ready to get into my car, when I heard a rattle and two thumps of another vehicle coming into the lot. I turned. A battered red pickup pulled in and parked across three spots. It was an older model with a boxy cab and sharp corners. An aging F-150, maybe. Sitting in the passenger's side was the fat kid from the convenience store, the one I'd elbowed in the face. A butterfly bandage stretched across one cheek and he sported the blackest black eye I've ever seen. It was probably exaggerated by the contrast with the pale, freckly skin of his face but, still, the effect was impressive. The blue-green discoloration went from below his cheek all the way around the socket. His eye, when he turned toward me, was filled with burst capillaries and gave him a baleful, mean look. Then again, a black eye like that would give Mother Teresa a baleful, mean look.

That eye widened and he turned in his seat to say something to the driver, who was obscured. After a second the kid got out, as did the driver and someone from the backseat on the driver's side. The three of them came around the front of the truck. The skinny kid from the convenience store—the one who liked slushies and who, when last I saw him, couldn't breathe—was the passenger from the backseat.

The driver wasn't anyone I'd seen before. He was slender, maybe five ten with messy, sandy-blond hair just shy of shoulder length. A threadbare, baby-blue T-shirt with a Camel cigarette logo on the left breast showed broad shoulders. Jeans with the knees ripped out, aviator sunglasses, and a three-day beard completed the California stoner imitation.

The three of them walked over to me. The fat kid slid his eyes away and to the right, not meeting my gaze, while the skinny kid glared at me from behind his hair. The driver stared right at me, though I saw his head turn and glance once at the SUV and Caddy, then back. From the corner of my eye, I could see the booth full of suits watching us through the window.

The three toughs stopped and glared at me. I glared back at them. I wasn't scared, but if Fat Man and Skinny Boy had planned their revenge, they might be carrying more than a ten-dollar flip knife this time. And I'd handled two of them, but three was a different story.

"So, this is the guy?" the stoner said.

"That's him, Jay," the skinny kid said.

"You don't get free doughnuts, either," I said to the skinny punk. "So, if you plan to steal a bunch of crullers from the nice folks inside, I'm going to ask you to pay again. Probably with the same result. Especially if you make me spill my coffee."

Jay, the stoner, said, "He's kinda old. You let him kick your ass?"

"Asses," I said. "Collective plural. I kicked both their asses."

I thought it might rile him, but he just smiled. "You a cop? You sound like one."

"No," I said, and shifted my stance. My SIG Sauer P220 Compact was in a waistband holster and I wanted to make it easier to reach if they thought I was a softy.

Jay seemed to understand what I was doing and raised his hands open and waist high. "Easy, chief. We're just here to grab a couple of doughnuts."

"Fine," I said. "But if you think you're going to step on me while you're at it, that's not going to happen."

Jay was going to say something smart and amiable, I think, when the skinny kid gave a high-pitched yell and charged me. He'd been sidling closer as Jay talked and, like his move at the convenience store, he'd telegraphed it five minutes earlier. I took a split second to make sure he wasn't pulling a gun, then had half a split second to watch as he tried a bad rendition of a roundhouse kick.

I'm not as fast as I used to be, but I had plenty of time to duck, grab his foot with my free hand, and help it on its way. All the way, in fact, so that his body described a complete circle, like a helicopter crashing. He lost his fight with gravity and fell into a heap on the ground. He scrambled to his feet, grabbing for something in his pocket, but I'd had enough. I stepped forward and planted a right cross on the bridge of his nose. The cartilage gave way under my fist and the kid sagged back and hit the ground. I felt a sting in my other hand and I looked down. A burp of coffee had spilled out of the sip hole and scalded my wrist.

I backed away, watching the other two. They hadn't moved. After a second, Jay glanced at the kid on the ground, now bleeding from both nostrils.

"Dwayne, get off the ground, will you?" he said. "This is embarrassing."

The kid tried to stand, but one leg was bent underneath his body and his head was lolling around like a broken doll's. Jay looked at me.

"You mind if we give him a hand? Or you gonna shoot us?"

"Be my guest," I said and stepped back. My right hand was smarting, but I resisted the urge to rub it. Tough guys have to maintain appearances. I did flick away the coffee that had burnt my wrist, though.

Jay and his compadre got the skinny kid on his feet and poured him onto the backseat of the truck, then got back in their spaces and took off without glancing back, doughnut-less and a little worse for wear. I glanced at the guys in the window who'd watched the whole thing. One of them gave me a grin and a thumbs-up.

At least I'd made someone's day.

CHAPTER NINE

They say that homes, like pets, eventually come to resemble their owners.

It's an interesting idea. If you're a skeptic, you'd probably say it was fait accompli, that the house or the dog or the cat was selected because it resembled the owner in the first place. As time passed, of course it would increasingly come to look like its owner. If you're the more believing type, then you'd subscribe to the original premise and decide that there's a mystical force in the universe that tries to pair like objects together, no matter how disparate.

I was looking more closely at the Hope residence than I had the first time and I was finding, despite an innate cynicism that I never left home without, that I believed in the theory of a mystical, universal force. The home was grand and sweeping, austere from one angle and gaudy from another. The fieldstone foundation spoke of permanence and respectability, but gave way to plank siding that was in need of updating and repair. Several shutters were crooked and leaning off their hinges and the ornate architectural details I'd noticed before were peeling and in need of a coat of paint. It wasn't shabby, not yet, but it wouldn't be long before it started the downhill slide.

The owner of the house, who so closely resembled it—or it, her—was in the front garden deadheading flowers. Clad in lavender slacks, a white blouse, with a green pinstripe apron and a floppy hat for shade, Dorothea Hope was gardening at a sedate pace. Her decision to move slowly didn't seem so much surrendering to her age as it was her exact intention to move with purpose and efficiency. She wore diamond earrings and I'm sure I would've smelled her carefully applied rosewater perfume if I hadn't been watching her from across the street, parked and waiting in my car.

With few options open to me, I'd driven to the Hope mansion, parked catty-corner down the street, and waited for Mary Beth to leave. I was hoping that, if I could get her alone, Dorothea might reveal things to me that she wouldn't in front of her daughter. It was a long shot and, what that special information might be, I didn't know, but ninety percent of detective work is wading into the middle of a situation and seeing what happens.

I got lucky and, a few minutes after I arrived, Mary Beth came out of the house, got into her car, and took off down Beal at a good clip. Her brake lights winked at one, two, then three intersections before she turned left and disappeared. I waited another minute, then climbed out of the car and walked across the street.

Dorothea was carefully trimming a boxwood, sprig by sprig, with a pair of gardening clippers. She wore yellow-and-white gardening gloves and carried one of those kneeling mats that help protect the knees. I crossed the neatly manicured lawn—wondering if it, too, was maintained blade by blade—faking a cough to give her some warning as I approached.

She turned with that wide-eyed look older people are unaware they carry. But those same eyes narrowed shrewdly when she saw who it was. Was it my imagination that she pointed the sharp end of the clippers at me?

"Mr. Singer," she said, pursing her lips in distaste.

"Mrs. Hope," I said back. "Sorry to bother you. I was hoping you could spare a minute to talk to me about your son."

She tilted her head. "Perhaps I was not clear before, Mr. Singer. I don't want to help you and do not plan on doing so. Did I not make myself understood?"

"You did," I said. "But I'm a stubborn man, Mrs. Hope. And an optimistic one. I was hoping you could put away your dislike of me for a short time so we could talk about J.D. Surely you want to bring his killer to justice?"

"Of course."

"Then give me a half hour of your time. Tell me about J.D. Help me understand what kind of person he was."

"Should I list the pets he had as a child? His favorite toys, perhaps?" Her voice was mocking. "I fail to see how any of that might help. I did not involve myself in his criminal life."

"I understand. But all information has value. I don't always know the questions to ask the first time I meet with someone, don't always operate from a position of knowledge."

"And you think me telling you about my son's childhood will change that?"

"It's worked for me before," I said.

"What if I say no?"

"I'm pretty good at being incredibly annoying. I might keep asking. Like, for forever."

She sighed. "Will you leave me alone if I agree to talk for one half hour?"

"Yes, if I possibly can."

She peeled off her gloves and dropped them on the grass. "Very well. I was wondering when you were going to get out of your car. Come along."

She led me around the side of the house to a veranda that overlooked a spacious backyard with yet another perfectly manicured lawn. Hedges and the wilting remnants of azalea bushes formed a border that hid the neighbors from view, while more towering oaks like the one out front shaded most of the yard. It struck me how impressive the place must've been years before. Mint tea and cookies on the porch, maybe croquet or badminton on the green. My eyes followed the pillars to the roof of the veranda and noticed the same peeling paint and crumbling structure I'd seen in the front.

When I lowered my eyes, I saw Dorothea was looking at me archly. She had put her hat on the table, and sat with her hands folded neatly in her lap. "Does it meet with your satisfaction, Mr. Singer?"

"It does," I said, sitting opposite her in a vintage white metal lawn chair. "It must've been a lovely house."

"It still *is* a lovely house," she said tartly. "Ferris is a fine landscaper and can fix anything with moving parts, but he's afraid of heights, I'm sorry to say. So the paint will continue to peel and flake until nothing of the outer shell remains. But I'll be gone by then and it can be someone else's concern."

"Speaking of Ferris, I saw him not long ago, while I was having breakfast." I paused.

She raised her eyebrows. "Does your statement have some hidden significance?"

"Not particularly. Although I found it interesting that Ferris was, in essence, J.D.'s stepbrother."

She sighed. "Really, Mr. Singer? Do you think Ferris killed my son? His 'stepbrother,' as you say?"

"Not necessarily," I said. "But I find those kind of connections can be significant. It's what we ex-cops call 'need to know.'"

"Well, now you do. Is there anything else you *need* to *know*? Perhaps access to my tax records or a complete medical history?"

"No, I don't think that'll be necessary." I picked at a flake of rust on the arm of my chair. "But I'll get back to you."

"Are those the questions you came to ask?"

"No," I said, then framed my thoughts carefully before speaking. "I'm curious, Mrs. Hope. I want to know how a boy raised in a home like this, in a quiet, rural community with almost zero crime, with an upper-middle-class and perfectly law-abiding family, grows up to be a drug runner, crook, and thief."

I was hoping to shock her out of her shell of superiority, but she simply smiled frostily and shook her head. "I'm afraid I can't take any credit for that, Mr. Singer. There was a time when I would've told you nurture would triumph over nature, every time. Certainly, no mother wants to think that their love isn't enough to overcome a child's innate tendencies if they appear to be taking the wrong path. But I saw J.D. with my own eyes turn from a toddler to a mischievous boy to a rebellious teen and, eventually, into the criminal you knew."

"What was he like as a child?"

"The same as any boy, I would think. He liked snakes and frogs and rocks. He threw things for no reason. He ran when I wanted him to walk and wouldn't budge when I needed him to hurry. As he got older, he would hide in the house—you see how big it is—and I wouldn't see him for days. He would sneak around to get food and use the commode, but the only clues I had that he was even alive were crumbs on the kitchen counter and the sound of water running through those old pipes."

"You never saw him?"

She shrugged. "I was nearly alone in the house. It wasn't difficult to keep from being found."

I had no easy way to ask the next question. "Your husband was . . ."

"Dead, Mr. Singer," she said. For a moment, while recounting J.D.'s childhood, Dorothea's face had gone misty and introspective.

But her eyes came back to sharp focus as she spoke to me. "Charles died not long after I gave birth to Mary Beth."

"You raised both of them by yourself?"

"Yes."

"That must have been incredibly difficult."

"You can save your sympathy, Mr. Singer. My husband had done well with his investments and we were perfectly comfortable after he passed."

"How did he die?"

"Not that you're entitled to that information," she said, "but I suppose I should tell you in case you accuse me of obstructing your inquiry."

"If you wouldn't mind," I said dryly.

"Charles collapsed from an aneurysm. He lingered in a coma for some time until I told them to end his suffering. The doctors counseled me to wait, that there might be some small chance at recovery, but they were asking me to invest in a miracle. I threatened them with a malpractice suit if they wouldn't remove his life support and that was the end of that."

I was quiet for a moment, absorbing what I'd just heard. "That seems . . . harsh."

"Does it, Mr. Singer?" she asked. Her eyes were piercing. "To be decisive? To be strong in the face of adversity? Harsh is living for years with a vegetable for a husband or father. Or forcing yourself and your children to believe in a hope that doesn't have reason behind it. Or making the suffering victim suffer longer for you. Too many people confuse strength and willpower with cruelty. They don't understand that the nature of true love is the strength to do what is right, no matter how terrible it might seem."

A slight breeze that had soughed through the yard died and the morning was still and quiet. A green, verdant smell hung in the air, like fertile ground turned over in the sun.

"Is there anything else you'd like to know?" she asked.

"Who do you think killed your son, Mrs. Hope?"

She stared at me for a moment before answering. "Whoever they are, they'll get what they deserve, I have no doubt."

"I didn't take you for a religious woman," I said.

"I observe the Sabbath, but I didn't say anything about the day of reckoning being in the afterlife," she said. Her face was a tapestry of grief and anger and patience and something else. "There are many ways to suffer in this life, Mr. Singer, and many ways to pay. Whoever killed my son—or had him killed—will do both."

CHAPTER TEN

After thirty years as a cop, I know the sound of a police cruiser's engine like I know the sound of my own humming. It's not a field of study; just time logged driving, riding in, and being around the car. Given enough time, I could identify the year by listening to the way it shifts. I know whether it's an old-fashioned LTD from its throaty gurgle or a Crown Victoria P71 from the uniform purr. No matter what model and which year, few cars can make the sound of that 250 horsepower attached to a solid frame. A contained threat on wheels.

So, when I heard that deep-in-the-chest thrum behind me as I walked along Main Street, I knew what the car was. Who was in it was the only question. Cabbies like to buy old, decommissioned CVs since they're reliable and the body is easy to fix. But I'd be around for the Second Coming before I saw a taxi in Cain's Crossing. That left cop wannabes trying to live the law-enforcement life vicariously and old ladies who had driven Crown Vics all their lives and happened upon a secondhand police model at auction. It was an interesting thing to ponder without turning around.

The mystery was solved when the driver goosed the gas to pull alongside me. I heard the whine of automatic windows, then, "Mr. Singer." A statement, not a question.

I looked. Chief Palmer was leaning across the middle console so he could look at me through the passenger-side window. The cruiser inched along to keep pace with me. Eventually, he was going to plow into a telephone pole, so I stopped and walked to the car. I bent over so he could talk to me without breaking his neck.

"Chief," I said.

"I'd like to have a word with you."

"Okay."

He jerked his head. "Hop in."

I opened the passenger-side door and slid in. Palmer glanced in the mirror and wheeled back into traffic, heading through town at a steady twenty-five with one hand on the wheel and the other propped on the door frame. The AC was on low despite the windows being down. Chief Palmer wasn't a green sort of guy. What he did seem to be was relaxed but ready, more comfortable and proficient driving a beat cruiser than I would've given him credit for. Not that he'd struck me as a desk jockey, exactly, but he'd certainly given the impression he was more spit-and-polish than Shane Warren. Who had seemed more like just spit.

"You know, when I came to Cain's Crossing four years ago," he said, watching the road, "it was like stepping into another world. The town that time forgot. Folks were kind, if slow, and crime was all but nonexistent. Just a dot on the map."

I waited. He wanted to get to something, so I figured I'd let him get to it at his own pace.

"Now, I came from Philly. Twenty years busting goombahs and cokeheads and a whole sewer-full of lowlifes that had somehow decided my city was the best place to take root. Though, to be fair, most of them were homegrown. Just a couple of transplants from New York and Atlantic City. Whatever. I'd had my fill. I don't have to tell you what that's like, I know. You've had your fill, too."

Palmer made a slow, arcing turn onto Pickett Street, a pretty lane much like the one that Dorothea Hope lived on. The scene was peaceful.

Shutters and white fences and shady lawns were the norm. A breeze that I couldn't feel at street level made the treetops sway. The sedate pace at which Palmer was driving and the cool, serene environment started to put me to sleep.

"So, you can imagine my delight when I found Cain's Crossing. Low crime, no drugs. Last murder was in 1967 and that was right at the corporate limit, so you can almost give that one to the next town over. All this place was missing was a police chief. Totally ripe for the picking." He looked over at me. "For someone looking to retire, I mean."

I knew the story. Police work is a mobile skill. Crime is universal, so fighting it is, too. But after the thrill of the big city wears you down, organizing parades and pulling cats out of trees in a quiet, rural town starts to sound pretty good. If you weren't ready to cash it in a hundred percent and head for the Caribbean, or if you still needed the work, Cain's Crossing would look like Shangri-la.

"Problem is," Palmer continued, "city work will make you arrogant. You figure, what could this pissant little town possibly throw at me that I haven't seen a thousand times before? You're thinking the biggest challenge is not falling asleep in your office after lunch. Then something shows up that you didn't expect."

Even at twenty-five miles an hour, we were heading for the edge of town, so Palmer made another lazy left. A sign said we were on Little Run Boulevard. I didn't recognize where we were. We could've been in any burg in America. A kid passed us going the other way, pedaling furiously on a bike with a low seat and high handlebars. He seemed oblivious to the heat, his head bowed to get as much thrust as he could from his legs. His crew cut, jeans, and gray sleeveless shirt could've been straight out of 1953.

Palmer had gone quiet, so I asked, "What was the something?"

"Hmm? Oh, it was a bunch of things, really. J.D. Hope was one of them, of course. That erased the nice run of non-murders. There were some other things, issues that you're probably discovering as you poke around. My point is, these things took me off guard at first. I was a big-city cop, right? I could enforce the law in this whistle-stop with both hands in my pockets. But when this latest situation got out of hand, I was a little surprised."

"Okay," I said.

"I probably don't have to tell you that surprise leads to anger. Leastwise, it does for me. So, after I got over my initial setbacks, I took steps to set things right. No way I was going to let a couple of punks or an unsavory situation push me around. It didn't happen in twenty years in Philly and it wasn't going to happen here."

We made another left, past a school. The chief took his time going over the speed bumps. The CV's suspension took it in stride, jouncing gently up and down as we rolled over the rise. Palmer raised a hand and waved, smiling, to a pair of spandex-clad ladies out power-walking. They smiled and waved back enthusiastically.

"And, quite frankly, I like it here. This is my home now. My wife's gotten used to the heat and we don't have to plow the driveway in the winter or fight traffic on the Blue Route for two hours just to see our daughter. We've settled in Cain's Crossing, and that means something to me."

Palmer made one more smooth turn, hand over hand, and then we were in familiar territory, not far from the Mosby. I smiled to myself. Despite the fifteen-minute drive, I'd made it precisely one block. He stopped in front of my hotel and put the cruiser in park, then turned to me square, his eyes drilling into mine. The jovial, glad-handing chief of police dropped away, replaced by someone harder, professional, and dangerous. I hadn't been fooled by the chummy pleasantries back in the police station, but now I saw the steel under the soft façade.

"You're probably wondering why I'm telling you all this."

"You could say that."

"I wanted you to have some background. You were a cop, so I owe you the courtesy. But make no mistake. This town is mine. I've taken possession of it and it's under my protection. That means, no matter how it might look to you, things are under control. I'm sure you mean well and plan to do good by the Hopes, but the help isn't needed. And it's not wanted."

"So, this is my warning?"

He smiled and shook his head. "I don't do warnings. A warning would imply that you might do the wrong thing. And I know you'll do the right thing. Won't you, Mr. Singer?"

III.

Through the glass, the kid is skinny, feral-looking with a patchy blond beard and hollowed-out eyes. The bony tips of his collarbone are bumps in his red-and-white faux-vintage Lucky Strike T-shirt. I blink and he's pumping gas or working on cars or driving a tractor in some whistle-stop a thousand miles away. Not sitting at a table across from Stan, about to get leaned on for multiple counts of first- and second-degree homicide. With nothing much to pin on the kid, Stan's going for the rollover.

"So tell me again," Stan says with exaggerated patience. "You come up from Hicksville looking to find work and fall in with the wrong crowd. You got no money and start running errands for this guy Maurice."

"Yeah."

"And he pays good and you don't want to rock the boat, so you do whatever he says."

The kid looks down at his hands.

"Dropping off baggies, right? Picking up cash?"

The kid says nothing.

"Look . . ." Stan glances down at his sheet. "J.D. We already know that part. Friend of mine's been watching you for the last two months. We don't care about any of that. You coulda delivered a pickup truck worth of crack *and we wouldn't give a shit. We're Homicide. We want the guy who's snuffing people. Who killed that little girl."*

"I didn't have anything to do with that," J.D. says. His hands squeeze the edge of the table and his shoulders bunch.

"Relax. I didn't say you did," Stan says soothingly, and J.D.'s body unclenches fractionally. For all his faults, Stan had a touch in the room that I'd never acquired. "But here's the problem. For you, I mean. You are the only white guy working in an all-black gang. Maybe they're paying you well. Maybe you think you're going to climb the corporate ladder there or something. But someone's killing homeboys left and right. Now, guys like Maurice are smart. They know too many bodies bring guys like me around. That's not going to keep them from knocking off whoever they want here and there, but they know better than to go on a killing spree. So, why would they do that?"

J.D. says nothing.

"I'll tell you why." Stan leans forward. His patrician face is concerned, sympathetic, eager to help. "They got the perfect fall guy. A white kid from the sticks who does whatever he's told. Who's afraid of getting cut out of the loop. Who no one would miss if he happened to go up the river for half a dozen murders."

"I told you, I didn't do any of that."

"You think that matters?" Stan asks. He slides his coffee mug into the middle space between the two of them, waves his hand over it. "You know what this is, J.D.? It's my crystal ball."

I sigh, close my eyes, open them. J.D. says nothing.

"You know what I see in it? I see us finding you in some shitty apartment or some shitty alley or in your shitty car a few months from now with two bullets in the back of your head. And you know what we'll find on your body? A couple bucks, some rock, and the nine millimeter that's been used in every one of these killings. Will we like it? Hell, no. But you know what? We'll take it. One homicide to solve five? We'll do that deal all day long, my friend."

J.D. swallows, his Adam's apple bobbing up and down.

Stan spreads his hands, palms up and pale. "There's one easy way to keep that from happening. And you know what it is. Now . . . what're you going to do?"

J.D. stares back at him.

CHAPTER ELEVEN

With its high turrets and crooked frame, the Cain's Crossing Municipal Library could've been the backdrop for a horror movie, but it had a peaceful side garden with a sundial and a trio of marble birdbaths. I took a seat on a wrought-iron bench in the shade of a crape myrtle and tried to move and breathe as little as possible in the heat. I thought about Eskimos and penguins and polar bears, but sweat still formed between my shoulder blades and trickled down to the small of my back.

Mary Beth turned the corner of the library ten minutes later, wearing a white pantsuit and a floppy sun hat. Her makeup was in place and gold earrings gleamed from under the hat. There was something about Southern women, I thought. They dressed to the nines no matter what the occasion. Mary Beth probably had an outfit to clean the bathroom and another one to do the laundry. Despite the high fashion, the look on her face was unhappy and unwelcoming. Probably the one she wore when she cleaned the bathroom.

Her eyes scanned the garden until she spotted me in my little patch of shade. I stood as she came through the gate of the white picket fence and walked over. We sat down simultaneously, though she crowded herself against the far arm of the bench. Her back was stiff and her movements overly precise.

"Thanks for coming," I said. "I know this isn't easy for you."

She stared straight ahead for a moment, mouth pinched, a younger version of her mother. I let her handle the silence. Finally, she asked, "Do you remember me?"

"What do you mean?"

"At the trial. Do you remember me?"

I looked down at my hands, thinking about lying to her. "No, I'm sorry."

Her mouth pinched again and she breathed out a long breath through her nose. "I watched you and that other officer the entire time. You seemed so bored, so weary of the process. I don't think you even knew how you sounded. You were barely awake during J.D.'s testimony."

I hesitated. "I don't have any nice way to say this, but your brother's trial was one of about a dozen arraignments, hearings, and trials that I went to that week. Maybe the same day. Not remembering the details of his trial or your presence at it doesn't say anything about me. It doesn't mean anything."

"It meant something to him," she said. "It cost him twenty years of his life."

I took a deep breath. "Look, Mary Beth. You can be mad at me for helping put J.D. away or for zoning out during his trial. But you can't change the fact that he was a crook. I can't tell you that he got what he had coming to him; that was for the jury to decide. But what I can tell you is that it's all spilt milk. Now, you can keep raking me over the coals for doing my job decades ago, or you can help me find your brother's killer *now*."

She was silent.

"You have information that could be important to finding J.D.'s killer. Crucial. But, in order for it to help, you have to give it to me. If you don't want to give me a hand, that's fine, but then all I've got is wandering around town, questioning random strangers, which I can tell you so far hasn't been all that useful. And, if that's the way it goes, in another few days I'll give up, get in my car, and go home."

"Why would I care if you left?"

"I saw your face at your mother's house. You wanted me to stay. To help. And you need it. You're still paying for that billboard. And judging by how uncooperative the police were, I think I'm your last, best hope."

She was quiet for a moment. Then, "You went to the police?"

I shrugged. "You obviously weren't getting anywhere with them, but I wanted to see what their attitude was, what progress they'd made."

"What did they say?"

"That J.D. was hiding out in Cain's Crossing from the gangs that he ticked off in DC. And that they finally caught up with him and killed him."

"What do you think about their theory?"

I wiped a trickle of sweat away. "I think it's phony baloney."

"Why?"

"Because they wouldn't have waited. If there's ever a time to kill somebody that's pissed you off, it's in prison. Especially if the hit's coming from a gang. They've got guys lining up around the block to make their bones. Believe me, if J.D. made some boss angry—on the inside or outside, doesn't matter—they would've gotten to him in the first month. They wouldn't have waited twenty years and they sure wouldn't have waited until he came back to Mayberry to do it."

She smiled when I said Mayberry and I felt a tiny sense of victory. "Who did it, then?"

"I have no idea, Mary Beth. That's why I called you. I don't even know how J.D. died, where he died, who found the body. Hell, I only just found out he was married."

Her head snapped toward me, her mouth open with surprise. "J.D. was married?"

I looked at her. It was my turn to be nonplussed. "Yes. Didn't you know?"

Matthew Iden

"I . . . no. I didn't know," she said, swallowing. "To whom?"

"Ginny Decker."

"Good Lord. I suppose it makes sense—they dated in high school—but I had no idea he'd gone and married her."

"Dorothea not forthcoming with information of that sort?"

She shook her head and kept shaking it as she leaned forward and put her face in her hands. Her shoulders shook with small spasms while I looked on, afraid to say anything. Besides my natural reluctance to bother people while they were grieving, Mary Beth was my last chance for information on J.D. If I tipped her over the edge, I might as well get in my car and start driving north, like I'd said.

Slowly, she got ahold of herself and sat up straight on the bench. I fished out a tissue and handed it across like a flag of truce. She took it and nodded before blowing her nose.

"She's such a bitch," Mary Beth said, wiping the tissue across her nose. "I shouldn't be surprised she didn't tell me."

I said nothing.

"Dorothea Hope has had her own way since she was old enough to walk," she continued. "No matter who gets hurt, run over, or abandoned in the process. It's no accident that J.D. ran off to DC or that I ended up in Baltimore for most of my adult life. The real question is why we didn't end up farther away."

"She tough at home?"

"You have no idea. I haven't had kids yet, but I've seen parents who live through their children. My mother took that idea one step further, pulling our strings until both of us—at different points in our lives—felt we had to leave or go crazy."

"J.D. was older?"

She nodded. "Five years. It wasn't his fault he was born first. He made all the mistakes and I got to learn from them. If our places had been reversed, you probably would've arrested me instead. As it was, by the time I even thought about getting in trouble, J.D. was in jail."

74

"And that was enough to keep you on the straight and narrow?" I asked.

"That and my intense dislike of confrontation," she said. "Which I demonstrated from the masterful way I handled my mother when you came by. I'd make a lousy crook, I'm afraid."

"If it's any consolation, J.D. wasn't a criminal mastermind himself."

She smiled sadly. "Friends used to call him Bounce, because he got himself into so many scrapes that he had to learn how to come back from them. This time, though, Bounce didn't come back."

We were quiet for a moment, then I said, "Can you tell me anything about J.D.'s life here? Friends, lovers, associates? When did he come back to Cain's Crossing? Did he get together with old high school buddies, make new friends, hang at the same old places?"

"I don't know," she said, shaking her head. "It sounds like you know more about him than me. I'm embarrassed to say it, but I knew him better when he was in prison. We corresponded more, that's for certain. When he was released, he came back here and I assumed it was to start over from the beginning, you know? But from what I heard from the police after his death, apparently he started over, all right."

"I wouldn't necessarily trust their opinion," I said. "Didn't your mother tell you anything? Surely she came clean with you?"

Mary Beth picked at nonexistent lint from her slacks. "Not really. I got the impression from her that he asked for some money when he first moved back, dropped in every few weeks, and otherwise kept himself as far from her as he could and still live in the same town." She looked pained.

"You said you don't live in Cain's Crossing?"

She shook her head. "I've lived in Baltimore since my husband and I separated. When J.D. was killed, I took a leave of absence. But I can't stay here forever and need to make some kind of headway before I have to return. We need an answer."

I watched as a butterfly came through the garden, alit on a leggy, flame-red bush, and began opening and closing its wings slowly. "I know this hurts, but can you tell me how J.D. was killed? And where?"

"J.D. was found in a motel room that he'd been renting long-term. He'd been . . ." she took a deep breath, "he'd been hit in the back of the head. A tremendous blow, the coroner said."

When she paused, I asked, "Just once?"

"Yes."

"That was the only wound? He wasn't beaten?"

"The police told us that he hadn't been hurt in any other way before he was killed. His death was probably instantaneous. No one else was injured. No one heard a struggle. There were no witnesses and his . . . body wasn't discovered until several days later, so memories were fuzzy and no one remembered seeing anyone suspicious entering or leaving. It was also a motel, so . . ."

"Lots of coming and going," I said. "Every room has its own entry."

She nodded.

"What else did the police say?"

She squeezed her hands together. "They don't give a damn. The detective in charge as much as said so. When we heard nothing after the first month, I started calling him. After the second month, I went to the police department every few days. Before that happened, he would simply shrug and say they didn't have the resources to chase everyone who might've wanted to kill J.D. It wasn't long before he refused to take my calls and stopped letting me back to his office."

"Were there any personal effects?"

"You mean like a box of his stuff?" she asked. I nodded. "One suitcase, I think. Just clothes. A few odds and ends."

"There were no other leads?" I asked. "What about coworkers, friends, girlfriends, drinking buddies?"

She shrugged helplessly. "J.D. couldn't keep a job, his friends were probably people you don't want to meet, and I wasn't around enough to know about the others."

"Where's the motel J.D. was staying at?"

"It's a cheap place on the outside of town. Just the kind of place you'd expect to find an ex-con." Her voice was bitter. The butterfly took off from its perch, zigzagging to its next destination. "Does that help?"

"It does," I said. "I'll go out there, see if there's something someone remembers. The color of a car or a glimpse of a face."

She looked at me. "That's not much."

"No, it's not," I said. "It's a start, though."

"Why are you doing this?" she asked suddenly, as though she were trying to shock me into a truthful response. "Why look into J.D.'s murder?"

Twist. "Like I told your mother, I'm curious. I was a cop, I like to see rights wronged."

"Bullshit," Mary Beth said.

I paused. "Okay. Maybe it's because I helped put him in jail. I feel responsible for J.D. and what happened to him to some extent. He served his time and deserved a fair shot at things." I was quiet for a second, then shook my head. "I don't know. Those aren't very good reasons. Maybe I'm not the best person to help you after all."

She reached out and touched my arm, a shy and curiously intimate gesture. "You have to be. You're the only one who's called."

CHAPTER TWELVE

Mary Beth gave me the address to J.D.'s motel and the instant after she got in her car and left, I jogged over to mine, punching in directions to the motel on my phone. In five minutes, I was heading out to the Dixie Inn. It turned out to be a bank of one-story ranch-style motel huts not far from Route 29, just farther north than the exit I'd taken to get to Cain's Crossing. Each hut of the motel was painted maroon with white trim on the windows and doors. Unfortunately, the nails in the trim had rusted, giving each a rusty dot with a corresponding rusty smear heading south. There were three cars parked in front of a total of fourteen huts. Business was booming.

Across from the motel was an abandoned ice-cream stand. A sad and badly out-of-date price list hung in the window and a humongous cake cone still adorned the peak of the roof. I cruised by once to look the motel over, did a U-turn a quarter mile up the road, then came back. I eased the car off the road and pulled in tight against one wall of the ice-cream stand. My car could be seen by someone really looking for it, but I was modestly shielded from the first hut, the one that said "OFFICE" in large white letters. A shiny new silver Tahoe was parked in front of the office door. It looked like a designer tank.

A portion of the ice-cream stand was boarded up, but one dirty corner of the front window was untouched. If I ducked my head down,

I could just sneak a peek through and see the office's front door. All of the huts with cars in front of them were visible.

I settled in to watch. I didn't know what I was looking for, but I figured some reconnaissance and a little bit of patience wouldn't hurt. The name of the motel was the first hint of a lead I'd gotten since rolling into town—I hadn't actually said "Hot damn!" when Mary Beth had given me the address to the motel, but I'd been tempted—and I didn't want to squander it. So, rather than running pell-mell into the office, why not hang out and see if anything crawled out of the woodwork?

Two hours later, with the sun beating down on the paved lot and nothing to show for my patience, I started to wonder. I hadn't brought anything to eat or drink and the car's AC was fighting a losing battle. Drowsiness and boredom set in, relieved only when a flatbed truck hauling tomatoes bumped down the road to my right. It passed out of sight, things calmed down, and I returned to contemplating pulling my hair out one strand at a time to stay awake.

Around four thirty, the door of hut number seven opened and a pale figure appeared in the doorway. It was a stick-thin woman with brown hair just past the shoulders and skin so pale she glowed. She wore a ribbed tank top and red panties with no pants. Her thighs had no muscle tone and she had knobby knees that nearly touched. She was lighting a cigarette, but her hands shook and had trouble keeping the lighter steady. The tip eventually caught on fire and she took a long drag, then gazed out over the road. She looked as bored as I felt.

The hut roof's narrow overhang kept her from contact with direct sunlight, which was a good thing, since I was pretty sure it would turn her into a steaming pile of goo if it touched her. She stayed there until she'd smoked the cigarette halfway down, then blew out a big lungful of smoke and tossed the butt into the parking lot. She leaned out to check the modest row of parked cars—one last attempt at garnering excitement, perhaps—then pulled her head back in and shut the door.

I could barely get my breathing under control. Something had actually happened. The little bit of action carried me through until just after five, when a white Dodge Caravan came down the road and pulled up directly in front of number seven. My angle let me see both van and hut door. I watched as a man slid out from behind the wheel. He had on dress slacks and a dress shirt that had been purchased several years earlier, based on how taut the material was over belly and butt. He took his time getting out, leaning back in the Caravan and fiddling with the glove compartment and the door. Behind him, the blinds twitched for a second, then the door opened and the skinny woman appeared in the doorway again.

She said something to the van guy, who looked up, then slammed the door shut and tried the handle to make sure it locked. He walked toward the woman and they had a brief conversation that involved her shaking her head a lot. They eventually resolved their disagreement and went inside, closing the door behind them. Twenty-eight minutes later, the man came out looking just as he had when he'd gone in. He jumped in the van and took off without looking back. It was all I needed to see, but I hung out for another hour and was treated to a second man following roughly the same procedure, though he and the woman didn't seem to disagree about anything. When that guy left, I was sure I had what I needed—or would die of old age waiting for more. I got out, did a few stretches, then got back in the car and drove over to the office.

I parked and walked in to the jingle of a little bell above the door. A too-small AC unit was doing its best to pump cool, Freon-tasting air into the room. Small foil ribbons on the unit's louvers fluttered to prove its struggle. The office walls were paneled in faux-walnut strips and a chandelier made of deer antlers hung from the center of the room. The floor was linoleum and the whole place smelled like a urinal mint. The room rates, posted on a bulletin board behind the counter, wouldn't have paid for overnight parking in DC.

A small man in his fifties looked up from behind a wide computer screen at the counter. He had a mustache shaped like a comb and was balding. He'd grown his hair long in the back to compensate and it trailed over the collar of a dingy, short-sleeved dress shirt that once had been white. Glassy brown eyes drifted up from whatever he was reading on the screen, registering neither interest nor surprise.

"Can I help you?" he asked unenthusiastically.

"Yes, sir," I said, smiling. "I'd like to see J.D. Hope's room, please."

He paused. "Who?"

"J.D. Hope," I said. "About forty, dirty-blond hair, missing some teeth. Killed in one of your motel rooms."

"Oh," he said. *That one?* "Are you a cop?"

"Once upon a time, yeah," I said. "Right now, I'm looking into his murder for the family. And looking into a killing usually starts with the crime scene. Mind if I take a look?"

"You're not a cop," the man said, though he seemed to ask it.

"Like I said, no. Used to be. Before you start citing the Bill of Rights, though, let me point out that there's probably not much in the room to see. You've had it cleaned and I bet it's as neat as a button. So, it should take you less than ten minutes to stand up, unlock the door to Hope's former room, let me look around, then lock it back up again. Or, we could stand here and argue about your inalienable rights for twice as long."

He looked at me like I was some kind of fish for about ten seconds, then shrugged and said, "What the hell." He got up, came out from around the desk, and led the way outside, preceded by a potbelly. He had on Bermuda shorts, black socks, and leather sandals.

I hid a grin as I realized we were probably about the same age. I might be sweating through my clothes, but I was wearing jeans, a white short-sleeved polo shirt, had all of my hair, and weighed less than I had when I'd entered the police academy. I could thank cancer for the severe drop in weight, but I'd beaten that so far and felt fit and trim. I wanted to buy this guy a beer. It was the first time I'd felt good about myself physically in more than a year.

But I resisted hugging him and we trooped down to hut number three. The door had a simple, old-fashioned lock, not an electronic key card. The manager unlocked it with a master key, then led the way inside. The sun was too bright to make out any details, so I shut the door and turned on the overhead.

It was about as mean and dreary as I'd pictured it. The walnut paneling motif from the office continued here, and mottled brown-black carpeting made the room look twice as dark as it had to. A queen-sized bed with a ratty green coverlet took up the majority of the floor space. Flanking the bed were boxy particleboard nightstands, each with a lamp. There was a long, low dresser with a TV bolted to it. A wardrobe squatted in a corner and there was a tiny bathroom done in grimy, salmon-colored tile. The light in the bathroom took four bulbs but only one worked.

I turned to the manager. "You know where the body was?"

The guy gestured vaguely at the floor beside the bed. "Here, I guess. Blood everywhere. Glad I had that carpet or I would've had a hell of a time cleaning it up."

I looked in every drawer, peered behind every piece of furniture, and checked under the bed. I opened the wardrobe, looked on top of it, and tapped its sides. I opened the medicine cabinet, poked around the toilet tank, felt underneath the sink. I avoided the carpet next to the bed when I got down on my hands and knees to look under the bed. I found nothing.

The pudgy manager had watched me from just inside the door as I examined everything. As I straightened up from looking under the bed and wiped my hands on the legs of my jeans, he said, "Guess there was nothing to find."

"I guess not."

He opened the door and I walked out into the sun, waiting for him to lock the door. I followed him back to the office, where he took up his post behind the counter.

"Mind if I ask you a few questions?"

He raised his eyebrows as if to say *If you have to.* Apparently he thought he had been handed the moral high ground when I'd come up empty on the search.

"You own this place?"

He nodded.

"Were you here the night Hope was killed?"

"Yep."

"I know you told the police all of this, but would you mind giving me the rundown of that night? Did you see anyone? Hear anything? Who found the body and when? That kind of thing."

He sighed. "I'm the owner, janitor, chief cook and bottle washer, so I guess I was working that night. I didn't see anything or anybody. I didn't hear anything. I turn in around eight every night and live down the road, so if something happened after then, I wouldn't have seen it."

"You don't live here?" I asked. "What about late-night check-ins?"

"Mister, look around. No one's pulling in here after dark. I don't even know why I stay open until eight."

"How do guests get ahold of you if they have a problem?"

"There's an after-hours number if they need me."

"And no one called that night, I take it?"

He shook his head.

"Who found the body?"

"Cleaning girl. Started screaming . . . well, bloody murder, when she saw it." The man grinned at his own joke.

"And then the cops came."

"Yep."

"Were there any possessions or effects?"

The man slipped a finger into his mouth along the gum and fished around for a minute. "A suitcase. The family took that."

"Nothing else?"

"Nope."

"Sure about that?"

The first sign of worry, a little crease over the brow. "Yeah. Of course."

I leaned my elbows against the counter and looked down on him. "I ask because I'm curious how a person—even a single man—leaves nothing but clothes behind. See, I talked to the next of kin and they told me they'd gotten the suitcase, but literally nothing else. No credit card statements, no bank cards, no day planner. Not even junk mail. Isn't that strange? I mean, who doesn't get junk mail?"

The man started fidgeting with a paper on the edge of the ink blotter on the desk. "How the hell would I know what he did with his mail?"

I didn't answer, just walked over to the window and pulled the curtain back. The cold air from the AC unit hit me in the face like a slap. "Help me figure this out. You own a motel five miles from the middle of nowhere. You don't have any help except the cleaning lady because no one's coming in. But you've got a brand-new Tahoe and a pretty slick computer on the desk. Where's the money come from?"

"This is a business expense," the man said, unable to help himself from glancing at the computer screen. "I saved up for the Tahoe."

"Good man. Not enough savers in today's economy," I said. I paused, trying to get the timing right. "But how about the hooker in number seven? She a business expense, too?"

His mouth bobbed open and shut, but he didn't have anything to say. I pressed on.

"Here's the funny thing. The happy hooker is still not enough to explain the Tahoe. You can't be pulling in more than a fraction of whatever she makes and, no offense to her, but I just don't see your cut of her earnings being enough to pay for a car that's as expensive as some of the houses down here. Can I guess what else is going on?"

The man stared down at the countertop in front of him like it was a Bible or a schematic for getting out of a bind.

"I'm going to go out on a limb here and guess that credit cards aren't just accepted here, they're downright encouraged. Am I right? And if your guests were smart enough to track their statements, they might notice something's amiss. But if you're careful and keep the charges small, then they almost never notice. And, hey, if you pull in a bonus once in a while—like a dead guy's private paperwork—you could make a nice living for yourself, emptying his bank account and setting up dummy credit card accounts under his name. Which is a good thing, since you're losing your shirt on the motel and I bet the money you get from the hooker doesn't even net you gas money."

"What do you want?" he asked hoarsely, still staring at the counter.

I rapped a knuckle on the countertop until he looked up. "I want everything you got of J.D. Hope's room. All of it. Now. You leave anything out and I'll drag you to the police myself."

I expected a struggle, but maybe the guy had been waiting for someone to drop the hammer on him. Some crooks expect it from the minute they break a law. He stood and waddled to a back room behind the counter. I heard some things being moved around and dropped on the floor, then he came back into the office with a large cardboard box, about two feet to a side. He wrestled it up onto the counter and took a step back, like he expected a cop to pop out of the box.

"If you turn me in," he said, getting a little gumption back, "I'll deny it. I'll just say I forgot about it after I cleaned the room."

"Sure," I said. I was still going to hand him over to the Cain's Crossing PD when all this was done. He could be their problem. "Thanks for your cooperation."

I picked up the box and turned to go. I left him that way, looking forlornly at his computer screen, wondering if his identify-theft ring of one was destroyed forever.

CHAPTER THIRTEEN

A quick peek in the box revealed a pile of unorganized paper junk that was going to take some time to work through. I felt simultaneously elated and bored. Paper was a great way to chase down leads, but it took time and patience.

It would be nice to have some help tackling the job. I chewed on that the whole way back to town, then decided Mary Beth made the most sense. Not only was it polite and might endear her to me, she might recognize something that I wouldn't. Even though she'd lived in Baltimore for years, she could still have an eye for local names, businesses, and addresses. Chick was another possibility, but I had an inherent aversion, going way back, to giving reporters anything but heavily sanitized information. Since the cops couldn't have been less interested and Dorothea would no doubt refuse to talk to me, there was no one else in town who qualified.

We met at Lula Belle's. Mary Beth walked through the door five minutes after I'd sat down, looking flushed and harried. She slid into the booth opposite me.

"Is this it?" she asked, lifting the lid on the box and wrinkling her nose.

"Yes."

"Where did you get it?" she asked.

"I'd rather not say," I said. "Let's concentrate on what's in it instead of who had it."

"I don't like the idea that someone held on to something of J.D.'s. Even junk."

"I understand how you feel, but we can fry those fish later," I said. "Right now, we're better off using it to dig for information on J.D.'s killer."

She sighed, unhappy, but nodded and said, "All right. Hand me a stack."

We sat at a corner booth, drinking burnt coffee and sorting the paper record of J.D. Hope's life for the next three hours. Shopping lists and Walmart receipts lay atop fast-food wrappers and fliers for rock shows that had probably been slipped under the door or hung on the knob. We removed each one from the box, smoothed it, and placed it carefully into one of three piles I'd created based on whether they were personal, financial, or random. Nothing was absolute junk. You never knew when the date on a gas receipt was the magic clue or a doodle on the back of an envelope was actually a decent portrait of the guy you were hunting.

Naturally, I was hoping for something more straightforward, but nothing leapt from the box and danced on the tabletop, waving its arms. A bank envelope looked promising, but contained only some sample checks and a Virginia state map with hand-drawn circles on it. The circles got me excited until Mary Beth gently pointed out that they were *printed* hand-drawn circles, put there by the gas company that owned the stations circled on the map, which they'd sponsored.

By the time the last piece of paper was stacked on the pile, I felt fuzzy and cross-eyed and I could tell Mary Beth, unused to this kind of tedium, was feeling it, too. I put the box on the floor and pushed the piles to one corner of the table, then waved a waitress over.

"Let's eat," I told Mary Beth. "I'm going to start crying if I have to look at one more sheet of paper."

We ordered. I got vegetable soup, Mary Beth a tuna-salad sandwich. The food was unremarkable, but our minds were somewhere else.

"Not much for an entire life, is it?" she said, glancing at the piles.

"Twenty years in the joint doesn't leave you with much," I said. "Not much call for Pottery Barn catalogs in the pen."

She nodded, distracted. "Still, it's sad."

We finished and pushed the plates to one side, then I stacked each pile neatly on top of the other, until I had a super pile.

"Okay, if you don't mind, I'm going to hold on to these. I didn't see anything worth chasing just now, but you never know when something we've got here—a date or a time or the name of a fast-food joint—will break things wide open."

"Missed one," she said, reaching deep into the box. She pulled out a very thin, very small piece of paper that had gotten stuck under one of the flaps.

"What is it?"

She frowned. "It's a prescription."

"May I?" I asked. She handed it to me. The handwriting was atrocious, so I couldn't begin to decipher what the medicine or the amount was. But the name of the doctor who had written the prescription was printed legibly at the top, like a letterhead. *Dr. Joel Raycroft.*

"Does this tell us anything?" Mary Beth asked.

"I don't know," I said. "But Dr. Raycroft will."

Cain's Crossing Medical Arts was located just outside of town on a plot that had probably been a horse farm or a meadow last year. The small hillock it sat on was rounded just so, hinting that nature hadn't formed it quite that way, and the brickwork, signage, and fresh-out-of-the-box landscaping told me that Raycroft and Associates had moved in since last baseball season.

Mary Beth and I parked and walked through the foyer and into the waiting room. I should've been prepared, but my mind was on the case, not myself. Just a single step into the foyer and the smell, look, feel, and sound of the place rolled over me like a wave. I balked like a horse being led through a gate and almost tripped as we approached the registration window. The antiseptic bite of the medical environment had taken me back to every one of the doctors' appointments I'd had over the last year. Things were trending better in that department, of course, but this wasn't a part of the brain under my control. Feelings of fear, pain, and confusion were interwoven with doctors' offices and hospitals and there wasn't much I could do to stop it.

"Are you okay?" Mary Beth asked. A young woman reading a magazine in the waiting room glanced in our direction.

"I'm fine," I said, lying. I took a deep breath and moved to the window.

A scruffy twenty-something guy with blond hair and a beard sat on the other side, tapping away at a keyboard. He was heavyset and I could hear his asthmatic breathing through the glass. His gaze never left the monitor screen. I waited patiently. When thirty seconds had gone by and he hadn't so much as glanced at us, Mary Beth elbowed me to one side.

"Excuse me, sweetie," she said. The young man raised his head, blank of face. No one had called him "sweetie" since the third grade.

"Yes?"

"Is Dr. Raycroft available?"

He blinked. "Do you have an appointment?"

"I'm afraid not."

"He's booked for the rest of the day."

Mary Beth got a worried expression on her face. "Do you think he's got a teeny bit of time for a few questions? Detective Singer here would like to talk to him regarding a murder case he's involved in, you see."

"What? Shit. I mean, sure," the kid said, pushing away from the desk. "Hold on a sec."

Out of the corner of my eye, I could see the young woman raise her head from her magazine again at the words "murder case." Words carry well in waiting rooms. The receptionist disappeared through an office door, banging it shut behind him.

It opened a minute later and the scruffy kid waved us back. We followed him down a hall to an office. Sitting at a small desk was a trim man with a mane of silver hair and just enough color in his cheeks, wearing a white coat over a blue striped dress shirt with perfectly knotted scarlet tie, the very picture of a successful physician. He was writing something on a pad as we walked in, but bounced to his feet as we came near.

"Joel Raycroft," he said, coming around the desk. He offered his hand and we introduced ourselves. "Billy said you're investigating a murder?"

"Nothing to worry about, Doctor," I said. "Well, not too much. We're looking into the death of J.D. Hope."

"Oh," he said. He sat on the edge of his desk. "Terrible thing, the way he died."

"How did you know J.D., Doctor?" Mary Beth asked. "Was he a patient of yours?"

"May I ask what your interest is?"

"I'm J.D.'s sister," Mary Beth said, sweetly but with steel under the words. "I've asked Detective Singer to help me get to the bottom of his killing. Which I very much doubt you had a hand in. I just would like to know as much as I can about J.D., whether it had to do with his murder or not. I'm sure you understand."

"Of course," he said, hesitating. "Certainly I want to help. But, you know I can't speak in much detail, I hope? My patients retain their rights to privacy, even in death."

"Feel free to speak in generalities, Doctor," Mary Beth said, pouring on the sugar.

Raycroft smiled. "We don't have to be cryptic. Just careful. I can tell you John was referred to me by a colleague in DC. I'd been seeing him for almost a year. He was a good listener, engaged in the process, wanting to know about how to improve his health. A model patient, really."

"I understand you have a responsibility to respect your patients' confidentiality, even deceased ones, but would you mind taking a look at this?" I handed him the prescription we'd found. He took it from me delicately, as if afraid of touching my hand. A glance seemed to be all he needed, as he nodded and handed it back.

"Did you write this prescription, Dr. Raycroft?" Mary Beth asked.

"It appears to be one of mine," he said. "Though I would want to check our records before I laid ownership to it."

"Are you afraid it's a forgery?" I asked.

He smiled weakly and the confident patrician image wobbled a bit. "Not really. But I'm the defendant in two malpractice cases right now. You'll forgive me if I don't admit to anything I can't independently confirm. Or I'm not subpoenaed to confirm."

"I understand," I said. "Hypothetically speaking, even if it wasn't one of yours, could you tell us what drug the prescription is for?"

"Riluzole," he said. "A rather heavy dose of it, in fact."

"What is it used to treat?"

"Well, the use of it is still rather controversial. There are reported side effects that many patients claim are as damning as the disease, though I personally think that's a stretch."

I sighed. "What disease is that, Doctor?"

"ALS," he said. "Amyotrophic lateral sclerosis. Lou Gehrig's disease."

Mary Beth stiffened beside me. I asked, "What does Riluzole do for the disease?"

"It's not a cure, if that's what you're asking," he said. "ALS is fatal. The disease often progresses quickly. Patients lose muscle control and, eventually, respiratory function. Pneumonia sets in and eventually respiratory compromise leads to death. The best we can offer is relief for the worst of the symptoms. In a nutshell, Riluzole delays the need for a ventilator or a tracheotomy."

"For how long?"

"Three to five months. There are some rare instances of it increasing patient survival for up to a year, maybe slightly longer. The data is not encouraging beyond eighteen months."

Mary Beth was quivering like a bowstring. Raycroft, engaged in his clinical element, was oblivious.

"Can Riluzole be abused?" I asked. "Is there a market for it?"

"Dealing it? Like, on the streets?" he asked, surprised by the question. "No. It wouldn't do a thing to a healthy person. Or for them."

I asked, "How long had this particular prescription been in use?"

At that, Raycroft shut his mouth with a near-audible snap. We weren't dealing with hypotheticals anymore—this was a direct question about J.D. I could imagine the advice of his malpractice attorney echoing in his head.

"Please, Doctor," Mary Beth said. "I don't want to sue you. I don't care about money. I just want to know about my brother. What his life was like. What he was going through."

Raycroft looked at her, suddenly seeming to realize the effect his words had had on her. The struggle between sympathy and self-preservation played across his face, plain to see.

"How long, Doctor?" I asked.

He sighed and closed his eyes. "Almost seven months."

Mary Beth made it through the waiting room, but once outside she made a sharp right-hand turn, walked five steps, then leaned against the hot brick and began sobbing. I went over and put a hand on her shoulder, but she shrunk away, so I went back to the car and sat on the hood to give her some time. It was hot and the sun beat on me in the blacktopped parking lot, but the least I could do was suffer a little.

It was all over in five minutes. She disappeared back into the office, wiping her eyes. I got in the car and started it to get the AC going. In the time it took me to fiddle with the controls, she was on her way back to the car, put back together almost as if nothing had happened. Only a red swelling around the eyes gave her away.

She slid into the passenger's side and we sat there for a second. I sat as still as possible while she took several deep, shuddering breaths.

Finally, she asked, "Does this change anything?"

I sat back. "I don't know. It depends on whether his ALS factored into the drug dealing."

"But the doctor said that the . . . the Riluzole didn't have any value."

"He said it wouldn't have any recreational use," I corrected. "There's still a market for pharmaceuticals simply because they're expensive as hell. Granted, they don't have a street value like run-of-the-mill narcotics, so I'm skeptical. But it's something we have to consider until we can prove otherwise."

She stared out the window. The blast of cold air was condensing around the edges of the glass. "It hurts. To know he was going through this and not know how or why. Maybe the doctor will tell us more later."

"But?"

"But, in a way, what does it matter? J.D. was killed by a person, not a disease. All of this information is useless in the face of that. We still have to find the person who killed him and bring him to justice."

I didn't say anything, just started the car and eased out of the parking lot. Her voice had gained strength in just a few sentences, sounding nearly normal by the end. I didn't want to do anything to wreck that, but after hearing about J.D.'s ALS—and with the consequences of my own disease fresh in my mind—I couldn't help wondering if whoever had killed J.D. had done him a favor.

CHAPTER FOURTEEN

Things hadn't changed at Woodland Corner trailer park. Kids were still splashing and screaming in the stream, toys and grills littered the side yards, and the same lady was yelling for Jack again. One change, however, was that instead of knocking on Ginny Decker's front door, I went right around back, where I found her sitting in a chair, smoking and drinking beer. She was staring out over the treetops, the smoke from her cigarette curling into the sky.

She didn't see me until I was nearly at the steps to the deck. When she did, she made a quick motion to get up. I raised a hand to stop her. "Just give me a minute, okay? One minute." She froze with her hands on the arms of the chair, neither moving nor settling back.

"I know you don't want to talk to me," I said. "I know you're scared. I'm not trying to push you into anything or make your life any harder. That's the last thing I want."

She didn't say anything, so I kept going, my voice low.

"Problem is, it might not be up to me. Or you. I've talked to a crowd of people who all seem to agree that J.D. was still involved with something dirty back here at home. The local police think it caught up with him, that he was done in by a mysterious hit man from Washington, DC."

The look on her face told me what she thought of that. I rushed on. "I know. The story's so fantastic that I think they either don't know or won't say what's going on. I'm betting you've got some ideas. I know you're afraid of where that might lead, but I can tell you from experience it doesn't matter if you don't tell me."

I waited. Finally, like the words were being dragged out of her, she said, "What do you mean?"

"It's simple. If whoever you're afraid of thinks you have information that could hurt them, it won't stop them from taking an interest in you. Tell me and at least I can do something about it, maybe even stop whoever it is that's got you so scared."

"What the hell is it to you?" she asked, her voice strained. "Why do you give a damn about J.D.? About me?"

I took a deep breath. If I didn't give a real answer, or at least part of one, this conversation was over for good. "I owe him, Ginny. It's as simple as that. I let something happen to him that I shouldn't have."

"J.D.'s dead, mister," she said, blunt as a bullet. "Whatever debt you owed is gone with him."

"It's not about him, really." I stared at her as I spoke, realizing it was true. "This is about me. About what I think of myself. About who I am. If J.D. were here himself and told me to give it up, it's okay, I don't think I'd do it."

"We're all just along for the ride. Is that it?"

I considered, then nodded slowly. "Yes, I guess you are. I'll help you out if I can, but I'm going to find out who killed J.D. and why for myself."

She took a long drag from her cigarette and blew it straight up. "Might not like what you find, mister."

"Probably not," I agreed. "I'm not here to clear his name. For all I know, J.D. came back home and picked up where he left off before he went to jail. The guy wasn't a saint. But I don't care. He still gets justice. And I get peace."

She shook her head. "Sounds nice, but there still ain't nothing you can do."

"Try me, Ginny. I'm a son of a bitch when it comes to finishing what I started."

Slowly, glacially, she settled back into her chair. I climbed the short steps to the deck and eased myself into a rickety-looking lawn chair across from her. I looked at her over a battered white plastic bistro table. We stared at each other for a minute, the tension high enough to taste. I felt like I'd cornered a wild cat.

Apparently, I passed some kind of test. She sighed, and said, "What do you want to know?"

"Let's start easy," I said. "How did you and J.D. meet?"

"High school. Nowhere else to meet anyone around here. He was two years ahead of me and made all the girls squeal with this black Trans Am he bought off his uncle. We used to peel around the school parking lot and haul ass into the country. We drove the hell out of that thing."

"You get married after high school?"

She shook her head. "Later. Before he went to the big city."

"What was he like before he left?"

She sighed and stubbed out her cigarette in the ashtray, where it joined a forest of others. "J.D.'s dreams were always two sizes bigger than he was. Which is all right, that's most everyone's problem. But he couldn't focus on any one of them. I told him he must have ADD, the way he picked up and dropped ideas. First, he was going to open an auto body shop, then he was going to get into construction—even though he didn't know what end of a hammer to grab—then he told me he was about to sell vacation property in the Carolinas. J.D. did everything but sell Amway."

"All that sounds aboveboard."

"Yeah, well. Those were the dreams. The reality was, from high school on, J.D. was always hanging with the wrong crowd. We both were, I guess. I was there because he was, but J.D. was there because he wanted to belong to something. Problem was, he was willing to do pretty much anything to impress. And some of them were lowlife shits, so J.D. did a lot of stupid things just to get on their good side."

"Running dope? Stealing cars?"

"Not that bad. Not yet. He'd lift beer from the store or break into people's houses. Wouldn't take anything. He just wanted to see if he could."

"That's it?"

"He smoked weed. I mean, we both would. But he wasn't into dealing it."

A man and a woman walked by on their way to the stream. I could see them shooting glances back at us. They waved when they knew they'd been seen. Ginny waved back with a weak smile. I raised my eyebrows.

"Donna and Fred Ray," she explained. "From three trailers down. They wouldn't set foot in that stream if their hair was on fire, so the only reason they're walking by is because my next-door neighbor phoned them and said she'd seen a tall, dark, and handsome stranger sitting on my back porch with me. Nosy sons of bitches."

"Glad I could provide today's entertainment for Woodland Corner," I said.

Ginny reached for her lighter and pack where they rested on the table. "Honey, you provided this *month's* entertainment for Woodland Corner."

I waited for her to light her cigarette, then asked, "What happened to make J.D. want to leave Cain's Crossing so bad?"

"Even J.D. could see he was going nowhere fast with the scum he was hanging out with. And he had no prospects. Work didn't suit him and he'd never been much in school. He thought he might be able to make something of himself in DC, so off he went."

"Well, he certainly made something of himself," I said. "A felon."

She sighed. "I told him not to go, told him DC was going to grind him down to nothing. But he wanted to prove something to me, to his friends. To his mama."

"You two split when he went?"

"Well, we weren't together. And when he went and got himself arrested, I figured the courtship was over. I had to move on. The papers for the divorce came through around the time the door to his cell slammed shut."

"But then he came back," I said.

She nodded, blew a plume of smoke toward the sky. "Surprised the hell out of me. Just showed up one day, knocking on the door. He had seventeen dollars and a duffel bag full of old clothes. He smiled and said, 'Hey, Ginny,' and next thing I knew he was in my bed."

"Did he move in?"

She shook her head. "He was here most nights, but kept a room out at that shitty motel where they found him."

"Any idea why?"

"Why what?"

I gestured at her home. "Free place to stay, the woman he loves. Why get a motel room?"

She laughed. "Maybe I scared him. I told him if he wanted the two of us to be an item again, he needed a plan."

"He already had one, though. Headed right back to the dark side."

"It didn't start that way. Jail made him a different man. Harder, meaner. I didn't like all of it, but can't deny it was nice to see him stick up for himself for once."

"How?"

She tapped the ash from the end of her cigarette. "Some smart-ass was razzing him at Jackie's bar one night not long after he came home. Said something about him being some bad man's girlfriend when he heard J.D. had done time. Well, my sweetie hit him in the throat with a bottle of Rolling Rock and that was the end of the jokes."

"Who was this guy?"

"Name's Jay."

I thought back to my run-in at the doughnut shop and described the surfer wannabe to her. "Is that Jay?"

She nodded. "He runs around with the Brower brothers."

"Tell me about them."

She paused and I was afraid she was going to clam up again. But she blinked a few times and continued. "Three rednecks like you read about in a bad book. They tool around in pickups, bad-mouthing the Mexicans, the blacks, college kids, don't matter. They spit and cuss and run over old people."

"And hassle people at gas stations," I said. "So they're racists and have a bad attitude. They do anything more serious?"

"Anything bad happens in Cain's Crossing, you can pin it on them."

"Do they run dope? Hookers? Chop cars? Rob banks?"

She gave a little shake of her head, which could mean *no* or *I don't know*. I dropped it, afraid it might make her skittish. "So. These Brower boys. They hear through the grapevine that J.D. was back in town after pulling time in the big city, and . . ."

She nodded again. "Buck is the youngest. He was in the bar the night J.D. nearly killed that guy with the bottle. I guess Buck was impressed and tried to get J.D. to talk to the other two."

"Darryl and his other brother Darryl?"

She tried a small smile, shook her head. "Tank and Will."

"Tank?"

"His real name is Harold, but everyone's called him Tank since grade school. He'd twist your nose off your face if he caught you calling him Harold."

"What about Will?"

She shrugged. "He ain't bright, but the others do what he tells them. Just a mean son of a bitch. Spent some time in the army, then got out and worked in Norfolk before giving it up to come back here."

"You said Buck 'tried' to get J.D. to talk to his brothers," I said. "He didn't want to?"

She shook her head and took a sip of her beer. "I think he wanted to try something legal for once, but he couldn't get work anywhere. Tank and Buck took to coming by at night, talking him up, until finally he agreed to do some jobs for them."

"That bother you?"

She closed her eyes briefly, opened them. "It didn't matter what I thought. He was always making the wrong decisions. Nothing I was going to do or say would turn that around. And I couldn't feed us both on what I was bringing home, so he needed to start making money. Maybe I should've told him to straighten himself out first, get a real job, keep his hands clean. But what job was that supposed to be, exactly? He couldn't all of a sudden decide to be a doctor or an engineer. J.D. was born a small-time crook and always would be. I could love him the way he was or tell him to leave, but change him? Wasn't going to happen."

"What did the Browers want him to do?" I asked.

"It wasn't washing their cars, I can tell you that," she said, taking a drag and blowing out the smoke.

I scratched the back of my neck. "They might grow weed, but the margin on that's a little light these days. And if they weren't into robbing banks or chopping cars, seems like the only thing J.D. might know that they didn't would be something more hard-core," I said, thinking out loud. "Which is drugs. When I busted him back in DC, he was working for a crack dealer, but these bumpkins wouldn't know how to get their hands on that. You need connections and business relationships and it doesn't sound like these guys have been outside the county in twenty years. Plus there's no market for it here."

"Maybe you could figure this out on your own time?"

"So, weed is too light. The action for coke and crack are too hard to elbow in on, there's no way to get a source, and there's no market. Same thing with heroin," I said, going down the list and ignoring her attempt to cut off the conversation. "There's oxycodone, but that's all on its way up from Florida. Dealers might pass through here, but they're not sourcing it here."

Ginny didn't say anything, tapping nonexistent ash from her cigarette several times in a row.

"How about a shot in the dark? Rural farm country, a bunch of tough guys, and a huge profit margin," I said. "I'll take crystal meth for a hundred, Alex. They can make it easy enough if they learn how, but then who do they sell it to? The big money is in the city. Enter J.D. Hope, right?"

Ginny gave a humorless laugh. "Mister, I like the way you look and you seem nice enough, but you're not going to be around later if one of the Brower boys decides to throw a gallon of gas on my trailer. I'd just as soon you learn that on your own."

"How about if I guess and you just nod if I'm right?" I asked. She shook her head, but I plowed on. "The Browers are the local badasses since time began. They grow some weed on the side, but then they hear about how easy it is to make meth. You need space to cook it, but there're lots of farms and empty barns out here in the boondocks. Then J.D. comes home after a few years pulling time and they say to themselves, Hey, I wonder if good old J.D. learned a few tricks working with those crack dealers in DC? Maybe he's got some connections we could use."

Ginny kept shaking her head no.

"But then J.D. made a play of his own or got caught skimming off the top or just said the wrong thing at the wrong time and Buck or Tank or Will decided they didn't need J.D.'s big-city experience after all."

Ginny stood and started gathering the ashtray, lighter, and beer cans with quick, jerky motions.

"But the question is," I said, into the air, "the way J.D. was killed. From what everyone is telling me, the Browers aren't the type to hit someone once and call it off. So, did they hire someone to do it for them or was it not the Browers at all?"

Ginny finished gathering her things and, without a word, went into the back door of her trailer and shut the door.

IV.

"He won't roll?"

Stan slams his mug down. Coffee sloshes out and a dark puddle spreads across his desk until it's stopped by a stack of folders. He swears and snatches at a stack of fast-food napkins to mop up the spill.

"No, he won't fucking roll. He thinks he's got a better chance with a crack dealer who's killed four of his best friends."

"We got anything else on Maurice?"

"No," he says, sulking.

I try to bridge the gap. "Want me to pick him up again? Try my charms?"

"Be my fucking guest. I see him again, I'll punch him in the face. He could help us put away the whole crew. Wants to be a stand-up guy for a crack dealer. Jesus."

I grab my car and head over to Southeast. Territories are tight here, measured by half-streets and storefronts, but even knowing where to look, it still takes me all day to find J.D. He's slouched in the driver's seat of a beat-up white Accord at the corner of Benning and E Street, hand draped over the top of the steering wheel, staring off into space. Wondering, maybe, if Stan was right. Wondering if he's going to get shot in the head.

I pull up, roll down my passenger-side window, lean over the seat. "J.D."

He looks over, uninterested. Maybe a slight lift of the eyebrows. "Yeah?"

"You know who I am?"

Eyes sleepy, too street-slick to care. "Should I?"

"I'm a friend of Officer Lowry's. We need to talk."

He gives a start, then catches himself and settles back in his seat, trying to salvage some of that cool. "No, we don't."

"Yeah, we do. Stan says you're not interested in helping out."

He shrugs. "Y'all are fishing. Otherwise, you would've pulled Maurice in already."

"Who's Maurice? I didn't say anything about a Maurice."

J.D. sits for a second, quiet, then says, "Nobody talks, y'all don't have shit."

"That's not the way it works, J.D.," I say. "If someone talks, that's nice, but if nobody talks, we just find another way to get it done. And if you had a chance to help but didn't, then you go upstream with the rest of them. Even if you didn't do anything."

He looks at me for a long second. "I didn't kill nobody."

"J.D., you're in way over your head. We got five bodies, including a little girl that was going to start first grade in about a month. You either pulled the trigger, know who pulled it, or work for the guy who did. Sooner or later, we're going to round everyone up, and you're going to be in with the rest of his crew. Help us out and maybe you wiggle free."

He stares straight ahead and says, "I didn't kill nobody and I ain't going to jail for something I didn't do."

I try to wait him out, but an old lady in a Lincoln pulls up behind me and lays on her horn. "Don't bet on it," is the best I can come up with. I yell it through the window and pull away.

CHAPTER FIFTEEN

I went back to the Mosby, said hello to the night clerk who I think was alive, and headed to my room to take a cool shower. I made it cool, not cold, because chemotherapy had given me a sensitivity to cold bordering on the excruciating. My last treatment had been months ago and the doctors had said I should be over it by now, but either they were wrong or I had one hell of a psychosomatic complex, because anything colder than tepid made me wince.

But it was August in south-central Virginia and I'd just sweated my tender parts off walking and talking to people for the previous eight hours. Daredevil that I am, I turned the "C" knob in the shower an inch further counterclockwise than I was used to, took a deep breath, and got in. I hissed as the spray bit into my skin, but in a minute I was groaning enough to make even me self-conscious as the day's heat was washed away.

I stayed in there for fifteen long minutes, toweled off, and threw on a robe. I grabbed a glass of water and my cell phone, then dragged the single chair in the room over to the window so I could look outside while I talked. I sat and went through my cell's contact list until I found the number I wanted.

It was answered after two rings. Before the voice on the other end could say anything, I whispered into the phone, "Bring zee money to zee train station at midnight."

A pause. "Singer?"

"Goddamn it," I said. "I can't fool anybody anymore."

"You don't try hard enough," Lieutenant Sam Bloch said. "How's it going, Marty?"

"Not bad. How's life in HIDTA?" I asked, pronouncing the acronym like *hide-uh*. The High Intensity Drug Trafficking Area program was the Washington, DC, area's premier interdepartmental drug task force, meant to bring federal, state, and local law enforcement together so they could share drug intel in what was a very fractured jurisdictional environment. In a relatively small area, DC came together in three states, one district, and a dozen federal pieces of turf. Without cooperation among law-enforcement entities, dealers would only have to drive a mile in any direction to set up shop in another jurisdiction, thereby complicating law enforcement immensely. HIDTA was supposed to provide the interagency cooperation that nullified that problem. Sam was a medium-level honcho with the organization. I'd helped him out with a tangled case earlier in the year, which I hoped made him beholden to me, at least a little.

"It sucks. You back in DC?"

"Not exactly," I said. "I've had a detour that's proven . . . interesting."

"And interesting is what's got you calling me, I guess?"

"Afraid so," I said and outlined the situation for him. He listened without interrupting, though over the phone I could hear him drumming on his desk, the victim of Sam's wicked nicotine habit. Working in a smoke-free environment gave him world-class jitters.

"So, this murder. These Brower brothers are looking good for it except that's not how they like to off people down in the heartland. You want me to sniff a bit and see if they're everything everyone says they are."

"Yep," I said. "And was J.D. their link to something or someone in DC? If so, you might be doing yourself a favor as much as me."

"What kind of favor is that? If it doesn't start with 'd' and end in 'rugs,' then it's not in my corner."

"Oh, there's d-rugs, all right," I said and explained what I'd pieced together after talking to Ginny Decker.

"Meth, huh?" he asked. "This favor is the kind where I pull over-time? Thanks a lot."

"Hey, if J.D. was setting up a network between crystal-making rednecks and a bunch of gangbangers in Southeast, then the work's coming your way whether I tell you or not," I said. "Wouldn't you rather be in front of it instead of playing catch-up?"

"I'd rather be on a beach in Cabo," he said. "Anything else I can do for you?"

"Now that you ask, yeah." I told him about the four suits I'd seen at the doughnut shop. "While you're nosing around, mind seeing if any three-letter federal agency is doing some work here? It would be nice not to get pinched in a government investigation while I'm trying to do a nice lady a favor."

"I can do that. Most of them don't tell me shit if it isn't happening in the Metro area, but I can make some calls, see who's willing to talk. DEA's got an office in Warrenton."

"Thanks," I said.

"Don't mention it," Sam said. Then, hesitating, "How are you feeling?"

There it was again. The "C" question. "Not bad. The surgery was successful. I'm in remission. I can jog a half mile without passing out. Even gained a few pounds back, so I can stop putting new holes in my belt."

"I'm not going to pretend I know what I'm talking about," he said, "but it's better than the other thing."

"True. I stopped feeling sorry for myself a while ago. I do what the doctors tell me to and let the rest run its course."

"That's all you can do," he said.

I was feeling pretty good about the work I'd done so far. I should've called it a day and watched SportsCenter until I fell asleep, but the shower had given me a burst of energy that seemed a shame to waste, so I shucked the robe and put on a pair of jeans and a T-shirt I normally wore to mow the lawn that said "Pobody's Nerfect" on the front. It hung on me more than it used to, but it worked out, since it was loose enough to cover my SIG that rested comfortably in a holster at the small of my back.

I didn't know how to do half the things on my phone I knew I could, but one thing I could do is look up an address. I punched in a few words, fiddled a bit, then found the object of my search. I trundled downstairs past the night clerk, who was asleep with a Danielle Steel novel in her lap, and headed for my car.

Jackie's was outside of town on a narrow lane named Ashland Road and was the first right after the town dump. It looked just like I thought it would, kind of a converted smoke shack with two or three generations of aluminum-siding additions tacked on, a few neon signs in the window, and a couple of tin pipes sticking out of the roof for ventilation. Every window had an AC unit and even from the gravel parking lot, the hum they made almost drowned out thought. An old Chevy pickup and a severely dented Jeep dripped oil onto the cinder lot. I expected that. Two brand-new, top-of-the-line Ram trucks with all the fixin's, on the other hand, were something special.

I parked and went inside. It was dim, no surprise, with most of the lighting coming from three TVs and a Budweiser sign on the wall. The main room had a horseshoe-shaped bar with taps on the far left side and a few bags of potato chips tacked to the wall near the register. Faded pictures of race-car drivers and feed store signs were attached to the wall with whatever had been handy: a nail, duct tape, staples. It smelled like every bar I'd ever been in—smoke, spilled beer, and a rubber-mat stink that reminded me of breaking up fights. Cool, moist air from the AC units intensified the odors rather than dissipated them.

Some cowboy on the digital jukebox in the corner was warning people not to touch his pickup truck or else. The slide guitar and gid-dyup percussion made me wince. Then again, I personally thought a good musical lineup consisted of the Ramones, Iggy Pop, and Patti Smith, so what did I know? A small room in the back—one of the additions I'd seen from the outside—was the game room, complete with pool tables, foosball, and a dartboard that looked like a nest of termites had been hung from a wall. All were lit occasionally from the flash of a pinball machine. A few shadowy figures paced between the tables.

Four or five Cain's Crossing citizens sat at the bar, all of them drinking solo, staring straight ahead or watching the NASCAR action on one of the TVs, barely blinking. Two geezers played checkers in a corner. Unhurried, automatic moves suggested they'd been playing each other for years. Two girls, incongruously, were sipping wine at a table near a window overlooking the parking lot.

I walked to the bar, put my elbows up on the counter, then took them off again when I felt how sticky it was. A tough-looking, thirty-something bartendress came over. With the cutoff jeans and perma-nent cynicism etched into her face, she could've been Ginny Decker's younger sister. She raised her eyebrows.

"Sam Adams?" I asked.

"Bud, Bud Light, Coors, Coors Light. Some kind of lemonade thing in a bottle."

"Will I get my ass kicked if I order the lemonade?"

A tiny smile came and went. "Probably. Maybe by me."

"I'll take it," I said.

That got me a full laugh and she went to grab my drink. I smiled and nodded to anyone who would make eye contact, but the most I got in return was a half nod before sleepy eyes went back to a point on the wall or the flickering blue screens.

"Here you go," the bartender said as she came back and put my drink on a paper napkin. "Do you want your ass-kicking now or later?"

"Later, maybe," I said. "Can I enjoy my clear malt beverage first?"

"I'll let it go this time. Where're you from?"

I took a pull from the bottle and sighed. Citrusy, light, cold. "I'm down from DC to visit some folks."

"Who's that?"

"Mary Beth Hope. You know her?"

The woman's eyes grew guarded. "Not really. I know the name. But I don't know her directly, you know what I mean."

"I tried to find her," I said. "But ran into her mother in that mansion."

The guarded look faded a smidge. "Old Dorothea. We used to skip her house on Halloween."

"No candy? Or afraid you wouldn't make it out alive?"

"Both," she said and then moved to the end of the bar to fill a mug. She came back. "Did you find her?"

"Well, you know," I said, hunching my shoulders, trying to keep a secret. "I wasn't really looking for Mary Beth; I was trying to find her brother, J.D. I thought maybe one of them would know where he was. But I got the cold shoulder from the mother and can't find the sister. You know anything about him?"

The mildly suspicious, guarded expression was replaced by a steel wall. But her head turned, involuntarily, toward the pool tables before she stopped herself. I could've guessed as much, but I wanted to test the waters, see if anyone was interested in talking. I put a twenty on the bar, thanked her, and sidled toward the game room.

The room was empty except for three guys at the farthest pool table. The lighting was more generous than in the main room, turning the shadowy figures into distinct people. The guy currently taking the shot was thick, with chunky, sunburnt arms that could've been mostly muscle or mostly pork rinds. His green T-shirt had dark spots under the arms and a silver-dollar-sized blot of sweat at the sternum. Pink skin showed through his crew cut. His eyes, flicking back and forth from the cue ball to the six, were an antifreeze blue.

Watching him were two skinny guys. One sat on a bar stool, his elbows on his knees, not playing. He had on a tank top and long, shiny soccer-style shorts that nearly met tall white tube socks pulled almost all the way up his shins. His head was shaved, the hair shorter even than that of the guy at the table, and he wore giant sunglasses that swallowed half his face. Veins stood out under the ghost-white skin of his arms and neck like blue snakes.

The other toothpick I recognized. It was Jay, the stoner who'd braced me at the doughnut shop. He was leaning on a cue stick but had his back half turned to the doorway, so he didn't see me. He was still wearing the grimy Camel T-shirt and ripped jeans.

I took a spot against the nearest wall and watched the farm boy. He was a nervous shot, the kind who pumps the cue stick back and forth two dozen times before trying to smash the balls into outer space. Sure enough, he slammed the stick into the cue ball off-center and barely clipped the six, which went careening off in the exact opposite direction he'd hoped for. By some miracle, it dropped into a corner pocket.

"Shit shot," the gangster on the stool said.

"Mother*fucker*," the farm boy said, straightening from his shooter's crouch and slamming the butt end of his cue stick into the floor. When he stood, I saw his neck was as thick around as my thigh and shoulder muscles that bunched up and down. So, he was at least fifty-fifty muscle and pork rinds.

"Leave it in, Tank," Jay said. "You're going to need it."

"Go fuck yourself," Tank said.

Jay moved to the table and settled smoothly into a hustler's stance, hips low and feet wide. In three quick, economical movements, he sank the ten, the fourteen, and the eleven. The table, crowded with balls when I'd walked in, was thinning, but somehow the remaining solids were all crowded around the eight ball.

Jay lined up on the nine ball, his posture a little crooked. "Eight ball, off the nine, corner pocket."

Tank laughed *huh, huh, huh* and my eyebrows jumped. I could feel the skinny gangster's eyes on me as I watched. Jay's eyes flicked up, down, up . . . then he shot. The cue ball kissed the nine and caught the eight perfectly, sinking it dead in the corner. But the combination took a bad split on the nine and everyone watched as the cue ball went straight in the side pocket—a scratch. Unless they played a different version of eight ball here, Jay had just lost the game.

They didn't. Tank whooped and Jay hissed his disappointment. The gangster said, "Jay, you do that every time. Why don't you try winning the old-fashioned way?"

Jay shook his head. "Can't help it. Always got to take the trick shot."

"Pay up," Tank said, snapping his fingers.

Jay pulled a meager wad of bills held together by a rubber band from his pocket and made a big show of slapping two bills in Tank's hand. "I shouldn't even pay you, Tank. I'd win every time if we played straight pool."

"Do it then, asshole," Tank said.

"What do you think, mister?" the gangster—who had to be Buck, the youngest Brower—suddenly said to me. "Think my brother could ever beat good ol' Jay-bone?"

The heads of the other two snapped around, surprised, like I'd just fallen from the ceiling. I saw Jay straighten up as recognition kicked in.

I shrugged. "I think Jay-bone could beat Tank in eight ball or trick shots or tiddlywinks if he weren't trying to throw the game."

No one likes to be accused of sandbagging, so I expected Jay to come zooming around the pool table and into my grille, but he just stood there. Tank, on the other hand, was ready to bite. An ugly look spread across his face—not easy on a face like his—and I could see him swell, gearing himself up for a brawl. Buck smirked. He'd waved a red cape and Tank had gone for it. I tensed, getting ready for the fireworks, when all three heads swiveled toward the doorway.

"Fuck is going on?" a voice from behind me said.

I turned and backed away from the door while trying to keep an eye on Tank at the same time. Standing in the doorway was a guy my height, in his forties, with broad shoulders and black hair slicked straight back. I could still see the lines his comb had made. His face was pockmarked and craggy, with a deep brow that hung over brown eyes like a shelf. A blue, short-sleeved work shirt revealed thick forearms covered in blurry tattoos the color of his veins. He smelled fake clean, like motel soap and drugstore aftershave. Everything about him screamed hard-time con.

"Hey, Will," Tank said. The other two were dead silent, as if they expected him to bite all the pool cues in half. The con ignored them and walked over to a stool next to Buck. He sat, then reached into the breast pocket of his shirt, pulling out a pack of cigarettes and a steel lighter. He fished a cigarette from the pack, lit it with a *plink*, and took a deep drag. The smoke poured out of both nostrils.

"Jay," he said, but kept his eyes on me. "Dwayne told me some asshole who talked like a cop beat the living shit out of him the other morning. Said you were with them when it happened."

"Yeah," Jay said.

"Yeah?" Will mocked in a falsetto. "Well, we got an asshole standing right here who looks like a cop. This him?"

"Yeah," Jay said, uncomfortable.

Will continued to stare at me, squinting as smoke curled around his face. "So. You a cop?"

I shrugged.

"No answer, huh?"

I stared back at him.

"What if I beat the living shit out of *you*? You got an answer to that?"

"I guess you could try," I said. "You that eager to head back to the can?"

Buck, emboldened, piped up. "Maybe he was a mall cop."

Will smiled, but said, "Buck, shut your fucking mouth. Well, mister? You here in some official capacity?"

I smiled back. *We're all friends, right?* "Just doing a buddy a favor. Somebody killed an old acquaintance of mine. J.D. Hope. Maybe you heard of him?"

"Nope."

"That's strange," I said. "Because all I seem to hear is how J.D. hung out with a bunch of losers. And the reason they let him is because they thought he owned some big-city drug connections they thought they might be able to use."

"That so?" Will said. Tank shifted in place. Jay was very still.

"Yeah. But what he didn't know was that they were even bigger losers than he was."

"You thought you'd come down and set him straight?"

"Yeah. But I'm not from around here, see, and I didn't know where to start. So I just tried to find the shittiest bar with the biggest losers in it."

"Think you found it?" Will asked, his smile getting wider. But not friendlier.

"To tell you the truth, I wasn't sure," I said. "Until you showed."

Slowly, Will stubbed out his cigarette against the wall, then leaned over and plucked the cue stick from Tank's hand. With a sharp twist, he unscrewed the two halves, then tossed the lighter end on the pool table. He stood and tapped the butt end in his hand a few times, watching me. The smile hadn't left his face.

I cursed my big mouth silently. Things had gone south, fast. I straightened up so I could reach the butt of the SIG. Four against one were not good odds and, with his reach, one step was all I could give Will Brower before he planted the cue stick upside my skull.

Then we froze as a voice with a deep Southern twang said, "You're not about to put holes in my favorite bar, are you?"

CHAPTER SIXTEEN

I'd been handcuffed before during "sensitivity" trainings when the brass wanted us to understand what it was like. The idea was to make sure you didn't overdo it. Containment was the idea, not punishment. It was never really something I enjoyed, even when it was done kind of jokingly, like at the academy, but I especially didn't like it now, when it had been done to me for real.

Warren had gone through the entire protocol—putting me against the car, frisking me, confiscating the SIG with a grunt, and slapping the cuffs on me before stuffing me in the backseat of the cruiser that was parked—with lights flashing—in Jackie's cinder lot. He left at a sedate pace, giving the locals who had piled out of the bar to watch a real nice view of me hunched over like any old crook. Tank and Buck Brower hooted and pointed me out to each other while Will looked on impassively, still smoking his cigarette. It was a novel experience, and I liked it even less than being cuffed.

We drove for fifteen minutes in silence, heading back toward the center of town. Warren took a few lefts and rights, though, until I was thoroughly lost, finally stopping in another dusty cinder parking lot. He shut the car off and turned around to look at me, with one arm flung over the seat. He didn't say anything for a minute, just stared at me with a sour expression, like he was rolling a lemon seed around in his mouth.

"You're a goddamned idiot, you know that?" he said finally. "There were only two ways that was going to end. Either I'd be trying to get someone to identify your body cuz no one would recognize you after the beating you were about to take. Or I'd be hauling you in for a quadruple homicide after you got done ventilating an entire generation of Browers."

I didn't say anything. I'd come to the same conclusion. Not my finest hour.

"What is it about 'not getting involved' you failed to understand?"

"Seemed like a good idea at the time," I said. "But I'm coming around to your way of thinking."

He shook his head. "You're not a cop anymore, Singer. This ain't your town and it ain't your place to go around trying to right wrongs or wrong rights or whatever the hell it is you're trying to do. You had your shot in DC and that was it."

"I'm not saying the way I handled things back there was all that bright," I said. "But there are still questions that need to be asked, Warren."

"No, there *ain't*," he said, exasperated. "Don't you get it? J.D. Hope got exactly what was coming to him. And the world is a better place for it. No one gives a good goddamn if he got whacked by some hit man from DC or Will Brower or the tooth fairy."

"His family does."

Warren groaned. "Dorothea Hope was so sick of him herself that she's probably the one who done it. And Mary Beth will forget the whole thing as soon as she gets back on the highway and points her car north. Hope was a waste of space and I'd shake the hand of the man who did him in if I didn't think it was useless trying to find the fucker."

"So, what happens now?"

He rolled out of the car instead of answering, then opened my door and helped me to my feet. He made a spinning motion with his hand. I turned around and he unlocked the cuffs. It was clichéd, but I rubbed my wrists. I couldn't help it.

"Here it comes," he said. "You ready?"

"The speech?"

He nodded. "You're goddamned right. Stop the amateur-hour bullshit or I'll run you in. This one's a courtesy. After tonight, you're out of aces."

"Why not dig up some answers instead, Warren? Why not give the family what it wants?"

"They already got their answers, dumbass. Just like you." He handed me back my SIG and climbed back in his car, leaving me standing there.

"Where are we?"

He pointed. "The Mosby is three miles that way."

"Don't want to give me a lift?"

"Why the hell do you think I drove out here?" he said. "This way I know you ain't heading back to Jackie's. It's gonna take you an hour to get back to your hotel."

"Great."

He shot me a look. "I'm not bullshitting you, Singer. If I see you around town, I'm slapping you with jaywalking, loitering, swearing in public, whatever it takes. Don't think I won't throw your ass in the can."

"How would I leave town, then?" I said. But he'd already pulled away.

CHAPTER SEVENTEEN

The phone woke me at six the next morning. I answered without opening my eyes. "Singer."

"Hope I'm not waking you." It was Chick Reyes.

"It's all right," I said. "I had to get up to answer the phone anyway."

"Well, you might want to rise and shine for real," he said. "Ginny Decker's trailer got firebombed this morning."

My eyes snapped open. "Tell me."

"S'all I know, compadre. I got a tip ten minutes ago."

"She alive?"

"Dunno," Chick said. "No one's been admitted to any local hospital for burns, I know that."

"I have to get out there," I said, swinging my legs over the side of the bed, then stopped as I remembered something. "Shit. You're on your way, right? Can you give me a ride? Or, uh, get me out to Jackie's bar?"

"Leave something behind, Singer?" Amusement colored his voice.

"You could say that."

"I'll pick you up in front of the Mosby in ten minutes."

A shower would have to wait. I stood, winced at the pain in my feet—three miles was a long way to walk—and did what I had to do in the bathroom. A change of clothes later and I felt just above subhuman, but that's as good as it was going to get, so I left the room and headed downstairs.

Chick was already in front of the Mosby as promised, idling a canary-yellow Camaro. A pair of fuzzy dice hung from the rearview mirror. His head was bent over some papers and one hand dangled outside the driver's-side window, as though still holding a cigarette. It wasn't six thirty yet, so the breeze was cool and the sun lit storefronts and windows in a cheerful light, but already I could tell it was going to be ninety-nine in the shade.

He raised a hand in greeting as I got close. I hopped in and he handed me a small coffee in a paper cup. I nodded my thanks, took the top off, and blew the steam away.

"Anything more over the scanner?" I asked, nodding to a little box that squawked and hissed. "Bodies? Arrests?"

He shook his head as he put the Camaro in gear and we took off, the muscle car's engine growling. "Not that I've heard. Cain's Crossing doesn't have a forensics or arson team, so they might be waiting for help to come over from Warrenton or from Richmond before they go tramping around."

"From what I've heard, there's one group that's good for it," I said.

"Yeah," Chick said, taking a turn smoothly. "Who's that?"

I glanced over. "The Brower brothers. Seems like they're the main force for evil in the area. Surprised you haven't heard of them."

"Oh, I know about those boys. They stir up trouble, make life miserable for some folks. But firebomb some lady's trailer?" He made a face, shook his head. "No way. They're just a bunch of local fuckups."

"That's all, huh?"

Chick glanced my way. "Someone get into a little trouble last night?"

"Sort of."

"Care to share? I like to hear about Anglos getting in trouble at bars."

I gave him the abbreviated version of my night on the town. He was quiet, listening intently as I spoke. His driving was precise and economical.

When I got to the point about provoking the three brothers, he laughed. "So, that's why you asked about the Browers. Some criminal syndicate, huh? A bunch of redneck brothers looking to kick some ass at a dive bar."

"Ginny Decker thought they were more than that and now her trailer's gone up in smoke."

He waved that away. "We don't know anything yet. By the way, I like your investigative style. Don't know anything? No problem. Just go to Jackie's and start calling people names."

I made a face. "I wanted to rattle some cages and see what fell out. Which was fine, while it lasted. I thought I had things under control until Will showed."

"He's hard-core, man," Chick said. "The only one of them who did real time."

"I figured as much from the prison ink," I said. "Who's this Jaybone guy with them?"

Chick shrugged. "Regulation-grade ass-kisser. Hit the scene maybe a year ago and started hanging around the brothers. He's just their kind of loser, though he doesn't have their reputation for busting skulls for fun. Oh, and he and J.D. got into a scrap when Hope came back from DC."

"He's the one J.D. hit with a bottle?" I asked.

"Yeah. Ginny tell you? They made their peace after that since they were both working for the Browers. Jay'd only been in good for a couple months when that all happened."

I nodded, but was quiet. Something Chick had said tickled the back of my brain, but I couldn't put a finger on it. Whatever it was sank back into the muck, however, as we pulled into Woodland Corner. The stink of burnt rubber and vinyl hung in the air and a blue haze sat over the top of the trailer park like a dark cloud. There were no sirens, but the flash of lights from fire trucks and police cruisers showed us the way.

We parked next to a white-sided mobile home a half dozen lots away that was succumbing to algae or moss or something green working its way up the walls. A middle-aged Latina was half in, half out of the door watching the action. She started to disappear inside when she saw us, but then Chick called to her in Spanish. She shook her head and slipped inside, shutting the door behind her.

"What was that about?" I asked.

He shrugged. "She's the one who phoned me about the fire. Guess she doesn't want to talk anymore."

"Hard to argue with that," I said, "when the reasons for not talking are floating in the air around you."

He grunted and we walked toward the blackened rubble that had been Ginny Decker's home. Hoses led from the fire trucks to the edge of a charred circle that still popped and hissed. Two cops and three firemen stood a discreet distance away, hands on hips, talking and occasionally shaking their head. Warren was one of the cops and I slowed, giving myself a chance to check the scene before I went toe-to-toe with him. Judging by what he was wearing—the same clothes I'd seen him in when he'd dropped me off the night before, now rumpled and askew—he'd clearly worked a double, at least. He'd be tired and angry and ready to blame me for all kinds of things. And maybe he'd be right.

There were none of the witnesses or bystanders you'd expect to see hanging around the scene, though maybe they'd come and gone since there was very little to see that wasn't charred, stinking, and over two feet tall. None of it was recognizable, though a slightly larger lump might've been a refrigerator and some twisted metal that looked like a snake's nest might've been what was left of a set of box springs. The fire, though obviously intense enough to have melted almost the entire trailer, had been contained. So, by some miracle, the propane tank that had probably heated the trailer hadn't blown. In fact, the black smear that marked the fire didn't spread more than a few feet away from the plot in any direction, and none of the other mobile homes had been touched.

I felt a lump twisting in my gut. Ginny Decker had been alive this time yesterday, hoping to go unnoticed by me, by the Browers, by whoever had killed her ex-husband. I'd told her I'd be able to do something about the people or person who had killed J.D., with the implication that I could keep them from doing the same to her. Not only had that not been the case, there was no way to escape the fact that it was probably my visit that had caused her death.

I didn't have long to think about it, though. One of the cops nudged Warren, whose expression turned nearly as black as the smudge on the ground when he saw me. He stomped over to the two of us, then let me have it.

"Happy, you son of a bitch?" His face was flushed and blotchy and a line of perspiration dotted his upper lip. "Anything else you want to cross off your list? Want to blow up a hospital, maybe shoot a couple of orphans on the way?"

"Was Ginny in there?"

"What's it to you?"

"*Was she in there?*"

"What the hell do you think?" he asked. "Lady's trailer goes up in smoke at six in the morning, she's probably in there."

"So you don't know," I said, feeling the first stirring of relief. Even if it was faint.

"When we find her body—if we can tell it apart from all that—your ass is mine," he said, putting a finger in my face.

"I didn't set this fire, Warren."

"You might as well have," he said. "In twenty-four hours you've done more to wreck this town than anyone since the goddamn Civil War."

"You find a body, Detective?" Chick asked.

"You go to hell, Reyes," Warren said, his eyes flicking over to the reporter. "Singer wouldn't have had a clue to come here except for you."

"What you mean is, the Brower brothers wouldn't have had a reason to torch Ginny Decker's trailer except I had the guts to talk to her about J.D.," I said. "Still, it's a pretty important question, Warren. If there's no body, we're talking destruction of property. But if Ginny's at the bottom of that pile of ash, then we're talking homicide. Even the Cain's Crossing PD could make a case from that, I hope."

Warren's face purpled and I was pretty sure he was going to take a swing. And, if he did, I'd just have to take it, because I'd be lucky to avoid a night in jail with what I'd said already. But instead of smacking me in the mouth, he stomped away, jerking a thumb for me to follow him. Chick started to follow, too, but Warren barked, "Not you."

Thirty feet away from the scene, Warren stopped and rounded on me. "You dumbass. We know damn well the Browers did this. And loads more over the years. We're not all hayseed morons, no matter what you think after your thirty years in Wash-ing-ton Dee-See."

"So, prove it," I said. "I'm asking questions that a freshman in criminology would want answers to. What's the big deal?"

He shook his head. "Haven't you been listening? Remember that little bit about how we don't have the luxury of a twenty-man department to take this on? That ring a bell? We have to go slow and do things right."

"This isn't enough to get you started? You've got a clear case of arson. I mean, that's smoke I'm smelling, right?"

He poked a finger at me. "This ain't a case we can make a mistake on. If we put Buck away but not Will or Will and not Tank, then whoever's left is going to burn down this town like they did Ginny Decker's trailer. If one goes, we gotta make sure they all go."

"So start the process. Nail them for J.D., trace this fire back to them, start racking up charges," I said, confused. Warren was making excuses. And not very good ones. "You know they're good for some of it, probably all of it. Do your damn job."

"You want to eat your teeth, boy, you keep telling me how to do my work."

I took a breath. "Fine. How about showing a little bit of effort, then?"

"Who said some of us ain't trying, Singer?" he said. Close up, I could see bags under his eyes and a slackness to his face that spoke of sleepless nights. "Maybe some of us are trying to do it the right way."

"What do you mean, 'some of us'?"

Warren started to lay into me, then caught himself. "If it was any of your damn business, I'd tell you. If you've got a brain in your head, you'll drop it."

"So, you're not going to lock me up?" I asked.

He sighed and took his hat off to wipe his brow. Some of his anger seemed to have fizzled away. "You know as well as I do there's nothing to lock you up for. You start any more trouble and I'll find something. But I would appreciate the hell out of it if you would just go home, Singer. I can tell you that going around pissing people off don't make it any easier for us. And now a good woman is dead, thanks to you."

Warren turned away and headed back to the site. Chick had gotten statements from the firefighters and remaining cop while Warren and I had our come-to-Jesus moment, so it seemed like a good time to make an exit. I retreated to the far side of the burn site, staring at the grotesque pile of slag. The air still wobbled and curved from the heat rising from the fire, a testament to how intense the blaze had been. It was hard to believe that the body of the woman I'd talked to yesterday was intertwined with the industrial mess in front of me.

"Hey," a voice said. I looked up. Chick was looking at me, eyebrows raised. "You all there?"

"Yeah."

He raised his notebook. "All done. Want to vamoose?"

We were quiet as we walked back to his Camaro. I got in, still thinking. Something about the burn site was bothering me.

"Looked like you struck a chord with Shane," Chick said, interrupting my thoughts as he backed the car up and pulled onto the road. He reached into a pocket, took out his tin of mints, and popped one in his mouth as he drove. The mint clacked against his teeth. "You long-lost brothers or something?"

I shook my head. Whatever was bothering me floated away. "Was it the screaming in my face or the fact he almost took a swing that gave it away?"

"Actually it was the fact he even talked to you," Chick said. "All I ever get from Shane is a dirty look and a 'Talk to Palmer, Reyes.' Then again, I can't get in his face like you did, either. I guess that's how you get people to open up. I mean, it worked at Jackie's, right?"

"You have to try. You never know what happens when you push people, make them uncomfortable."

"Sometimes you get your dick shot off."

"That's true. Good thing I haven't needed mine in a while."

"Mother of God, don't tell me that," he said, making a face. He rubbed the fuzzy dice hanging from the mirror. "You might be bad luck. It's hard enough to get laid in this town without you killing my chances."

"The Latin lover thing isn't doing the trick for you?"

"You've been to Jackie's," he said, glancing over. "What do you think?"

I thought of the all-white, nearly all-male clientele at the roadside bar. "I guess you swarthy types aren't considered the marrying kind around here."

"Not really, fucker."

"Try shaving the Pancho Villa mustache off. You might get somewhere."

"Like I'm going to take advice from an old man who doesn't even use his junk," Chick said, but he straightened as he checked himself in the mirror, running a hand over his mustache. "Why don't you just donate it to science?"

I've already made my contribution, I wanted to say. But I said, "It was just a thought."

He grumbled for a half minute, then, "Seriously, did Warren give you anything?"

"No. They're not even sure she was there," I said, wanting to believe it.

"But she hasn't called? I mean, your house goes up in flames, you're going to show up or call the cops or something."

"Yeah," I said, shifting in my seat. "In any case, kind of puts the Browers in a new light."

"You think they did this?" he asked, jerking a thumb behind us.

"Well, yeah. Unless she really pissed somebody off at work. It's pretty obvious, don't you think?"

He shrugged. "Seems outside of their comfort zone. Punch a nosy ex-cop's lights out in a bar? Sure. First-degree murder? I can't see it."

I thought of Will Brower's stony look as he'd slapped the cue stick in my palm and had no trouble seeing him tossing a Molotov cocktail on a mobile home. But, to be agreeable, I just said, "Either way, Warren will know more when the fire marshal's report comes out."

He made a face. "In three weeks? How does that help me now?"

"You'll think of something, Chick," I said. "There's a lot of news to cover in the world."

"That's a nice thought. Not sure how it helps me pay my bills, though."

We pulled into Jackie's gravel lot. The bar was like an old hooker, looking even more forlorn and weathered in the daylight than it had last night. My car was the only one in the lot. Seeing as how I'd essentially left it in the hands of the Browers five minutes after pissing them all off, I half expected it to look a lot like Ginny Decker's trailer, but it appeared to be untouched. Miracles do happen.

"Here you go, Singer," Chick said, putting the Camaro in park. "Keep your nose clean."

"How am I going to do that? I thought you wanted to get a story out of this."

"I do. But I need something longer than an obituary," he said, then pulled away.

V.

Stan is sweating. His b.o. and the smell of stale coffee are stifling in the car and I crack the window to pull in some fresh air. What comes in, though, isn't much better and I put the window back up.

"So, you got a tip fingering J.D. for all the shootings," I say. "And that he held on to the gun."

"Yeah."

I take shallow breaths. "Any trouble getting the warrant?"

"Nope. Signed, sealed, and delivered," Stan says, patting a breast pocket. The action seems to remind him of something and he reaches in for his tube of lip balm.

"Got any doubts?"

"Nope. We tear his place apart, find the gun, then put this piece of shit away."

I open my mouth to say something, but drop it. If Stan's made up his mind, nothing I say is going to change it. We wait in silence for the MPDC badges that'll be our backup on the warrant. There's not much to see in Southeast that I haven't seen a thousand times before. People, mostly black, going about their business. Trying to make ends meet in a hurry. Quick word to a neighbor or a scowl for a car running a red light as they try to cross the street. There's a special on chicken thighs at the Safeway. Three guys sit *on a low wall on the street side of the store, elbows touching knees, passing a bag back and forth.*

"My grandson," Stan says out of nowhere, "will be starting second grade this year."

"That's great," I say out of habit. When family comes up, responses are limited and automatic.

"He's four months older than the little girl this punk shot over in Fort Dupont."

"Where's he go to school?"

"Not around here," Stan says. "If my daughter tried to raise her kids in DC, I'd put them all in a truck and drive them to Iowa. This place is a fucking hole."

"It's got its perks."

"Like what? Getting shot in your living room?"

"Museums, galleries, theaters. Birthplace of a nation. The world's capital."

He makes a noise. "DC is a fucking hole and you know it, Marty. MPDC is just here to kill the rats and take out the garbage. And that's what we're going to do with J.D. Hope."

A cruiser comes down the street and we drop our dead-end conversation to get out and meet the two cops. Introductions all around, then we cross the street to bang on the ground-floor apartment door of a sagging redbrick town house. Peripherally, I see the winos in front of Safeway get to their feet, casual, and ease down the street away from us.

In a minute, the door opens and J.D. Hope stands there in boxers and a tank top and widening eyes. Stan explains what we're doing there, flashes the warrant. Over J.D.'s protests, we muscle our way into his apartment. It smells of corn dogs and chili. A cardboard case of Bud Light, open and spilling beers, sits on a kitchen counter. One of the beat cops moves J.D. off to the living room and watches him while the three of us each take a room. Stan heads back to the bedroom. I snap on a pair of plastic gloves and start sifting through the coins and receipts and envelopes stuffed into plastic cups or lying on side tables, the debris of a listless life. J.D.'s time in DC has been short and unproductive. I'm done in five minutes and head back to the bedroom.

"You need a hand?" I ask as I walk into the room. "There's nothing out there."

Stan is approaching the far side of a rumpled double bed. He looks startled, like he just fell from the sky. "Sure. Take the closet?"

I open the flimsy doors and start going through the handful of T-shirts and jeans hanging there. Most of the clothes have been worn and are on the floor. I'm glad for the gloves as I gingerly pick up the clothes, search them, and drop them in a pile by the door.

After a minute, Stan says, "You want to give me a hand?" He points to the headboard of the bed.

As we move it, I hear the muffled thud of something hitting the floor. I kneel and reach into the gap we've created between the wall and the bed. Something heavy wrapped in a towel. I grab it and pull my hand out. I unwind the towel carefully, exposing a handgun, a chunky 9mm.

"Well, lookee that," Stan says. He holds his hand out and I give it to him carefully. "Looks like a Hi-Point. Cheap little sucker, but good enough for the job, I suppose."

"Not much of a magazine," I say, thinking of the spread of bullet holes peppering our first scene.

Stan gives me a look. "Ever hear of reloading, Marty?"

We walk out to the living room, Stan holding the gun in both hands like an offering. J.D. looks at us, a carefully fabricated expression of boredom on his face replaced in a flash by one of disbelief when he sees the gun.

"Want to tell us about this?" Stan asks.

And the protests begin.

CHAPTER EIGHTEEN

After Chick drove off, I got in my car and thought about my next move.

Maybe Chick was right and the Browers were just a bunch of big troublemaking goofballs and nothing more. Maybe Shane Warren and the Cain's Crossing PD had everything under control, despite my feelings to the contrary. Maybe Ginny had been wrong and J.D. hadn't been involved in anything criminal. Maybe he'd been killed by a lunatic passing through town. Maybe he'd tripped backwards and crushed his own skull on the plywood end table by the bed. Maybe Ginny Decker's trailer had spontaneously combusted while she'd gone on vacation.

I kicked the floor of the car in frustration. Maybes didn't get me anywhere. I'd learned as a cop that there was rarely any "maybe" about homicide. The question was, how did I make the maybes go away?

I didn't have any solid sources of information. No snitches, no leads. The cops were a dead end. Chick seemed as clueless as I was. A frontal assault like my stunt at Jackie's had produced less information than it had headaches and potential jail time.

Speaking of headaches, maybe I could beat someone up for information. The spinster managing the Mosby might know something. Or, hey, maybe there was another bar in town that I could go to and learn something interesting this time before I got thrown through a window? Throw a punch, dump a beer on someone, smash a bottle over somebody's head—

A bottle?

I put the car in gear and headed for town.

Over the course of the next seven hours, I experienced more of Cain's Crossing than I'd ever wanted to know.

I cruised every back street and alley, every fast-food joint and gas station, every driveway and auto repair shop and parking lot looking for a red pickup truck in need of some cosmetic work. I learned that the lights on Maple were timed their entire length while the ones on Walnut were not. Intrepid detecting informed me that there were five salons in town but only one gym, leading me to believe one gender valued its appearance more than the other, which wasn't really news. I noticed that drivers in Cain's Crossing drove at approximately half the speed that DC drivers did, causing me to white-knuckle the steering wheel. I saw mothers with strollers, old-timers with walkers, young studs in hot rods. I even saw a Cain's Crossing PD cruiser with what looked like Shane Warren's profile behind the wheel. I pulled a quick right turn and got out of his line of sight.

I was coming up empty and was about to cash it all in when I talked myself into doing one last run along Market Street. It was a main thoroughfare that would eventually lead back to my hotel anyway, so it didn't really cost me anything to try.

And there it was. A beat-up old truck next to five or six other cars in a grocery store parking lot. A huge red-and-white sign over the entrance spelled out "Dollar-Sav." I whipped into an empty space and headed inside.

It was small as modern groceries go, hardly big enough to fit an airplane. The produce section was as wide as my two outspread arms and from the entrance, I could see down almost every aisle. A teenage girl with frizzy hair and too much aqua-blue eye shadow leaned against the only open register. Her head was bent, examining bright orange nails, while she talked to the bagger, a nerdy-looking teen with greasy black hair, wearing a maroon apron. He gave a start as I walked in, as if he wasn't supposed to be talking on the job. Or maybe the cashier was the high school football captain's girlfriend.

The one aisle that I couldn't see was marked "Beer and Spirits" on the end. I had a pretty good idea where my target was. I worked my way over to the beer aisle and found my man squatting, one hand on the shelf above him for support, while he compared prices on the cases of cheap beer stacked on the floor. He looked up as I walked toward him, did the classic double take, and slowly got to his feet. His stance was casual, confident. No fear. I wondered if he was packing.

"Hey there, Jay-bone," I said. "Remember me?"

He took his aviators off and hung them from his shirt collar. Lines in his face and blue smudges under the eyes aged him ten years.

"How you doin', chief," he said, cracking a smile. "You interested in shit beer, too, or you still mad about the scene out at Jackie's? Looking to get even?"

"Don't try stealing the beer and we won't have a problem."

He snorted. "I ain't Dwayne. I pay for what I drink."

"Glad to hear it," I said. "Actually, I just thought I'd ask you a couple questions, see if you're more, uh, forthcoming without the Three Stooges hanging around."

"Yeah? About what?"

"I'm curious. I heard you and J.D. had your differences when he first came back home, but were able to patch things up since you both ended up working for the Browers. But what, exactly, is so worth doing that you're willing to play nice with a guy who hit you with a beer bottle?"

He rubbed the side of his neck, maybe in subconscious memory. "Jobs are tough to come by in Cain's Crossing, chief. You take work when you can get it."

"Things tough enough to take it away from someone else?"

He laughed, a short bark. "You think I wasted J.D.? Because of a bar fight? Over some work? Sorry, chief. I got better things to do."

"I don't know," I said. "It makes a kind of sense, if you ask me. Payback for getting smacked, plus narrowing down the competition."

He shook his head. "Try again."

"All right. Maybe the Browers didn't like something about J.D. You're their go-to guy. You'd put J.D. in the ground if Will Brower told you, wouldn't you?"

"Bud, I know this is going to sound like it's straight out of a movie, but you don't know what you're fucking with," he said. "Don't get caught up in something you can't get out of."

"See, you told me there's something to look out for," I said. "Now I'm curious."

He shook his head, as if he were more sad than anything. "There's nothing to look into. And why would you want to? What's it to you?"

"Let's just say I have a habit of wanting to do the right thing. Finding out who killed J.D. is one of those things. And if the Browers get a bloody nose in the process, that's okay with me. And they're not the only ones. Maybe you're the one who's caught."

Jay slipped his aviators back on again, transforming himself into someone cooler and more dangerous. "You're not a cop, right? I mean we got that out of the way when Deputy Dawg cuffed you and put you in the back of the squad car. So I'm pretty sure I don't have to stand here and shoot the breeze with you all day while you try to pin J.D.'s murder on me. Now, if you'll excuse me."

He grabbed two boxes of Milwaukee's Best and headed down the aisle, brushing past me on the way.

"Jay?" I called. He turned. "You hear what happened to Ginny Decker this morning?"

He waited, motionless.

"Someone burnt her trailer to the ground. Nothing's more than ankle-high by now. You willing to take the fall for that, too, when the cops finger the Browers for it? You willing to go to jail for something you didn't do?"

He stared at me for a second, then shook his head and kept walking.

CHAPTER NINETEEN

I hadn't learned anything from Jay-bone, although hopefully I'd given him some food for thought. It wasn't much, but maybe I could drive a wedge between him and the Browers that could be exploited later.

There'd better be something. Until something blossomed on that front, I had nothing to go on. All I could do was go back over J.D.'s paperwork and hope for a break. Mary Beth and I had read through it once already, of course, but finding J.D.'s prescription and the surprise behind it had put a different spin on things. Maybe there was another nugget of information if I dove in again. First time through, eyes glazed over, numbers crowded together, information was lost. A fresh going-over always had the chance of turning something up.

I headed back to my hotel room and began laying out all the paperwork from the super pile, deconstructing it into their smaller groups across my bed. Jotting down dates, amounts, and locations, I started with the receipts and any bills I could find, then moved to the miscellaneous lists and one-off pieces of paper. Small piles became larger ones as I cataloged each scrap, pouring myself into the mundane details of the paper trail. The world outside faded away. The sun set, throwing cherry-red slabs of light through the windows that I only noticed when I raised my head to give my eyes a break. The sound of traffic swelled and relaxed as regular folks quit work, went to dinner, and abandoned the street. Occasionally, a random honk or shout would reach me over the rattling of the air conditioner, but soon the sounds stopped altogether. It wasn't until I found myself holding a piece of paper two inches from my nose that I realized I'd worked well into the night.

I glanced at my watch, wincing at the zing that went through my neck. After nine. I yawned and fell back against the pillows, looking over the carnage of paper strewn across my bed. The only thing that stood out this time was the bank envelope that I had originally thought held sample checks and deposit slips. Mixed in with them were three deposit slip receipts. They'd been for deposits made in February, April, and May, each for five hundred dollars. Nothing on the slips gave even a hint where the cash had come from.

A deep growl from my stomach surprised me. I hadn't been truly hungry for a long time and it had been even longer since my body had independently let me know it. I found myself inordinately pleased at the thought. When cancer takes such simple pleasures as eating away from you, it's a treat to be reminded of even the most basic needs. I tossed the bank statements on the bed without a second thought and went to find some grub.

The streets were quiet and clean and dark. Traffic was nonexistent and the two or three forlorn stoplights I could see went through their green-yellow-red loop, unneeded. A dog barked a few blocks away and I listened in wonder when I heard actual crickets. It was after dark in the middle of the week and people were already long at home. They'd eaten a meal with their family, watched and laughed at their favorite sitcom, and gone to bed.

I wasn't envious. I'd spent most of my life in isolation of one kind or another, and it'd been thirty years since I would've considered going to sleep at nine and rising at six a normal routine. But I could still feel melancholy without wanting to trade places and so I did, sauntering down the dusky street, finding my way by sodium streetlights, past Lula Belle's—closed for the evening—until I came across a late-night eatery.

"America's Best Chili—Easy as ABC!" Glaring white light spilled onto the sidewalk from the diner's windows and, combined with an aqua-and-white-tile décor, it had all the charm of an operating room, but it was either chili or a cold glass of water back at the hotel.

I went in, ordered from a silent man in a stained apron, and had a steaming bowl in my hands seconds later. Tucked in a back corner booth with my chili and corn bread, I let my mind wander a bit on what I'd learned so far . . . and quickly decided that I was more at sea now than I'd been when I'd stopped at the foot of the highway billboard.

Take the money, for instance. Three months of the same amount in deposits over two quarters implied a routine payment, like a salary or a disbursement or a payoff. No one had mentioned J.D. having a job, and ex-cons who'd served time for manslaughter normally didn't find employment that easily. He wasn't being paid disability or didn't have a government check coming in the mail—surely Mary Beth or Ginny would've told me. He'd been working for the Browers, of course, so payoffs seemed the most likely source, but even in Cain's Crossing, five hundred dollars a month was chicken feed. And how many meth dealers pay their flunkies exact, consistent amounts on a regular schedule? Dealers didn't run payroll.

I drummed my fingers on the table. Maybe the amount wasn't so small. I was used to the obscene mounds of cash I'd seen when we'd busted DC crack dealers, stacked on kitchen tables like paperback books. Maybe crime didn't pay out here in the boondocks. And J.D. was, despite being a native, the new kid on the block. Maybe the Browers had paid him in dribs and drabs until they felt he'd proven himself.

Maybe, maybe, maybe. The problem with the money thing was that I didn't have enough data. I needed more deposit slips or access to his account if I wanted to get any kind of traction on the issue. I sighed and pushed away the unfinished chili, full on food, if not answers. It was probably more than I'd eaten in one sitting in a year's time.

Hopefully, I wouldn't pay for it later. I left two bucks on the table, paid the tab, and left, distracted and thinking hard.

The streets were still dark and serene. The dog had ceased barking, but no one had told the crickets to stop. I walked along, enjoying the silence until the peace was interrupted by the far-off, ripsaw sound of a hemi cutting through the air. Someone letting loose on a backcountry road, trying to set a land-speed record. The sound held on for about ten seconds, then faded in a burble of downshifting gears. Night noises covered by the industrial ruckus came back: the crickets, the buzz of a neon sign, footsteps in the distance.

Footsteps?

My pulse bumped up a notch, but I kept my pace measured and steady for a minute, trying to pick up the sound again. The idiots with the hemi had turned around, however, and were trying to beat their previous record, coming in my direction. Even from half a mile away, all sounds around me were obliterated by the scream of 400 horsepower. I allowed myself a quick glance over the shoulder and, when I didn't see anyone, slipped into the doorway of an old-timey drugstore, fronted in glass with wide, swirling gold letters on the door. I backed into a wedge of shadow and slipped my SIG out, waiting.

The roar of the hemi disappeared, hopefully for good. I cupped a hand around one ear and tilted my head this way and that, trying to pick up any stray sounds. Crickets. And neon signs. And the dog again.

I stayed that way for ten minutes, trying to outwait my tail. If there had been one. The sounds had been so innocuous and I'd been so distracted that now I doubted myself. I tensed as an approaching car was preceded by the hum of tires on asphalt. An old man driving a brown Chevy Impala—hands at ten and two, head barely clearing the steering wheel—cruised down the street at a stately twenty miles per hour. He passed my doorway without so much as blinking. Then, looking neither left nor right, neither slowing nor speeding up, he sailed through the red light at the intersection.

I counted to five hundred for good measure. No sounds, no cars, no bodies to match the footsteps. Finally, I slipped the SIG back in its holster, shook my hands and feet, which had gone numb, and continued back to the hotel. The night clerk was awake and I gave her a courteous nod as I headed up the stairs to my room. I was tired and cranky and a little on edge. My stamina wasn't the best it had ever been, I was getting so paranoid that I was hearing sounds, and I wasn't sure I had any business stirring up trouble in this little town anymore. I unlocked the door, threw the keys on the desk—then fumbled for my gun as the bathroom door opened. A figure sauntered into the shaft of street light coming through the window and my finger squeezed down on the trigger . . . then I relaxed, easing out of my shooter's stance and dropping the bead. But I didn't put my gun away.

"That ain't no way to greet the dead," Ginny Decker said, walking toward me with a sad smile on her face.

CHAPTER TWENTY

"Surprised, Mr. Detective?" she asked, pushing papers out of the way and sitting on the corner of my bed. Her voice was uneven and her movements overly precise. She was trying very hard to maintain a thin, coy look over the top of a deep pocket of fear. And failing.

I stared at her as my mind raced to put things together. A tickle I'd felt at the trailer park blossomed into a full-fledged deduction; things clicked into place. "The propane tank."

She nodded but looked worried. "You figured it out?"

"I saw that the tank was missing from your trailer, but I didn't think through why." I slid my gun back in its holster. "You didn't want an explosion that would hurt your neighbors."

"Didn't look like an accident, huh?"

"Your trailer had burnt to the ground evenly. That only happens if it's lit in more than one place—not just one end where, say, someone might've chucked a gallon of gas on it. It wasn't the Browers. You set that fire."

She bit her lip. "If it was that easy to piece together, then I don't got much time."

"You can probably relax. I imagine I'm the only one in this county that's gone through FEMA arson training. The locals might figure it out in a week when they go through the scene and don't find your body, but not before."

She shook her head. "I can't take the chance."

"So . . . you didn't torch your trailer for the insurance money, I guess?"

She put a hand to her mouth and shook her head again, looking lost. I walked over to the desk and turned on the table lamp, then pulled out the chair from the desk and settled in. "Was I right? You didn't want to hurt anyone else, so you . . . what? Drained the lines and unhooked the propane tank?"

She nodded.

"You did it to beat the Browers to the punch and maybe hamstring them with an arson investigation. To give you time to run?"

"All I did was get to it before they did," she said in a whisper. "Couple hours after you and I talked, Tank and Buck came by the trailer park. I heard that damn huge truck of theirs on the road and hid in a neighbor's house while they pounded on my door."

"So what are you doing in my hotel room? Why aren't you hauling ass out of the county?"

She plucked at the strings of her fraying cutoff jeans. "I am. Everything I own is in the trunk of a car down on the corner. By this time tomorrow, I'll be in the west end of Kentucky."

"But?"

She looked at me, her eyes meeting mine. "You said you owed it to J.D. to find who killed him. What happened to him."

I nodded.

"No one else gives a shit, which means you're the only one who can hurt whoever killed him. I want to tell you everything I know before I get the hell out of Cain's Crossing."

"Okay," I said.

"There was things going on, reasons for J.D. to come back. And something important about him I want you to know."

"His ALS?"

"How the hell . . . ?" she said, stunned, then glanced at the papers on the bed. "Oh."

"I found a prescription in a box of stuff from the hotel room he was staying in. Ran it down, found his doctor, and got the news," I said.

She gave a little moan and started to cry. I gave her time. I'm lousy at comforting people. I know it helps to pat a shoulder or make the right noises, but I can't quite bring myself to do it. I suffer in silence and assume others want to, too.

When her sobs died down, I said, "It must've been hard."

She got up and went into the bathroom, where I heard her clean herself up. When she came back, she sat down and took a deep breath that caught in her throat. "He didn't tell me at first. Didn't want to scare me, he said. But the truth is, *he's* the one didn't want to be scared. Alone. Sick. Fresh out of jail. Disowned by his own mother. His sister a million miles away."

I didn't say anything.

"When we talked the other day, I told you he rolled in, all cocky and full of himself. And he was. Same old charmer, saying things like 'My, you look good enough to eat, Ginny Decker,'" she said, eyes unfocused, remembering. "A week later, he was crying in my arms, telling me he didn't want to die."

The chair popped and squeaked as I shifted in my seat, uncomfortable. Her eyes gained their focus and nailed me. "J.D. was dying. But he told me he didn't want to go having done nothing with his life. He wanted to do some good in the world."

"He said that?"

She nodded. "He broke down once or twice, when things got to be too much. The rest of the time, he was driven by something. He asked special for that medicine from the doctor so he could hang on. Said he had a mission."

"But you don't know what he was doing? What the mission was?"

She shook her head. "He wouldn't tell me. But if it wasn't something to do with the Brower boys, what else is there?"

"Do you know what he did for them?"

"No. I don't know. He never wanted me to know too much, as if that would protect me. I know they was impressed with him doing jail time and all. They must've figured he'd made some powerful connections they could use him for."

"Browers are cooking meth? For sure?"

She nodded. "Everyone knows. They used to be happy growing pot, but then meth's all you heard about starting a couple years back."

"And they wanted J.D. to help them make it in the big city?"

She shrugged, palms up. "Only thing that makes sense."

I chewed on that for a second. "This mission of his. Was he getting close, do you think?"

Wiping a tear away, she said, "I don't know. Every time I asked him, he would just shake his head and crack a joke. But if he wasn't close to doing them some damage, why'd they kill him?"

I nodded, paused, then said, "Ginny, one of the things I found in the paperwork was a steady payment of five hundred bucks a month. Was that coming from the Browers?"

She shrugged. "I don't know what they paid him. He gave me what he could to help with the trailer and I know that motel room he kept cost him, but he never told me where his money came from."

"Did he ever say he thought the Browers were on to him?"

"No. But something he said stuck with me, something he let slip once or twice."

"What's that?"

"A few weeks after he came home and got in tight with those crooks, he said those boys couldn't find their way out of a paper bag."

"I think I would agree."

She shook her head, frustrated. "No, it was more than that. There's someone else involved, he said. Someone in charge."

"Who?"

"I don't think he knew. And he never told me who he thought it might be. But he told me he was getting closer to finding out. J.D. wasn't no rocket scientist, but even he could think circles around those boys. He was due to move up. But whoever this boss was, he was scared of him. So I am, too."

Ginny stood and walked over to me, swaying as she moved. She leaned over, kissed my forehead, then put her face next to mine and whispered in my ear, "Whoever it was, he took my J.D. away, mister. He took my heart away. When you find him, pay him back for me, won't you?"

CHAPTER
TWENTY-ONE

Ten minutes after Ginny slipped out, I cleaned myself up and packed both my modest travel bag and the box of J.D.'s papers. I tidied up the room, put everything on the bed ready to go, and checked my watch. It was just shy of eleven when I left my room and padded down to the second floor.

I took my time in the corridor, checking for lights under doors and other signs of life. But I'd already glanced at the registry at the front desk and was pretty sure what I'd find: a whole lot of nothing. I went to what I deemed to be the least likely room to choose—not near the stairs, end of the hall, or a corner room—pulled a few tools from a back pocket, and was inside in twenty seconds.

The room was a twin to mine, except that the window was pointed toward the back of the Mosby, with a view of a brick wall across the alley. Harsh sodium lamps somewhere in the alley lit the wall a sterile yellow. A queen bed, a decrepit desk, and a rickety chair comprised the extent of the furniture. Stale smells of old cigarette smoke and aging linen hung in the air. I padded over to the window and peered out. A fire escape was just outside the window, but it was only a ten- or twelve-foot drop in any case. Just what I wanted for either a quick escape or a back entrance.

Snooping turned up a complimentary copy of the *Sentinel*, with Chick's stories all over it, lying on the desk. I skimmed it by the light coming through the window. It was a July issue, indicating exactly what I'd hoped, that the place hadn't been rented or even cleaned in weeks. Perfect.

When people were willing to torch their own homes and leave town to escape the notice of a gang of crooks, things were getting dicey. And, whether she'd known somebody at the front desk or had found some other way in, it had been child's play for Ginny to get into my room. Which meant, next time, it might be Will Brower with a pool cue sitting in the shadows.

So it was time to relocate, albeit not far away. Switching to a different room in the same hotel wasn't much of a ruse, but it would let me sleep tonight. And if I planned to keep plugging away at J.D.'s murder, I was going to need plenty of rest—and not wonder if someone was going to cave my skull in while I slept.

One quick trip was all it took to move my stuff into the room. I didn't plan to turn on any lights, but I jammed a towel under the door just to be sure, then put the desk chair under the knob. Not much in the way of security, but at least it would make noise if anyone tried to break in. I took two Advil, turned the sound on my cell phone off, and crawled into bed. If the bad guys could find me after all those precautions, they deserved to get me.

On the way to breakfast the next morning, my phone buzzed in my pocket. I snatched at the phone, then glanced at the screen. It was Sam.

"Hey, Sam. Got something for me?"

"Yes and no," he said. His pencil tapped a staccato beat in the background. "You got some time?"

"Nothing but," I said. "Lay it on me."

"Okay, first thing. Neither of the DEA boys in Warrenton or Richmond want to talk to me."

"What, they're not picking up the phone?"

"No, they answer. But when I ask for a favor or some info, I usually get it. This time, I gave them a ring, asked some questions, and got a promise for a conference call that never happened. When I tried to follow up on *that*, I got dropped like I was trying to sell them real estate. Voice mail, phone tag, silence."

"That old interdepartmental cooperation thing isn't going very far, then?"

"It's going nowhere. So, I decided to do an end run and start doing some digging myself."

"Here comes the good news, I hope?"

"Yeah," he said. *Tap, tap, tap.* "Let's back up. What do you know about meth production?"

"Some," I said, casting my mind back. "I took some crossover training in Vice. High points, mostly. Not all of it stuck. The drug-motivated murders I saw were from crack, not meth."

"Want a crash course?"

"Couldn't hurt."

"Okay, you want to make meth, you need three ingredients. Pseudoephedrine, anhydrous ammonia, and lithium. I'm not going to bore you with how it all works together, but if you're missing one of those three, you don't have meth, you've got junk."

"Uh-huh."

"Pseudoephedrine's regulated. It's why you get tackled coming out of a Rite Aid with more than two boxes of cold medicine. The anhydrous ammonia is watched, too, but you can get it almost anywhere because it's what industrial farms use to fertilize crops with. So the guys who bake this stuff can find tanker trucks of it on farms, just sitting there waiting to be grabbed if the farmers don't lock it up."

"Dangerous?"

"The ammonia is dangerous to handle, though not volatile by itself. But if you make a mistake mixing it with the last ingredient, lithium—and you happen to be understaffed in the brain cell department—you can have an explosion, a fire, or a chemical disaster."

"Explains the rash of booms out in Wisconsin and Iowa."

"Right."

"So, the lithium," I said. "Where do they get that?"

"You won't believe this. Batteries."

"Batteries?"

"Not the regular kind. You can't buy enough store-bought batteries to extract sufficient lithium. So—you'll love this—one source is to break into the backup control systems at railroad crossings."

"Because the switch boxes need to be reliable and last a long time . . ." I said.

". . . so they're powered by lithium batteries," Sam finished. "Huge ones that supply enough lithium to make batches and batches of meth."

"But, without the batteries at the switch, the trains wreck, right?"

"The nice junkies make it obvious they've broken into the cases and stolen the batteries so that the railroad people will know and replace them before anything bad happens. The assholes lock the boxes like they were so they'll have more lead time to run."

"What happens when a train derails because of these guys?"

"If someone dies, it gets prosecuted as a homicide. Murder one."

"Not much of a silver lining, but it's something," I said. "So the ammonia is easy to get if you've got the guts to steal it, the lithium is there for the taking with a little bit of effort. That leaves . . ."

"The pseudoephedrine. Suzie. It's a synthetic drug itself, so it's hard to come by."

I searched my memory of trainings from years gone by. "Most of it comes up from Mexico?"

"Mostly. The smugglers get caught ninety percent of the time, so the border patrol is snatching most of the pseudoephedrine coming over the border. But production of it in China and other parts of Asia is on the rise and it dwarfs the amounts that the Mexicans can make. The stuff gets sent over here in shipping containers. We still catch most of it, mainly on the West Coast. It sucked when China beat out Mexico as the main source, but we're on top of it. It hasn't been easy, but the whole market is being taken away."

"Since production gets more difficult if you can't get all your ingredients from robbing a farmer or knocking over a railroad switch box."

"Right. These guys still need immense quantities of pseudoephedrine if they want to actually deal. When they only have small amounts of material, they're reduced to using this penny-ante method called one-pot, where you take bits of pseudoephedrine from legally bought allergy medicine to make tiny batches of meth. Get enough junkies and dealers and losers to do one-pot for you and you're a medium-level meth dealer."

"But not really enough to make it lucrative."

"Gold star for you," Sam said. "So that's the background. Meth production has been falling thanks to the wipeout on pseudoephedrine. And the fact that it's hard as hell to make any money using the one-pot method."

"Okay."

"The only place meth production's been holding steady is New Mexico, Arizona, Texas, where enough Mexican pseudoephedrine still makes it across the border to make it worthwhile despite the busts. Eventually, the product travels east, and we make our arrests, but we're netting users and low-level dealers, not the cooks who make it."

"Production is somewhere else in the country."

"Right. Here's the problem. After you called, I did some cross-referencing in some of the reports that come my way for DC and the mid-Atlantic. Busts, arrest records, intelligence from snitches."

"Let me guess. Illicit drug use hasn't gone down."

"Meth use is up three thousand percent in the last six months. Localized to DC, Baltimore, Richmond, Norfolk, Raleigh, and Charlotte."

He was quiet so I could figure it out. I pictured a rough map in my head of the cities he'd listed, then felt a tingle run up my spine. "Oh, shit."

"Oh shit is right," he said. "Geographically speaking, Cain's Crossing is dead center to all of them. Congratulations, Marty. You just found the new East Coast capital of meth production."

I chewed my lip, thinking. "Cain's Crossing is in the middle of farm country, so the ammonia is here. And lithium you can get if you try hard enough. You also need a fairly isolated location to cook the batch, since it stinks like hell. Pretty easy to come by down here in the sticks."

"So the question is?"

"Where are they getting the pseudoephedrine from?"

"Yeah. And that's the sixty-four-thousand-dollar question. There are plenty of places that fit the bill in all the other ways."

"And you don't have an answer for that."

"Nope."

"But you wouldn't mind if I happened to find out?"

"I'd love it. As long as you observe all the laws and statutes of this great nation of ours as well as the state of Virginia while doing so."

"If you figured this out, Warrenton DEA could, too. In fact, they should be all over it."

Tap, tap, tap. "No shit. If someone's found a reliable way to get pseudoephedrine into the country—and, specifically, the East Coast—in industrial amounts, it's not going to be confined to rural Virginia for very long. By this time next year, we'll have a meth epidemic that will make crack look like a walk in the park."

"That bad?" I'd been in the middle of my Homicide career when crack hit the streets in the eighties, and it hadn't been pretty.

"It's as bad as you can imagine," Sam said. "Good meth is three or four times more potent than crack. You can smoke it, slam it, snort it. Some people like to use it as a suppository, stick it up their ass."

"Must put a damper on the party scene."

"The point is, if there's a new channel for pseudoephedrine, the wheels are going to come off. We can't control the ammonia or the lithium. And you can make it anywhere. Kids do one-pot in two-liter Coke bottles, for Christ's sake."

"How much pseudoephedrine does it take to cook?"

"Two-to-one. Typical dosage is a hundred milligrams."

"You can get ten people high off a *gram*?"

"Yeah. At two-to-one, it takes just two grams of pseudoephedrine to make it. So, with the suzie you could hide in one footlocker—say, a hundred pounds . . ."

"You could make enough meth to supply a large city," I said, doing the math. "Five hundred would supply the whole East Coast."

"For a while," he said. "Until demand started to take off."

"I don't see the Brower boys having the imagination to initiate and maintain a meth empire," I said. "Though I was told they might be taking orders."

"You'd be surprised at how few brains it takes to make and sell this shit. And that's part of the problem, too. This new flood of meth is attracting attention. Your Brower boys are going to be in for a rude awakening if and when some real players decide that they want some of the action. Cain's Crossing will get wiped off the map if the MLA or the Aryan Brotherhood decides it's time for a change in management."

I was quiet, looking off into the middle distance, dimly aware of a few cars passing by, moving slowly through the quaint main square.

From here I could see the crown of the library poking up over the houses. The tall tops of oak and chestnut trees swayed in the breeze, nearly hiding the white church steeple. I could feel the slow, bucolic pulse of the town as it eased through a summer of cookouts and church picnics and Little League baseball games.

"See what you can find, Marty," Sam said. "I'm going to hold off until I hear back from the DEA, but someone's got to move on this. And soon. Or we're going to have one hell of a mess."

VI.

Two months later, we testify at J.D.'s trial. His defense attorney goes the obvious route: the gun doesn't have his fingerprints, his client claims it wasn't his. The prosecution is just as predictable—a habitual criminal, known to associate with criminals, is in illegal possession of an unregistered firearm. The surprise comes from Stan.

"I know he's killed someone," he says when asked for his description of J.D. "Maybe not with this gun, but with a gun like it. He ditched it or sold it and got this one as a replacement, but whatever else he did, I know he's killed somebody before."

The defense erupts. The judge tears strips off Stan when it's clear he can't prove any of it. But the bell's been rung. And when the mother of the slain six-year-old gives her testimony, everyone in court holds their breath.

It works. J.D. gets twenty years based on the flimsy evidence, Stan's outburst, and the mother's tears. The bailiff leads him out, wide-eyed and still disbelieving, trying to understand that two decades of his life has just been excised and removed like an organ from his body. He sees me watching and seems about to say something, but then the system pulls him through the door like water down a drain. The judge, the lawyers, the bailiff have *all forgotten about him and the courtroom fills with the small noises people make when they move on.*

"That's that," Stan says behind me, brushing his hands together. "Too bad they didn't really nail his ass to the wall."

I turn to look at him. "Twenty years is pretty good for an impermissible opinion from the cop who arrested him and a boatload of circumstantial evidence."

"The bullets that killed that little girl were real enough."

"Stan, we had next to nothing on this kid."

"That's not how the jury saw it."

I'm tired of Stan's mock superiority and his staged, exaggerated personality. "You really think that clueless hick killed five people? He was stupid enough to pick up a gun from somebody and we were lucky enough to find it. End of story."

"We don't have a confession, so just let him go?" Stan says, leaning back on his rhetoric. "Pat him on the ass and give him a ticket? Since when did you need an airtight case, Sherlock?"

"I don't," I say, not feeling good about where Stan is going. Not feeling good about any of it. "But I'm not stupid enough to confuse one thing with the other. This shit we put together barely limped into the courtroom."

"That's the problem with you, Marty," Stan says. "You want it by the book, all the time. Due process until we all choke on it. How about the fact that he had a fucking gun? You don't think he was going to use it? That, a year from now, we weren't going to pick him up for putting two in somebody's head over a wad of bills or a bag of crack?"

"When it happens, we deal with it, Stan. We don't put people away for things they might do," I say, looking at him. There's a stale, uneasy tone to his voice, like he's rehearsed all these lines, but doesn't believe them himself. "Unless you know something I don't?"

"What, now I framed him? This whole thing was a setup? Fuck you, Marty. I don't need to waste my time setting up little shits like J.D. Hope.

They do it to themselves." He turns and walks away, done with me. But then he snaps his fingers and turns around, like he's just remembered something. "Oh, yeah. I almost forgot to ask. I mean, as long as you're playing saint. If you didn't think he did it, why didn't you say something?"

CHAPTER TWENTY-TWO

"And do you plan to use our facilities for anything seditious, criminally inclined, or pornographic?"

"No, ma'am," I said. "Unless you want me to."

Ms. Hawkins, the Cain's Crossing head—and only—librarian, assumed an expression like she'd just smelled something unpleasant, but pushed a small slip of paper and one of those two-inch golf pencils across the counter toward me anyway. "Sign here, please."

And with that, I was permitted to use the one computer in the library—possibly the county—that had an Internet connection. I signed the slip, then went to the corner to park myself in front of the aging machine, armed with a brittle tablet from the Mosby, a pen, and my curiosity.

I wasn't an online research type of guy. The bulk of my Homicide career had consisted of knocking on doors and relying on face-to-face interactions. And not because I was inherently opposed to technology. I just found that even the phone got in the way sometimes when you needed information. People find it ever so hard to lie when they have to look you in the eye and tell you that they didn't shoot someone or run them over with their car.

But even I had to admit that the ease with which you could find hard facts online—not the dissembling of suspects or witnesses, but dates, times, places, maps—made it very close to the technological miracle that everyone else seemed to think it was. Amanda, fully plugged in, had given me some pointers over the last couple of months and I now felt better than completely lost when I pressed the ON button of a computer.

My first stop was to find a decent map of the greater Cain's Crossing area with aerial photos, if possible. I poked at the keys, making sure I got my spelling right. I blinked. The map and photos were on-screen before I'd raised my eyes from the keyboard. Keeping that window open in the background, I then nosed around in the local tax records and phone directories until I found the Brower family residence, which was six miles outside of town, give or take. That took half a minute. I leaned back in my chair, allowed myself a congratulatory grin. At this rate, I'd crack the case before lunch, sitting on my butt in the library.

Last stop, real estate listings. Despite the beauty of Cain's Crossing's pastoral simplicity, my guess was that property wasn't moving all that fast. It was too far for weekend getaways from Richmond or DC, not quite in horse country, hours from the beach, and not on the way to much of anything else. I did a filtered search for farms and ranches that had been on the market for more than a year. It took some back-and-forthing to get exactly what I wanted, but the final count was seven. The diminutive thumbnail pictures showed that four of them were old enough to include descriptions like "great DIY project" and "build your new dream home on this lot," which meant that the buildings were falling over. And thus, abandoned. Perfect for someone looking to start a homegrown meth lab. I jotted down the addresses of the four, then went back to my first screen and mapped them in relation to the Browers' home.

"Ta-da," I said, too loudly. From her desk, Ms. Hawkins hit me with laser-beam eyes. I ducked my head behind the wall of the carrel like a third grader.

Three of the four properties were just minutes away from the Browers' by car, the fourth too far out. Three old farms, almost certainly empty, and quite possibly abandoned. I drummed my fingers on the table, weighing things in my mind. Could it be this easy? Were they this dumb?

Maybe. Redneck crooks used to pushing everyone around. An ineffectual police force. A rural county where fertilizer was fairly common and could be bought or stolen, then transported a short distance away to make the product.

Okay, what would I do? I'd build my labs far enough away from my own house that I wouldn't kill myself or bring even a police force as lackadaisical as the Cain's Crossing PD around. But I'd also want to be able to check on my product, protect it, and make sure it got shipped out. Would I really want to drive to the next county to do that? Wouldn't I build the labs in the woods and hills and farms my family had known for two hundred years?

I went over to Ms. Hawkins and asked how I could access news and police reports for the last year. She pointed to the microfiche machine and I smiled. Compared to the computer, it was like something Howard Hughes had invented. I traded a monitor for an opaque screen, a mouse for antiquated dials.

It took me the better part of an hour to find what I was looking for. *Fire at Lentz Farm Burns Through the Night*. I skimmed the article until I found the address, then compared it to my list. It was the second of the three. I tapped the list in triumph, then went back and read the article carefully.

The abandoned, turn-of-the-century farmhouse had burnt to the ground after an explosion had ripped off the eastern half where the kitchen was located. The building had been reduced to ash before firefighters had been able to control the blaze. Given the remains of drug paraphernalia and bottles of alcohol in the debris, the fire was blamed on nameless teenage deviants partying too hard and playing with fire.

I frowned. No mention of meth. The good folk of Cain's Crossing were isolated, but even *they* had to have heard of meth labs going up in smoke. I scrolled to the top of the article. Written by Chick Reyes. Naturally. *Awfully light, Chick.* I'd have to rib him about it.

But that would have to wait. I had some snooping to do.

I sighed and squirmed in the seat. It had been a long time since I'd done a true stakeout and it was twice as tedious as I remembered it. The heat didn't help, since I couldn't really run the air conditioner and still stay hidden. So I sat with the windows down in the shade of a chestnut grove, squinting at my target, sweating through my clothes into the fabric of the car seat.

Since the Lentz farm had gone up in a blaze of glory, there were two farms left from my short list of three. My theory was based on a ridiculously unscientific process, and the likelihood that I had a fifty-fifty chance of finding a meth lab with some guesswork and an hour in the local library was small. But I had time and no better prospects other than getting one of the Brower brothers alone and beating some answers out of him, which was neither legal nor likely.

So, I'd grabbed some bottled water and a few pieces of fruit and decided to stake out one of the farms. It seemed as good a way to net some answers as anything else I could do. Neither farm appeared more likely than the other, so I'd chosen at random and headed for the property. The county was big, however, and even with my phone's map and a printout of the MLS map I'd made at the library, it took me four tries to find the dirt road that led to the farm.

I worried some that my tracks would be obvious to the next guy, but the road was dry and as long as they didn't come soon and see the plume of dust I'd left, I should be in good shape. I didn't approach the farm directly. Once I knew I had the right plot, I turned around and headed back out, then looked for nearby roads on the map. After some careful study, I found a tiny road that overlooked the farm from about five hundred yards away. I pulled off into the shade, grabbed a cheap pair of binoculars I kept in the car, and settled in.

The farm was nestled in a small valley formed by a trio of low hills that tucked into each other like the folds of a blanket. A two-story farmhouse, once white, now grayed and peeling, sat beside a clapboard barn. Wide double doors on the barn were secured with a padlock big enough to see from a quarter mile away and stringy black remnants of old electrical wire ran to the house from the road. Green creeper vine smothered half of the barn, the broad leaves waving from a weak breeze blowing across the valley. Deeper into the property, I could see the remnants of what might've been outbuildings or run-in sheds for horses once upon a time, but were now mostly rubble. Untended fields, high with grass gone from green to straw yellow in the August sun, were sectioned off with rusted barbed wire wound around the stumps of fence posts. Beetles and bugs buzzing past my car and through the fields were the only sounds.

I was in position by ten and was, reluctantly, ready to spend the next twelve hours watching the place. Watching for what, I wasn't really sure. Movement, visitors, strange smells, explosions? A Vice cop or DEA agent would've known exactly what to look for, but I figured since I was staring at a supposedly abandoned farmhouse, anything more than a bird flying overhead should count as suspicious. Except for the presence of the padlock—which could've been put on by a real estate agent or absentee owner trying to protect what little of value the place had left—the place looked exactly like a deserted farm.

One little visit by a Brower was all I needed and the gamble would pay off. The trick to catching them, however, was staying awake. Every few minutes, I swept the place with the binoculars. They weren't much better than my own eyesight, but it helped keep me awake and semi-alert when reciting multiplication tables and the list of US presidents started to wear thin.

Two hours in, I knew every cracked board in the barn, every crumbling brick in the house. I'd named every president in order three times except whoever came after James Garfield. I missed that one on each pass. Multiplication tables were too easy, so I started doing square roots and naming capitals of European countries.

I was nibbling on an apple and sifting my brain for the capital of Latvia when I heard the distant, deep-throated chug of a pickup truck. I grabbed my binoculars and got ready to zero in on the farm. Nothing was visible for a few moments; then I saw a kick of maroon dust in the air coming toward the farm, fast. A red pickup came into view, its sides and fenders dented and scratched. It pulled around the house in a wide circle, throwing up a wall of dust, and came to rest right in front of the ramshackle barn. The cloud caught up with it, enveloping the entire truck for a few seconds before the wind carried it away.

The driver waited for the dust to settle, then hopped out of the cab. The sound of the door slamming shut reached me two seconds later. Whoever it was, he was skinny and moved with an easy walk. He went to the barn door but paused in front of it, head bowed, playing with a phone or something in his hand before glancing up and doing a quick circle. Looking for trespassers? Seemed a little late. I had him centered in the glasses, so as he completed his pirouette, I had a great head shot of good old Jay-bone, he of the trick shots and thrown billiard games and poor choice of friends. I grinned. Putting your time in at the library pays off once in a while.

Satisfied that he was alone, Jay took out a set of keys and fiddled with the padlock on the barn door. He pulled the door aside just enough to slip inside. The time was 12:13. I lowered the glasses and waited. He had to come back to the truck sometime. I worked the apple over, nipping bites all the way to the core. Just as I bit into a seed, I saw some movement and raised the 'nocs in time to see Jay exit the barn.

His hands were empty. He closed and locked the door, then pulled out a blue handkerchief and wiped his face and blew his nose as if to get rid of something. He glanced at his phone again as he sauntered back to the truck. It rocked back and forth as he got in, then took off in another cloud of dust.

I glanced at my watch. 12:37. I looked back at the farm, thinking. The dirty red cloud of Virginia clay floated in the air, then settled to the ground. I had confirmation that my hunch was correct, that the Browers and their crony Jay were up to no good at an abandoned residence perfect for creating a controlled substance like crystal meth. I'd found the right farmhouse with some intuition and some basic detective work. And, now that today's inspection was over, there was a good chance that the farmhouse would be deserted for the next twenty-four hours.

This would be a great time to call the Cain's Crossing PD and give Warren my suspicions and deductions. He'd be so impressed, he might deputize me. Or run me out of town for continuing to stick my nose in places it didn't really belong. On the other hand, he *had* to know the meth labs were there. If he wasn't doing anything about them . . . well, I didn't like where those thoughts led.

Still, I didn't have any right to go snooping around. I'd already been explicitly told not to make trouble or play cop. So, the sane thing to do would be to call it in and let the chips fall where they may. Let the CCPD do their job—even if they did so in a lousy manner—and head back to town.

"Where's the fun in that?" I said into the silence, then got out of the car and headed across the high grass to the farm.

CHAPTER
TWENTY-THREE

If I had any doubts that I was approaching a meth lab, the smell clinched it.

It's funny that you don't have to own a cat to know what cat urine smells like. Ask anyone in the street and they'll be able to describe it. It's a pervasive, rather stunning odor that, smelled once, sticks. In my case, I didn't have to imagine it, as I happen to own a cat named Pierre. Or maybe it's more accurate to say he agreed to share living quarters. Pierre's a big cat and does whatever the hell he pleases, including living where he wants.

But even a cat his size didn't have a bladder big enough to make the smell reaching me. From forty feet away, the acrid smell of ammonia was enough to make me clamp a hand over my nose. Keeping an eye out for a cloud of red road dust, I backed off and did a slow circuit of the barn. The grass was knee high everywhere except in front of the door and it was slow going as I passed through the strong, early-afternoon sun and into the shade of the old building. Grasshoppers took off in all directions like tiny springs being released as I waded through the grass. I brushed a few ticks from my jeans, grimacing as I plucked one off that had already latched onto my ankle. A tractor, no more than wheels and a chassis, lay rusting in the yard behind the barn. Two large oil drums, empty and pitted, stood guard in the back, but there wasn't anything else to see until I found—as I thought I might—a burn pit holding the charred remains of rubber tubes and melted clumps of some kind of packaging. During my inspection, I'd come within ten or twenty feet of the barn itself and the smell went from nose-wrinkling to tear-inducing.

But you can't prove a smell in court.

I stopped, thinking. The original owners had either long since given up on the place or were so absentee as to amount to the same thing. So B and E charges weren't a problem unless a Cain's Crossing cruiser pulled down the driveway just as I was prying a board off the side of the barn. No, the real worry was that meth labs were notorious for their highly flammable contents creating explosions that would make an army ordnance engineer proud. I didn't relish the thought of having survived cancer to this point, only to be blown to bloody bits in the back-ass of Virginia. Or being poisoned. The labs that didn't go out with a bang were often filled with the toxic gas of the chemicals used to bake the meth. Gasses that were heavier than air and settled in your lungs, silently drowning you where you stood.

With these dangers in mind, normally I would've turned around and left. But I'd just watched Jay spend nearly twenty minutes inside and live to tell about it. That wasn't exactly a ringing endorsement—there were plenty of tweakers that weren't smart enough to keep from getting killed in their own labs—but it at least proved to me that it wasn't instantly fatal. And you don't get evidence by standing around.

Keeping an eye on the road, I walked around front and checked the padlock. It was a brute of a thing, a Chateau disc lock that weighed a pound if it weighed an ounce. A hardened steel chain wound through two steel eyebolts that were riveted to the old door, not screwed in. I wouldn't be getting in through the front.

I took another circuit of the barn, searching for weak boards, big gaps, anything while I rubbed the sting out of my eyes and tried to ignore the itch in my nose. Nothing. It wasn't Fort Knox, but without a radial saw or bolt cutters, I wasn't going to get in. On the second pass around the barn, however, I stepped back and inspected the building more critically, tracing the corners and following the pattern of the planks.

It was the back side of the barn that had been taken over by the lush green creeper vine. The vine was well away from the entrances so it hadn't needed to be trimmed, but on the back, it literally hid the planks from top to bottom. But jutting from the peak of the gambrel roof was an old beam with a rusting pulley, the old block and tackle the farmers used for pulling up hay. And where there was a block and tackle on a barn, there was a loft door.

I examined the creeper where it grew at eye level. The stuff had been there since before I was born and was a gnarled and knotted vine as thick as my wrist. I peered at the leaves suspiciously. What had they told me in the Boy Scouts? Leaves of three, let it be? These had five points. I took a deep breath, then reached out and grabbed one of the thicker vines, tugging at it, leaning back, letting it support my whole weight. It didn't budge.

I wedged a foot in a crotch of the vine, reset my grip, and started climbing hand over hand up the barn wall. There were plenty of spots to step as well, or I wouldn't have made it by arm strength alone. Moving carefully and testing every hold thoroughly, I was within arm's reach of the loft door in less than a minute.

Bracing myself, I tugged and pulled and pushed and grunted, trying to open the door even a few inches. But the same vine that had made my Tarzan impersonation possible had also entombed the door, keeping me from opening it even a fraction of an inch.

I swore. The plan had been genius. I tucked my head to my shoulder to wipe the sweat away. I started back down, reaching for a wider grip for security, when I suddenly wobbled in place as—not the vines—but the boards *underneath* the vines started to give way.

I scrabbled for a better hold, found it, then peered at the loose boards. The vines were barely holding on to a rotten section. I followed the line of the plank upward and carefully climbed until I was even with the loft door again. Reaching out ever so cautiously, I pushed at the plank. A whole section was punky and rotted, probably only held in place by the vines themselves. A thin shaft of sunlight poured through the gap I'd made, revealing that I was even with the loft.

I twisted and pulled and, with the sound of kindling being snapped, a three-wide stack of boards peeled off without giving away entirely. I slipped a foot from the vine I was standing on and got it wedged in the opening. With more finagling I got most of one hand and arm inside. Then, with a deep breath, I pushed off and slid through the gap.

Once inside, I grinned, pleased with my innovative method of breaking and entering, but the grin turned to a grimace real quick. The cat pee smell wasn't just strong, it was crippling. I pulled my shirt over my nose and mouth and held it there while I let my eyes adjust to the gloom. Vertical shafts of light squeezed through gaps between the wooden slats of the wall, providing the only illumination except for the hole in the roof, where a common household window fan had been duct-taped and clotheslined in place. A quick look around confirmed that I was, indeed, in the loft. Dust floated in the air and a scattering of hay still remained from years gone by of storing bales for the winter. But the real action was on the first floor.

Folding tables and plywood counters full of bottles, tubing, glasses, and funnels crowded most of the free space below. Propane tanks and kitty-litter jugs lay on their sides, while towers of coffee filters leaned at crazy angles on top of a cabinet. A huge red stain covered half of the floor. Hot plates connected to extension cords covered one side table.

I made my way along the loft until I found the built-in ladder leading to the floor. I climbed down and found myself in an end of the barn that had been given over to stalls unused in forty years. I poked my head in each, finding nothing but an ankle's worth of hay littering all but one of them.

The last had plastic wrap and empty cardboard boxes stacked almost to the ceiling, while black foam cutouts, like the kind that protects phones and computer parts, were scattered on the floor. Figuring it was the packaging for the tubes and glasses, I only gave it a glance and was ready to move on when something, a peeling paper label on one of the boxes, caught my eye. I picked up the box, careful not to tip the rest of them.

The label was wrinkled and stuck to itself, but the flared wings of the eagle and the round logo were hard to mistake. As was the big lettering spelling out "US Customs and Border Protection." I turned the box over in my hands, studying the other markings. They were all in Chinese or some other Asian writing, but the foam cushions all seemed to be made to hold electronic parts. Pictographs of red Xs through water droplets and lightning bolts appeared to confirm my hypothesis. I put the box back and kept rummaging. Forty more boxes, precisely like the first, were stacked in the stall. I took out my phone and snapped pictures of the lot.

I backed out and moved carefully to the lab. The ammonia smell was bad, but maybe the hole in the ceiling was doing its job. Either that, or my sense of smell had been obliterated. I swallowed nervously. Rationally, I knew that if the chemicals they used in the lab were of the kind that were going to kill me, there's nothing I could do about it. Probably couldn't detect them, even. But I took shallow breaths through my shirt anyway, trying to taste the air to give myself a minuscule chance of surviving if the place turned out to be toxic.

Very little light reached the floor and I squinted, trying to discern details. I wasn't really sure what more I'd find. A first-year rookie would know this was a sizable meth operation and would have beat a retreat by now so he could call in the cavalry. But I pressed on further. Maybe it was curiosity. After all, I'd been Homicide, not Vice. I'd seen some of the street-side results of meth use and meth dealing, but I'd never busted a lab before and only seen one in the flesh as it was being dismantled and scrubbed by a forensics team, long after the action.

I walked closer to the main production area, where the tables were spilling over with glassware, tubing, and strange contraptions held together by black electrical tape. I peered into a bucket filled almost to the brim with matchbooks and another one with the cardboard-backed strike plates that had been stripped off those same matchbooks. Sweat rolled down my back and stung my eyes. The air was stifling and I was getting a splitting headache from the smell and the heat. I lifted buckets, took pictures, and scrounged with the utmost care, but after another ten minutes, it was clear I'd found everything worth finding. It was time to go.

Moving carefully, I retraced my steps through the stalls, up the ladder, and out to the vine. Getting out was exponentially harder than getting in, and I was fatigued enough that, at several points, I simply held on to whatever was handy and closed my eyes to rest. If the Browers showed up, I was going to be about as easy to nail as a Marty Singer–sized piñata.

But no one appeared to knock out my stuffing and half an hour after I'd entered the barn, I was following my own trail over the driveway, across the yard, and back to my car. I thought about what confirmation of the lab meant and what I was going to do about it.

My hand was on the door handle when I heard a strange snapping sound from behind me, like popcorn just starting to pop. I turned and looked back. A lone second's void of silence made the hair on the back of my neck stand on end . . . then the doors, walls, and bits of roof exploded outward and upward, sending bits of hundred-year-old planks into the sky and across the yard with the sound of a bomb going off. None of the debris reached the car, but I ducked instinctively and a second later a small shock wave washed over me.

When I looked up, the barn had been reduced to one ragged level. The remains of the second floor that I'd labored so hard to reach were now tilted and had fallen into the stalls below it. Small flames licked what was left and a sickly gray cloud lifted off the pile like a spirit. It was no great conflagration, but the toxic chemicals released by the explosion were a bigger issue.

Fumbling for my phone, I jumped in the car and got the hell out of there. I dialed 911 as I navigated the dirt road, letting the nice dispatcher know she had a problem and where, then hung up. Hopefully, they wouldn't bother with a cell tower trace until I'd straightened out some things in Cain's Crossing. Or before the Brower brothers straightened out some things with me.

CHAPTER TWENTY-FOUR

I edged back into the shadows of the carport as the headlights of a green Camry washed over me. I'd squeezed myself behind a flimsy toolshed and a rusty rake was poking me in the kidney, but I had to ignore it. I was concentrating on the driver of the Camry. My SIG was out and, while it had a black matte finish, I covered it with my free hand anyway to hide any glint. The driver stopped short of the carport entrance, pulling in only as far as the driveway—a habit that I'd already guessed by the blotch of oil stains on the cement. A pause. Then the headlights winked out and a large, heavy man heaved himself out of the car with a groan. He slammed the door shut and sauntered toward the front door of the little house, briefcase in hand. A tight green shirt and pink tie warred with each other across his front, the shirt straining so hard over his belly I could see his white undershirt peeking through. Even without the terrible fashion sense I knew who it was, but waited until his face was lit by the feeble yellow porch light next to the door for confirmation. Moths and beetles flew in suicidal circles around the light, careening into the vinyl siding with a repetitive ticking sound. The man reached out to open the screen door.

"Warren," I called, just loud enough.

The detective froze. The hand holding his house keys was extended in front of him. Then, "Singer?"

"The same."

He paused for a half second, then said, "I'm going to reach in my pocket for my phone. Act like I'm checking my e-mail. No calls."

"Okay."

Warren placed his briefcase on the ground, then fished around in his pocket and came out with a smartphone. A sterile white glow lit his face from below, all highlights and shadows, like something out of a horror flick. He wandered closer to the carport, as though he was in a cell phone daze.

"Afraid someone is watching you, Detective?" I asked.

"Looks like somebody is," Warren said with his head bent, studying his phone. He played like he was fiddling with the buttons. "You gonna shoot me?"

"Waste of a bullet."

He grunted. "So. Did you mean to blow that old barn across the county?"

"It just happened that way. Though I'm not shedding any tears for the lost product."

He humphed. "Boys down at the fire station owe you. They got all excited, chance to pull overtime and put on their hazmat suits. Can't beat it with a stick."

"Glad I could help." I waited.

"What do you want, Singer?"

"We've got a problem, Warren. There's a gang in your town producing enough meth to rock the East Coast drug trade. In under a week, I fingered the members, made inroads with one of their flunkies, and found the location of one of their labs. But, as far as I can tell, I'm the only one looking into it. And I don't even work here."

He nodded, like he'd read something in an e-mail he agreed with. "You want a medal?"

"Warren, my cat could've done the work. It took me an hour in the local library and a morning to stake out a lab. That's it. You've had *months* to do the same. Which, based on some of the things you said out at the trailer park, leaves just two possibilities."

"Yeah?"

"Either you and Palmer have one hell of a case against the Browers and you're waiting for the right moment to drop the hammer on them."

"Or?"

"You're dirty as hell," I said.

I expected an explosive denial or a string of name-calling. He sighed instead. "Ain't no one going to believe I'm checking my e-mail for half an hour on the front stoop. Kitchen's around back of the house. I'll open the door. We'll talk through the screen."

"How stupid do you think I am?"

"Since you asked, pretty fucking dumb. But if you really want to know what it is you stuck your nose into, come round back. Don't matter to me none."

Warren clicked his phone off, picked up his briefcase, and went inside. Lights snapped on, illuminating the front yard in squares and rectangles. There was some banging around, then some classic country music—George Jones, maybe—filtered through the walls. It went on for a couple bars, then Warren turned up the volume.

Keeping my SIG out, I padded out the rear of the carport and around the side of the house. I knew the way from snooping out Warren's place earlier. By the time I got around the side, the back door was open and I could see him through the window over the sink. A spotlight bathed the yard in pools of light. I steered clear of the back door and crept to a far point in the backyard and watched the kitchen. The light snapped off, plunging the yard in darkness, then Warren appeared silhouetted in the doorway. He raised his hands, slowly turned in place, then leaned against the door frame on the other side of the screen door, looking out into the yard.

Circling to stay out of his direct line of sight, I sidled up along the house until I was next to the screen door. We'd be speaking almost at right angles to each other. I could barely make out his profile, but I could hear him breathing through his mouth, a fat man's sound. "I'm here."

"Yippety doo," Warren said.

"You were about to tell me how you're not taking money to ignore the chronic meth production in your county," I said. "Or how you were about to expose the whole operation and bring in J.D.'s killer. Or maybe how you didn't have a clue that any of it was happening."

"I know," he said. "I been over every inch of this piss-poor county. That's the Sampsons' family farm. My granddad used to help bring in the hay when it was a working concern. I could tell you the number of bricks in their house, how many fence posts they got around their property, the last day anyone ever lived there."

"So you knew about the labs?" I asked.

"Yep."

"You knew it was the Browers running the show?"

"Yep."

"And you've known how long they've been cooking meth? When they start, when they finish, when they ship it?"

"Uh-huh."

I paused. "You dirty, Warren?"

"Would I tell you if I was?"

"Maybe. In a weak moment. Or if you thought you could take me out."

"If I wanted to take you out, Singer, I would've brought you in for jaywalking and made sure you hanged yourself out of remorse. If I ain't done it yet, it ain't likely to happen now."

"That's the only reason I'm standing here talking to you."

He sighed. "All right, if we're done pulling each other's peters, what the hell do you want?"

"You know what I want. If you're not dirty and you knew about the labs, why haven't you shut them down?"

He didn't say anything. The night was quiet except for the buzz of the fluorescent kitchen lights. In the house, George was telling anyone who would listen about a woman who'd left him with nothing but love letters.

"Warren? Why haven't you shut the Browers down?"

He sighed. "The chief told me not to."

"Palmer?"

"Uh-huh."

"Why not?" I asked.

"Because he's in on it."

"What?"

Warren scrubbed his face with his hands. "We've known those clowns have been baking for a year or more. It don't take a Nobel Prize winner to deduce how they pull in their cash. They don't run numbers, they don't pimp or own a cathouse, they don't have the skill to chop cars, and they're too dumb to rob banks. What's left for your average unskilled country crook?"

"Used to be growing weed. Knocking over liquor stores. Now it's cooking meth."

He nodded. "They picked meth. Not sure how they figured it out."

"You don't have to be a genius to make the stuff."

"Nobody'd accuse them of that. You know that old line about walking and chewing gum?"

I smiled despite myself. "So someone had to hold their hand, teach them what to do."

"It probably took a paint-by-numbers set, but yeah."

"What about Jay?"

I heard a rustle, then Warren blew his nose. He muttered something about goddamn allergies, sniffled a few times, then inhaled noisily. "They were doing it before he showed. Jay's just happy to be their bitch, running around and checking on the batches, but he ain't no mastermind."

"And J.D. wasn't it for the same reason," I said. "Too late to start the party, but not too late to join."

"Uh-huh."

"Why do you think Palmer's part of this?"

"I told the chief a year, year and a half ago what the Browers were doing. Hell, I took him for a drive and showed him the damn labs. He said to lay off. And we've been laying off ever since. I haven't done squat but give the Browers a parking ticket."

"Palmer's the one teaching them how to cook meth? Come on."

"No. But he's part of it. Willing to give them a safe zone in return for a cut."

"No other explanation?" I asked.

"You got one, I'll listen."

"Biding his time?" I suggested. "Doing it right so he can put them away for good."

"That would be fine if we were doing legwork, getting background evidence," he said, his voice full of frustration. "But I've been told to do nothing. Zilch. I don't know when the magic hour is supposed to happen, but if and when it does, we'll be starting from zero. It ain't a matter of doing the case the right way. It's a matter of there ain't no case."

"Who's the mastermind, then, if not Palmer?"

He paused, sighed. "That's the question, ain't it? If I had a clue, I would've told Palmer to go screw and busted whoever it is. Instead, I get to sit on my ass and clean up after you."

"Why are you telling me this?" I asked. "What if I'm in on it? What if I'm the DC connection now that J.D. is gone?"

He made a rude noise. "You're a Class A meddler, but blowing up one of the meth labs takes you out of the suspect pool."

"I could just be incompetent. Took the lab out by accident."

"Then called it in to the local fire department? Kind of strange for a badass drug dealer from the big city."

Shit. "You trace the number?"

"Yep. Pretty sloppy, Singer."

"Had to be done," I said. "And, hey, now you trust me."

"I said you're probably not working with the Browers," Warren said. "Don't mean I trust you."

"Thanks."

"My pleasure." We were both quiet for a second, then he said, "You know, right, that if I can trace that call so can Palmer? You might want to take a pass on going back to the Mosby."

"I was thinking about that."

"So what's your next move, supercop?"

"Jesus, I don't know," I said. "I was hoping you'd tell me."

"Ain't nothing I can do from where I'm standing. You got any outside contacts?"

"Some."

"Anything they can do to help out?" he asked. "I ain't real keen on being found hanging by my own belt from a jail cell ceiling, either. If you catch my drift."

"A buddy of mine is getting stonewalled by Warrenton DEA. But he's working on it."

"Shit. Thanks for nothing."

"It's more than you've got right now," I said, then changed gears. "Where do you think J.D. fit into all this? Why'd they waste him?"

I could sense him shrug. "Who the hell knows? Maybe skimming off the top. Maybe he wasn't such hot shit after all. Couldn't hook them up in the big city like they wanted."

"Ginny Decker said he'd come back to Cain's Crossing to turn things around. That he was on a mission to take the Browers down."

"Bull. When the Browers decided he could be their connection to DC and offered him a cut of his own, he jumped quick enough."

"Once a con, always a con, huh?"

"Yep. I don't know why you think he deserved any more than he got. He must've made a hell of an impression on you up in DC."

"Maybe he got what was coming to him. Then again, maybe he didn't. I'm willing to dig a little to find out."

"Don't hold your breath. Personally, I couldn't give a shit about J.D. Hope. But if you're intent on taking the Browers out, I'll be happy to sit back and watch."

"That's a big help."

"I gotta think of the future, Singer. You could get in your car right now and be back home by midnight. I don't have the luxury. You find out your buddy can bring down something official on the Browers, I'm ready. But not until then."

Warren pushed himself away from the door, took a step back, then started to close it. Our rendezvous was over. Or almost over. I was tiptoeing away when Warren called me back. "How do you know I ain't in on it? I've known the Browers a long time."

I smiled. "A hunch. It's a small town. You know where I'm staying. You've had about a thousand chances to stop me or run me out of town or let me take a beating. You might talk a big game, but so far none of that's happened. Which makes me think you're happier about me looking into this than you've let on. A little push here, a little prod there, and I end up doing the dirty work. Not a bad strategy for a cop who wants to do the right thing but might get killed if he tries."

I listened to Warren's breathing, simultaneously whistling and guttural. "You ain't near as dumb as you look," he said. And shut the door.

CHAPTER TWENTY-FIVE

Lee's Auto Body and Repair was a two-stall garage shop with a dozen cars in various stages of repair and age scattered around its parking lot. White spotlights lit the ground in stark pools and cast long, razor-edged shadows over the asphalt. I'd remembered it from my daylong search for Jay-bone. It was late and they'd closed up for the evening. Since it was Friday in a small town, they might be closed for the weekend as well. I squeezed my car between a twenty-year-old Cutlass missing its front-right fender and a Tahoe with a dent in its grille about the size and shape of a telephone pole. I had to slide across to the passenger's side to get out. I backed off ten feet and checked it out. Too new. I scattered a handful of dirt on the windshield and hood, then looked it over again.

The dirt was a nice touch, but one of the spotlights lit my car like it was on a Las Vegas stage. I glanced around, looking for anyone taking a late-night stroll. When I didn't see any, I grabbed a chunk of tar-covered asphalt and smashed the bulb in one throw. I held my breath, listening for alarms or shouts, but Lee's was on the edge of town and I might as well have shot the light out with my gun. A ten-dollar bill, folded in quarters and slipped in the space between the shop's front door and the jamb, kept me guilt-free.

I walked across the street to wait in the shadows. Ten minutes later, a white Coupe de Ville rolled to a stop along the curb. The interior light flashed on for five seconds, then off, just like I'd asked. I walked up to the car, opened the passenger-side door, and slipped inside.

Mary Beth looked at me from behind the wheel. "Where to?" I gave her the address to J.D.'s motel and she frowned. "Why do you want to go there?"

"How about I tell you on the way?" I asked, looking behind us. She put the Coupe de Ville in gear and we glided away from the curb. It had been a while since I'd ridden in a boat the size of this one. It was like riding on a cloud.

Once I was sure we weren't being followed, I gave her the short version of what I'd found out about J.D., the Browers, and the situation in her hometown. I included the part about blowing up their meth lab but excluded my conversation with Warren. It might've put her mind at ease a bit to finally understand the nature of the detective's stonewalling and the weeks of noncommunication, but I didn't need her confronting him or otherwise kicking over the applecart while I was still trying to figure out what I needed to—or should—do.

"Aren't the Browers going to want to kick your ass for taking out their lab?" she asked. Then, "Oh."

"You understand now?"

"You hid your car and now you need a place to stay." She bit her lip, concentrating. "You don't think they'll look at J.D.'s motel?"

I shrugged. "They'll try the Mosby first. When they don't find me there, they'll drive around looking for my car. If I've got any luck left, they won't find it in a lot full of other cars. At least, not in a single night. And with you dropping me off at the motel, there shouldn't be any trace."

"What about the motel owner? He's the one who had my brother's things, wasn't he?"

"Yes."

"How does he feel about you?"

"Uh . . . not so great," I said. "Which would be a problem if I planned on checking in."

"What's that mean?"

"Don't worry about it. I'll be safe. But I could use a ride in the morning."

She didn't look happy, but dropped it and we agreed for her to swing by at eight to pick me up. We were closing in on the motel, so I told her to pull behind the ice-cream stand where I'd staked out the place before. She shut off the lights and turned in her seat to look at me. Her eyes were large and liquid. In the colorless night, they looked like black pools.

"I'm sorry," she said.

"For what?"

"For hating you."

"If it helps, I understand—"

She stopped me with a shake of her head. "I knew what J.D. was. I've always known. A good guy who made bad decisions. Pushing limits like a little kid. Until he crossed a line he couldn't come back from. It's not your fault that you were the one who had to stop him. Someone would've eventually. I should be glad it was you and not some junkie or crook with a gun years ago."

I said nothing. The crawling sensation in my gut was almost unbearable.

She was quiet for a moment, then said, "Anyway, I wanted you to know I appreciate what you're doing. And that I'm . . . I'm ready to face whatever it is you find out. There's a good chance that J.D.—I won't say he deserved it, nobody deserves that—but that he did something to cause his own death. I don't like thinking about it that way, but I'm not going to be blind to the possibility."

"Don't get ahead of yourself," I said, my voice rough. "Let's find out what happened first, then deal with it. It might be hard, it might be easy. But inventing things won't help."

She nodded and looked down at her lap. I took a deep breath and got ready to plunge into a confession of my own. "Look, Mary Beth. There's something you should know. J.D. did some bad things, he should've done some time, it's true, but he doesn't deserve to shoulder all the blame. There were things that happened, things I did—"

She reached across and placed a hand over my mouth. "Don't. Please. It took me a lot to get this far. Whatever you did, forget about it. For now, at least. We'll talk it out when you find J.D.'s killer. We'll make it fit later. Okay?"

I nodded and she took her hand away, only to slide it along my face. She looked at me like that for a moment, then leaned forward and kissed me gently on the mouth. I stared at her for another long moment, then opened the door and slipped out. The Coupe de Ville's lights came on and she drove away.

I watched the motel from the shelter of the ice-cream stand. A few cars passed in the night, including a truck that tore past at about sixty not long after Mary Beth had pulled away. There seemed to be no one in the office. A light flicked on in number seven, but no one came by to have their itch scratched, and by midnight the light went out, though the blue strobe of TV light played through the cracks of the blinds. The windows of the other huts yawned black and empty. I sank back even farther into the shadows and pulled out my phone. I dialed from my phone's memory. It picked up in two rings.

"Bloch."

"Sam, it's Marty," I said. "Things have taken a twist."

"More than they have already?"

"You could say that," I said, and brought him up to speed. He listened the way Sam always did—quiet, with an intensity that told me he heard everything I said and more.

"So, I was right," he said. "Meth is the game."

"It gets better," I said, and described the Customs boxes.

A long pause. Then, "They've got it. A source for the pseudoephedrine."

"I didn't want to say it."

He swore. "What else could it be? Four dozen empty boxes with Customs markings in a meth lab? All the other ingredients are local."

"And where's the nearest major Customs port?"

"Norfolk."

"Will Brower worked at the Norfolk docks after a short spin with the US Army," I said. "Want to bet it was with the Customs office or close to it?"

"Where he made a buddy who said, 'Hey, you know, I could smuggle a Jeep through here without anyone batting an eye. How about fifty pounds of suzie instead?'"

"Problem is, the Browers didn't dream this up on their own. These guys make rocks look smart."

"I'll dig around," Sam said. "Shouldn't be too hard to chase down where he used to work and with whom."

"Any word from the DEA?" I asked.

"No," he said, frustrated. "Total radio silence. Doesn't make any sense."

"Keep plugging away at that," I said. "And let me know what you find out about Will."

"What are you going to do?"

"Keep working on the Browers. Maybe this kid Jay will crack. Blow up another lab, if nothing else pans out."

"Local dicks going to let you play Lone Ranger for much longer?"

"I pretty much have a mandate from a cop down here to stick my nose into things. Though he'll deny everything if I get caught." I relayed Warren's suspicions about Palmer.

"Do you believe him?"

I sighed. "I want to. Some things fit the way he says they should. On the other hand, I don't know squat about Palmer and it's not like I can go and ask him if he's on the take. I'll just have to bull my way through this until something or somebody cracks."

"Sophisticated detective work at play. I love it."

"You got something better, I'll listen."

"If I think of something, I'll call," Sam said. "Watch your back."

I hung up and watched the motel until my legs were aching and my feet were almost numb. I was stalling. What had seemed like a brilliant idea earlier in the day now looked lousy. I sighed and shook myself. I was going to have to sleep sometime. I took a peek left and right, then jogged across the road at a brisk place, neither walking nor running.

The roof's overhang cast a narrow shadow along the front of the motel and I tucked into it as I worked on the lock of number three. The locks looked to be originals, at least twenty years old, so I took out a bump key that looked like it would fit and got to work. It had been years since I'd tried to bump a lock, but I'd always had a knack for it and I was inside the room by the fourth try. I stood and listened for a minute, waiting to see if anyone had heard my *tap, tap, tapping* on the chamber door. It was always good to be careful, but I was two units down from a seemingly empty office and four from a junkie with her TV on. The others were almost certainly empty. Nothing and no one materialized after several minutes. I let my breath out and concentrated on the room in front of me.

Must and damp filled my nose, something I hadn't noticed when I'd looked over the room in the heat of the day. A weak light passed through the windows, just enough to limn the corners of the bed and the nightstands. The room was exactly as I'd seen it before, but the night—and my imagination—suffused it with meaning. J.D.'s blood had probably spread in a kidney-shaped pool just a few feet away, and I imagined I could see it pulsing softly into the rug in time to his last hoarse breaths, soaking down into the fibers, into the pad beneath, into the wood below, down into the earth . . .

I sucked in a sharp breath, like I'd been shaken awake. I was here to avenge J.D. To see justice done. To dole it out myself, if I could. His ghost would just have to be happy with that.

I took off my shoes, pulled the threadbare coverlet down, and slipped under the covers, hoping for a single night's sleep in a dead man's bed.

VII.

They've given me a special room away from the Visitation Hall. It has two entrances: one for cons, one for cops and DAs. It's the best way to keep cons who want to talk alive. Petersburg is a federal prison, and the code regarding informants is just as strong, if not stronger, than it is in state penitentiaries. The guards can sneak a con in here, have a ten-minute conversation, and put him back in General before anyone knows he's gone.

A constable leads J.D. into the room wearing his Day-Glo jumpsuit and white socks, hands cuffed behind his back. Since I know why I'm here and he doesn't, I get a brief second to look at J.D. before he recognizes me. The change in him is astonishing. In three years, he's even thinner and more ascetic than I remember. Like a table knife honed down to a straight razor. The shaved head and tattoos are part of it, of course, but there's a coiled violence in him that the punk in the car didn't have.

When he sees me, the look is assessing, trying to place me. Then he breaks into a smile. He's missing his four upper front teeth. The constable takes the cuffs off him and walks him over to the chair.

"So, you're my surprise visitor," he says.

"That's me. Getting along on the inside?" I ask.

"Can't complain. I mean, if I have to be here, it could be worse. Course, I don't have to be here, do I?"

I shuffle some papers. "I thought you might be interested to hear your old boss Maurice is up on about ten counts of murder and too many drug charges to keep track of."

"Is that so?"

"Yeah."

"You drove to Richmond to tell me that?"

"We could use your help. We got what we need to get the ball rolling on Maurice, but a word from somebody who knows him could put him away for good."

J.D. smiles again, showing off red gums and the gap where his teeth should've been. "You want to know how I got my teeth knocked out, Detective?"

"Not really."

"About a year ago, I stood up for this old man that was about to get fucked to death in the shower here. Cost me my teeth and about sixty stitches but it felt good, you know, doing the right thing. I ain't never had that feeling before, cuz I never really did the right thing before."

"This would be doing the right thing," I offer.

"No, it would be doing what you want," he says, and the smile disappears. "There's a difference. The right thing is doing something without payback. Doing it when it ain't easy. Doing it when it'll hurt."

"You gonna lecture me on integrity, J.D.?"

"Somebody has to," he says. "I'd say you and your friend Lowry could use a lesson or two."

"What do you mean?"

He gives me an incredulous look. "What do I mean? What do I mean? I mean you planted that gun on me and you fucking well know it. When I wouldn't rat on Maurice, you put me away."

I get a wriggling feeling in my gut. "Bullshit."

"Fuck you. One of the homies I used to run with ended up in Petersburg and told me Maurice himself gave the Hi-Point to a white cop to set me up. It's the truth and you know it."

I shuffle the papers yet again, then stop, angry with myself. "Wasn't me."

"Didn't have to be," J.D. says. "You were there when he did. And if you saw it done, you could've stopped it. Either way, you missed the boat, Detective. You had your shot to do one right thing and you blew it."

Memories tumble together. I see Stan's face, his attitude, his little speech in the courtroom. Things make too much sense. I fumble for a way to pull this back together. "If things went down the way you say they did, then Maurice is as much to blame as we are. This is your chance to get even."

The chair scrapes the floor as J.D. pushes back from the table. He walks over to the door and raps twice. "Maybe so, Detective. But I ain't going to take it. I meet up with Maurice here in lockup, he'll get his. But I'll be damned if I let you use me to do it."

The guard unlocks the door. He sees J.D. there and looks at me for confirmation. I nod. The guard makes a motion for J.D. to turn around so he can cuff him for the walk back.

Hands behind his back, J.D. pins me with his stare. "You might want to think hard on this, Detective. I got another seventeen years to chew it over. Might be too late for me, might not. But there's going to be another time when you'll wonder if you got it in you to do the right thing. You gonna be up for it?"

The guard turns him around by the elbow and they walk out, their feet echoing down the long corridor.

CHAPTER TWENTY-SIX

I slept fitfully. I dreamt of the explosion and hospital smells and chemotherapy and Will Brower's grinning face. I heard the soft, wet sound of a bat hitting a skull. The last tapering breaths. The crash of a cell door being slammed shut. Felt Mary Beth's lips on mine. Tasted smoke and gunpowder and blood.

I was floating in the middle spaces, not sleeping, not awake, when my phone—stuffed in my shirt pocket with the sound off—buzzed, jerking me awake.

I answered it by the glum light of the predawn, bleary-eyed and sleep-stupid. "Singer."

It was Warren. "Time to wake up, bud."

"What's going on?"

"State police found Mary Beth Able's car by the side of the road last night. Empty, with the doors wide open."

CHAPTER TWENTY-SEVEN

Warren came around the curve fast, bringing his Camry to a skidding stop a few feet away from me where I stood in the shadow of the ice-cream stand. I opened the passenger door, slid inside, and he took off again.

"Tell me," I said.

"Trooper called it in around four thirty this morning. Plates and registration confirmed."

"What shape was the car in?"

"No body, no blood, no struggle. Purse on the front seat."

I swore.

"Yep. Someone convinced her to pull over, got her out of the car, and shoved her in their trunk."

"Any evidence it wasn't the Browers?"

"Like, did they find a business card at the scene?"

"No, like someone ID'd one of the Browers' monster trucks leaving the area."

"Nope. Didn't get that lucky."

"You got a plan?"

He shook his head. He drove fast, cutting curves where it made sense, pounding the gas on the straightaways. "The best I can come up with is to hunker down near the Browers' place and watch it 'til we see something worth moving on. I tossed a pair of binoculars, food, some extra ammo in the trunk."

"You got any friends in the department that could help out?"

"Only six of us are full-timers, including me and Palmer. The other four would either run straight to him with the news or hem and haw about procedure. And I wouldn't trust the part-timers to not accidentally shoot us in the ass."

I leaned my head back on the headrest and closed my eyes. "What's their place like?"

"Old farmhouse. Still in pretty good shape. Their mama died just a few years ago, so they haven't had time to run it into the ground. Two or three outbuildings, falling down."

"If it's farmland, is there any cover?"

He nodded. "The land hasn't been worked for fifty years or more. Woods have grown over most of it. They keep the yard clear around the house out to about twenty or thirty yards."

"Fencing? Dogs? Cameras?"

"No fence. No dog could stand 'em. And I'll eat my own gun if the house is wired with anything slicker than a doorbell."

I frowned. "Are they that dumb?"

"No, they usually got one of them flunkies guarding the place, twenty-four seven. Give him a shotgun and tell him to walk around the yard, peek out the windows once in a while. Folks around here know to give them a wide berth if they don't want to get shot or have one of the brothers beat up their grandma."

"For someone who wasn't going to touch this, you seem to know an awful lot about the layout."

He quirked a smile. "A man's got his hobbies."

We talked a little more about how we wanted to approach the house, what we thought we could expect, and how far we were willing to go. With no warrant in hand, no backup, and my status as a civilian, things were going to be dicey on a legal front, to say the least. But we'd have to throw caution out the window if we saw any sign of Mary Beth being held inside.

"I'm going to fly past their place so you can get a view from the road," Warren said. "Then we're going to circle up the east side along an old road that used to be part of the property. We'll have to bushwhack to get to a good spot, maybe a half mile in from where we'll park. Think you can handle it?"

"I can handle it."

"All right, then. Coming up on it in about a quarter mile."

We drove past the Browers' place just under the speed limit, hoping to get a quick reconnaissance in without being too obvious. Even with Warren's description, I'm not sure what I expected. A ramshackle farmhouse with goats chewing the hedges? A hillbilly rancher with living room furniture on the porch and a '76 Firebird on blocks in the yard? A walled compound with razor wire and a Confederate flag waving in the breeze?

What I got was a glimpse of a tidy, three-story brick home, with a wide front porch and expansive front lawn. While it wouldn't have placed in any *House Beautiful* contests, it didn't fit the profile of a family of meth dealers, either.

Two miles later, Warren slowed and turned onto a half-dirt track named Browers Mill Road that split a cornfield in half. An idle portion of my brain decided that the name might explain the beautiful family home. A prosperous ancestor builds the first mill in an agricultural county, makes a modest fortune and, after forty years of saving, builds a beautiful home on acres of land by the edge of an idyllic wood . . . just in time for automated mills and corporate farms to make the family business obsolete. The Brower name fades over the decades until all that's left is the brick home and a vague sense of self-importance. Ending with the present generation of drug dealers.

Warren slowed the car even more as we tested the Camry's suspension on the deep ruts and potholes in the road. The low speed helped keep the dust cloud down as well. Ten minutes later, he eased off the track and bounced into a cornfield. A two-year-old could've followed the trail from the road, but at least the stalks broke up the car's profile from a distance.

We got out of the car and went back to the trunk. Warren opened it and took out a pump-action 12-gauge shotgun, a box of shells, and his binoculars. He was wearing a green-and-white Hawaiian shirt with palmetto trees on the front—as good as camouflage—and a hunter's vest over the top.

"You still got that SIG?" he asked me. I nodded and he pulled out a box of 9mm shells from a tackle box. "Load up."

I slipped a handful of shells out of the box and into separate pockets to keep down the jingle they made. The extra bullets were comforting, but that was the extent of their usefulness unless we got caught in a siege. My SIG had an extended eight-round magazine, but I'd have to eject and load the magazine manually if I ran out. Unlikely in a firefight. Nine rounds—eight in the magazine, one in the chamber— would probably have to do.

Warren tossed some bottles of water and some granola bars into a threadbare camo backpack, closed the trunk, and looked at me.

"You ready to do this?"

"Got to," I said. "When they don't get any info out of Mary Beth, she'll be nothing but a liability. We've got a couple of hours at best."

He nodded and we set off through the cornfield.

We set up four hundred yards east of the house, looking down at the back and side of it from a small rise in the woods. Warren and I had played commando, crawling on our bellies for the last fifty feet of the rise before it crested and sloped down to become the back forty of the Brower property. I wiped sweat out of my eyes and tried to ignore the sticks and rocks jabbing into my stomach. Warren dug around for his binoculars and scanned the place before handing them to me.

Closest to us, where we lay sweating and dirty, was an old freestanding garage with boarded and black-papered windows. A ring of trash that always seems to accumulate around farmsteads and old homes surrounded the garage: ancient milk bottles, rusty cans, a tire. It seemed to be in decent shape, but abandoned and unused. A graying, decrepit garden shed, with a wild grapevine poking through one window, stood sixty feet from the back door of the main house. More debris formed a perimeter around the shed. Some of it—like bed frames and lumber— leaned against the walls, other bits polluting the ground, like empty buckets and wash rags that had been in the dirt so long it was hard to tell what was earth and what was cloth.

I shifted my attention to the house. From our vantage point, I could barely make out the front porch where it peeked around the corner, but I did have a decent view of the back, where a modest porch led to, presumably, a back door and maybe a kitchen. There was a walk-down trapdoor to the basement in the back of the house and an old-fashioned coal chute on the side. A familiar-looking Bronco with gray spots of patching compound sat in the side yard.

Warren nudged me and said, "Coming around from the front. Right side."

I swung the glasses to cover that side of the house, where the chunky blond kid that I had prevailed against so long ago at the gas station came swaggering around the corner. He was wearing the same cutoff jean shorts and tank top. There were two new additions to his wardrobe that caught my eye. The first was a black baseball cap. The other was an

AR-15, cradled in his arms like a black bug. Which explained some of the swagger. He headed back to the garden shed and walked a simple perimeter route along the edge of the woods, peering menacingly into the shadows. I lowered the glasses to avoid a reflection off the lens and watched him with my naked eye. He bobbed in and out of sight as he passed around the far side of the garage, making no effort to stay hidden, and eventually made his way back to the Bronco, where he leaned the AR-15 against a tire and opened the door. He leaned in and came back out with what looked like a fast-food bag, picked up the gun by its top handle, and headed back to the house. He skirted it, however, and passed out of sight, presumably to do a circuit of the front yard, too.

"Who is that kid?" I asked Warren.

"Toby Henderson. All-star tackle for the high school football team couple years back. The highlight of his time on earth so far. Why, you know him?"

"He and some skinny creep tried to jump me about a week ago out at the gas station by the on-ramp to 29. I introduced my elbow to his face before his friend tried to knife me."

Warren smiled. "That warms my heart. Toby's been beating on people his whole life. Always been a big waste of space. The creep is Dwayne Riggins. Burnout pothead. I been running him in for touching girls the wrong way since he was in elementary school."

"Looks like they've both graduated to something bigger and nastier."

"Yep." He nodded toward the yard. "How often you think our little soldier goes on patrol?"

I thought about it. "He loves toting that gun around, but he's got to be bored as hell. I mean, no way anyone around here is stupid enough to trespass on the Browers' land, right? So, he only does it because he's afraid Will or Tank will show up and kick his ass. Once an hour, tops. Or maybe if he knows they're on their way back, he'll pop outside, show them he's on top of things."

Warren nodded. "S'what I thought. Want to throw him a curveball?"

We talked it over, then wriggled our way across and down the four hundred yards until we were right behind the garage. We took our time and used all the cover we could in case Toby—or someone else in the house—was being extra vigilant and spotting from the second-floor window. In twenty minutes, we were crouched behind the garage, leaning against the wall for support. Neither one of us was young or in the best shape, and I know Warren was as glad as I was that we still had another twenty minutes to go before Toby came out for his rounds. A soft breeze swirled around the back of the garage and I closed my eyes, drinking it in.

Warren took longer to catch his breath. Eventually, when he got it under control, he looked over at me. "Why're you doing all this, Singer?"

"J.D.'s thing?"

"Yeah, and Mary Beth. I can understand *wanting* to, but actually doing it?"

I gestured toward him. "You're here."

"It's my job. In my hometown. You're retired and a hundred miles from home. You don't get off on the vigilante thing, do you?"

"No," I said. I scratched idly at the rough cinder-block wall of the garage. "Just unfinished business."

"Don't give me that vague bullshit," Warren said, surprising me with the edge in his voice. "I'm out here with you risking my neck. Even if I don't take a bullet, I'm probably out of a job tomorrow. You owe me something better than *unfinished business*." He said the last two words in a high-pitched, little girl's voice.

I stared at Warren, thinking about it, seeing the years slip backwards. Maybe another cop would understand. Finally, I said, "When J.D. was busted all those years ago, he was just a small-time loser that got in way over his head. Running crack, picking up cash. Sooner or later he would've done time. Who knows how much or when. But he was on his way."

"Sounds like his time down here."

I nodded. "The thing you probably don't see in Cain's Crossing are cops who snap. I don't mean pull a gun and go crazy. I mean the ones where the everyday consequence of what they do and see erodes who they are and what they stand for. When murders pile on top of one another with no end in sight—and for sure not stopped because of anything you do—you start to lose it. Look for shortcuts. Assign guilt and move on."

"We talking about you?"

"No. I understand it, but I never went there. No, this was a guy I was assigned to temporarily, help him out with a string of shootings in Southeast. He was a couple years older, had seen too many things. Some of them in Vietnam, so maybe that had something to do with it." I ran a hand through my hair. I didn't like talking about this. "Long story short, he saw a little girl get shot and that was it, the one that broke him. He knew who'd done it and knew he'd never catch up to him."

"Then?"

"Then J.D. fell in our laps. And Stan—his name was Stan—saw J.D. as our golden opportunity. He thought we could lean on him, get him to flip, and we'd pull the shooter in. But J.D. wouldn't budge."

I was quiet for a long minute. Warren said, "So?"

Signed, sealed, and delivered, Stan says, patting a breast pocket. I sighed. "So Stan framed him. We searched his apartment on a jacked-up warrant and Stan slipped the shooter's gun into a likely spot."

"How'd he get the gun?"

"He cut a deal with the crack dealer whose gun it was. Isn't that nice? J.D. wouldn't rat out the dealer, so Stan turned around and did exactly the same to him."

Warren frowned. "Why'd the dealer want to do that?"

"Got rid of a flunky, the weapon, and the murder rap all at the same time," I said. "Who wouldn't go for that?"

"Why'd this guy Stan do it?"

"He told me later he didn't care, he'd nail the dealer on something else. But the real reason was that he couldn't stand the idea that J.D. could've helped him put the dealer away . . . and didn't. So he punished him."

Warren was quiet for a second. I knew what he was going to ask. "You know about the frame?"

"No. Not then. But then I had my doubts. Stan was acting crazy. And the day we found the gun, it was like something out of a movie. He nearly said 'oh ho!' when he dug it up. I got more and more suspicious but didn't say anything. It almost came out after J.D.'s trial, but I think I didn't want to know, even though Stan damn near admitted to me that he'd done it. Gave me his reason right there in the courtroom."

"Which was?"

"He asked, Why? Why are you going to bother with this piece of shit who is *going to go to jail* anyway? Why delay the inevitable? And, maybe more important, why wait until something worse happens?"

"And you went along with it."

I closed my eyes again. "And I went along with it. And because I did, J.D. Hope lost twenty years of his life."

Warren was quiet.

"I know what you're thinking, because I thought it, too," I said. "That Stan was probably right. That we would've put J.D. away sooner or later. It's an easy argument to like. But the fact remains that J.D. *didn't* do it. And that's got to be enough. We're not in it to play God, we're not there to decide who *might* commit a crime. We're there to stop the ones we can and solve the ones we can't. And that's *it*. If you can't stomach the idea that some guys get caught and some guys slip through, then you're in the wrong business."

Warren said nothing.

"So that," I continued, "is why I owe J.D. Hope something. Even if he was a lifelong crook, even if I was doing my goddamn job, even if he would've wound up doing time anyway. Even if he's dead."

Warren picked up a pebble, tossed it into the woods. "Can't change the past, Singer."

"I'm not trying to. The fact is, it's not for him. It's for me. Redemption is selfish."

Warren thought about it, nodded once. "Sometimes the ends don't justify the means. Sometimes they surely do. Not sure how I would've handled it. I guess I'm more of a cut-and-dried kind of cop."

"You would've let him go to jail?"

He shrugged. "Probably. But I wasn't there. I didn't have to live with it for twenty years."

"Yeah," I said. "And now it doesn't matter. Mary Beth's the priority now."

In the distance, we heard the front door slam and all conversation was done. I checked my watch—on the hour, exactly. Warren tapped me on the shoulder and I crept around the garage to the opposite side. Once there, I took my phone and turned the camera function on, then placed it on the ground and propped it against the garage. I toyed with it until only the barest slice—enough for the aperture to remain clear—showed around the corner. From my hiding place, I could see the screen perfectly, but Toby would have to be looking for a half-inch sliver of black phone two inches off the ground leaning against a garage with debris scattered around it.

Through the camera, I watched as Toby sauntered around the yard, poking at the vine in the garden shed, taking his time. Body language told me he was as bored out of his skull as I'd predicted. He stopped to put a wad of chew in his mouth, spit, and continue. As he came closer I heard his footsteps, one foot crunching on gravel, one silently on the grass. When he got within twenty feet of the garage, I carefully pulled the phone back and speed-dialed Warren's number. After two rings, I pulled my gun and stepped around the corner.

It couldn't have fallen out any better. Toby, head bent like the first time I saw him, was looking at his own phone. He held the AR-15 by the stock and trigger guard, the barrel pointed straight down, as he checked his messages. He shuffled slowly toward me, oblivious.

"Toby," I called softly as I drew a bead. At about the same time, Warren rounded the corner behind him, unseen and silent.

The kid's head snapped up and he stared at me like I'd suddenly sprouted from the weeds. The phone slipped from his hand and his mouth opened to say something, or yell for help, but Warren cut off any sound he might've made as he whipped the butt of the shotgun forward two-handed and cracked it against the back of Toby's head. The kid dropped like a sack of laundry. The only sound was a rattle as the AR-15 dropped with him.

I slipped the SIG in the holster and ran forward to help Warren drag Toby's two-eighty around the corner of the garage. Warren patted him down and cuffed him while I listened for any sign from the house that we'd been spotted. When there wasn't any, we gagged him and made sure he could breathe.

"Sorry, all-star," Warren said, patting Toby on the cheek. He then showed me two sets of keys he'd taken from the kid. "That's to a Ford. The Bronco, I guess. Bottle opener. And a couple of house keys."

"Those are his, probably. What about the other set?"

Warren flipped through the other set. "A padlock. Two house keys."

"Those are for the house," I said. "Give me the binoculars for a second."

Warren handed me the binoculars and I slipped up to the corner of the garage. A quick glance told me what I wanted to know and I ducked back around the garage. "There's a shiny new padlock on those basement doors. So, we've got front door, back door, and basement, here."

"What now?"

I looked down at Toby. "If there's anyone inside, they're going to be expecting him eventually."

"What are you thinking?" I glanced at Warren, then down at Toby, eyeing their respective sizes. He shook his head. "You ain't serious, Singer."

"Don't be a baby. You only have to give an impression, Warren. It might give us three extra seconds we need."

It took another minute, but I managed to convince Warren that we didn't have much time—or many options. Grumbling, he swapped his jeans and Hawaiian shirt for Toby's shorts and cutoff tank top. The hat and the gun completed the look.

"Looking good, Warren," I said. I picked up his shotgun. "We ready?"

"Let's get to it."

Warren tossed me the back door key, then sauntered out from behind the garage, holding the assault rifle by the stock just as Toby had. Swaggering like he owned the place, he traced the path we'd watched Toby take before, veering toward the Bronco, then out to the front yard to do the rest of the circuit. I watched as he reached in a pocket and pulled out Toby's phone and pretended to thumb through it as he walked. I had to admire his guts. He had no guarantee that he was fooling anyone in the house. Bullets might start flying any second.

But there wasn't a peep from the homestead and, as he started to round the corner toward the front, I sprinted for the back door, shotgun at the ready. I crouched to a stop at the foot of the porch, training the gun on the door. Ten seconds passed. Then thirty. A full minute later, when no one kicked the door open to take a shot at me, I padded up the steps and hunkered down near the door, leaning the shotgun against the wall. A quick check showed the door was locked, so I slid the first house key in.

No luck.

I listened. Nothing.

I tried the next key. It slipped into place like it was greased. I grabbed the shotgun and eased the door open.

I'd entered a dusky and gloomy kitchen. Fried onions, old coffee grounds, and stale beer dominated the topmost layer of a deep stink that made me want to hold my breath. Beneath it was the ingrained odor of years ignoring basic hygiene. Pots and pans were stacked in the sink and fast-food bags and cups had been thrown on the counter. Aqua-tinged linoleum had come up in places, revealing the black, gummy adhesive that had been used to set it fifty years ago. Sunlight made gray and greasy by a filthy window couldn't improve the look of stains and caked bits of food on the stove.

I crept through the kitchen, moving with exquisite care so as to not step on the loose floorboards I knew had to be there, and into a plain old dining room. Once upon a time, the carpet had been removed, revealing a patchwork of plywood and subflooring, but the renovation couldn't hide the smell of mold and decay. Gun catalogs and car manuals were tossed on an old pine table with thick, knobby legs and four chairs around it. I sifted through the papers quickly but didn't see anything valuable. I pressed on.

The dining room gave way to a long hall with wainscoting and a chair rail. It led in a straight line to the front door and past the stairs to the second floor. I resisted the urge to head straight for the steps and forced myself to clear the entire first level. Crossing the hall, I eased open a swinging door and found myself in a room that once, long ago, had served as a parlor or drawing room.

As bare as the other rooms were, this one was chock-full of boxes and furniture, as if the contents of all the other rooms in the house had been piled in there for some reason. It smelled of cardboard, glue, and twine. The small noises I made sounded smothered and close thanks to the stacks of boxes. Dark wood paneling on the walls made the room especially dim and mournful. I stepped in the room and had just lifted the lid on the first box when, from behind me, came the unmistakable sound of a shell being racked into the chamber of a shotgun.

"You nosy son of a bitch," said a low voice. "You just don't know when to quit."

CHAPTER
TWENTY-EIGHT

"Drop it."

I took a deep breath and squatted, putting the shotgun on the floor. "Turn around."

Keeping my hands by my sides and away from my body, I did a slow pivot. Relaxing in an old rocking chair, hidden by stacks of boxes, was the by-now-familiar stoner face of Jay-bone. This time, however, instead of a pool cue or a case of beer, he held a pump-action riot gun. Twelve-gauge, based on the size of the black hole at the end he pointed at me, which looked as big as a drainpipe from where I was standing. Just like the one at my feet that I had no way of reaching. My fingers squeezed into fists, impotent.

Jay set the chair to rocking back and forth in place, the expression on his face amused. "Think you can reach your backup before I pull the trigger?"

I was ten feet away from the end of his 12-gauge. My SIG was in a waistband holster, but I'd never reach it in time; it might as well have been back home in Arlington. If I tried, the spread of shot from Jay's gun would shred me and just about every piece of paper in the room.

The coroner would need any untouched boxes to put all the little pieces in. "No."

"Good answer." He nodded. Or the rocking of the chair made it seem like it. "I guess if you're standing here, you must've put another dent in Toby's head?"

I forced myself to relax. If Jay wanted to talk, maybe I could keep him going until Warren made it in. "He'll live."

"Good. Maybe you jarred something loose in that moron's head."

"You expecting me?"

"It was the next logical step. Either you or Warren." Jay's voice had changed. It had lost its twang, gained a measure of self-assurance.

"You know, someone told me the Browers couldn't find their butt with both hands and a map," I said. "Which means someone else is the brains behind the meth empire taking shape here in Cain's Crossing. That wouldn't be you, would it?"

He grinned outright, showing crow's-feet around the eyes. "That's rich. No, I ain't the boss."

"You just run the errands, tote the bales? Check on the labs once in a while?"

"Yeah. And keep meth dealers from kicking in nosy ex-cops' doors at the Mosby and filling the room full of buckshot."

I raised an eyebrow. "What? You want credit for keeping the Browers on a leash?"

"Well, some fucking gratitude would be nice."

"You don't strike me as a softy, Jay. Why not score some points with the Browers?"

"I don't think my betters would approve."

"Are you kidding? Will would've given you a promotion."

"No, you idiot." He sighed dramatically. "Weren't you some kind of hotshot detective up in DC?"

"That's what they tell me."

"Well, can't you detect it? All the clues are there."

I stared at him, lost.

He rolled his eyes. "Singer, not every backwater cop is crooked or has their head in a bucket. Didn't you wonder why your buddy Bloch was being stonewalled by the Warrenton DEA? Didn't any alarm bells go off when Palmer told you he had Cain's Crossing under his wing? Asked you to leave things alone?"

My face flushed. I relaxed all the way and sat down with a thump on one of the boxes. I wouldn't need to talk myself out of anything. Unless it was obstruction charges. "DEA? Or FBI?"

Jay pulled the shotgun away and laid it across his lap, looking like some kind of modern Pa Kettle. "DEA, son. Special Agent Jay Shero. Warrenton office, as you might imagine."

"You've been all over this."

He nodded. "Palmer saw something change in the way things were being done around here. Busting some hillbillies for growing weed, a couple chopped cars, that's one thing. Epidemic levels of meth? Whole other prospect."

I shifted my weight and the boxes moved underneath me. "The chief knew he was in over his head, so he called you for help."

"Yep. Took a while to get anyone interested. Crank labs are in Iowa, Missouri, places like that. Not the Commonwealth of Virginia. Then a couple of cities started noticing a surge in tweakers with no good reason for it. Somebody remembered Palmer's call and we came down to nose around."

"So the chief gave you carte blanche to start an investigation. You took it from there, going undercover . . ."

"Hoping to find the brains behind the operation," he said. "Because, I can tell you, it ain't the Browers."

At that second, we both jumped as the front door banged open at the front of the house. Jay shot to his feet, fast, bringing the shotgun to a ready position. I snatched mine from the floor and whispered to Jay, "If it's Warren, he's with me."

"What the— Singer, Warren's one of our suspects," he hissed.

I shook my head. No time to explain. We could both hear cautious footsteps coming down the hall. Jay glanced at me nervously. I could understand why. If it was a Brower, Jay couldn't very well call the name of a local police officer out loud. If it was Warren, he couldn't poke his head out for fear Warren was in on it . . . or that Warren didn't think Jay was armed and dangerous. I only saw one option.

Jay hissed for me to stop as I moved to the doorway. I slipped my head around the corner to take a peek. It was Warren, holding a bead with the AR-15 straight ahead as he shuffled down the hall.

"Warren," I called. He jumped but kept from shooting me. "Keep cool. I got Jay-bone in here."

"That's a good fucking thing, bud," he said, jogging down the hall, out of breath. "Cuz all three Browers are back and they saw me hightail it in here."

Jay appeared in the corridor behind me, shotgun held at the ready. Warren yelled something and I managed to knock the assault rifle up.

"Hold it! Hold it!" I yelled.

"You son of a bitch, I thought you said you had him in there," Warren said, struggling with me to get the rifle free.

"Jay, goddamn it, tell Warren who you are," I said.

Jay didn't move the gun. "DEA, Warrenton office."

Warren froze, mouth hanging open comically. "What?"

"He's undercover," I almost shouted, trying to get through to him. We didn't need to shoot each other when the Browers might be seconds from opening the front door.

Warren dropped the barrel of his gun toward the floor. "Please tell me you're shitting me."

"Long story," I said. "Jay's DEA, been working with Palmer on the Browers. They cut you out of the loop; I'm guessing they didn't trust a native. We're on the same side."

"Speak for yourself, Singer," Jay said. "Warren here is still in the pool."

"I can prove I ain't in on it in about thirty seconds," Warren said, "when Will and Tank and Buck come through that door and start shooting."

"Jay, I trust him," I said quickly. "He's helped me out too much, too many things fit together, for him to be dirty. Same for you. Only you would know about my buddy Bloch and the call he put into Warrenton. Trust me on this."

Jay's eyes flicked back and forth between the two of us. Finally, he swore and lowered the shotgun, pointing to the kitchen. "Out the back. I'll head to the front and see if I can't stall 'em."

As Warren and I retraced our steps, we heard the front door open again. There was a long pause, then the door slammed shut. Heavy steps stomped down the hall. "Toby?" Tank Brower's deep voice called.

"Hey, Tank," I heard Jay call as he walked to the front of the house, where the voices became muffled.

Warren and I snaked our way down the hall, through the dining room, and into the kitchen. Keeping to a bent crouch, we were headed for the back door when Buck's head popped up like a jack-in-the-box on the other side of the half pane of glass. Without thinking, I jerked the shotgun up and pulled the trigger. Buck's face disappeared along with the glass and half the door.

The boom rocked the house. I dropped the stealth act and sprang forward, kicking the shreds of the back door free from the hinges. What was left of Buck was a mess at the bottom of the back steps. Without thinking, I racked another round into the chamber and was turning to tell Warren to cover me when we heard a matching boom from the front of the house, followed by a quick *pop-pop-pop*.

Warren yelled, "Circle around, find Will," and gave me a shove toward the open door before turning and running back to the front of the house. I scooted down the steps and circled Buck's twisted body in time to see Will's pickup roar around the corner of the house at top speed.

My perception slowed, stalled, and shrank to individual fractions of a second. I observed them almost impassively as they passed. I saw Will's face. He had the twin to Toby's AR-15 pointed out the window, balanced in the crook of his elbow. The dust from his tires kicked up in a plume behind him, obscuring the yard. There was an instant's recognition as he saw me, then a sick pause before the industrial rattle of the Armalite being fired filled the air.

It took a century for me to bring the shotgun up, aim at the truck, and pull the trigger. Stipples appeared broadside in the truck's driver-side door as it roared past. My body and mind processed the danger and the need automatically, shooting and pumping, shooting and pumping, until I realized I was out of rounds and the truck had slammed into the garden shed, knocking one wall down and getting beached on the brick foundation.

I dropped the shotgun and drew my SIG as I jogged to the truck. The side and back windows were shattered, as was the windshield. The door was mangled and through the hole where the window had been I could see Will, bloody, slumped over the wheel. I opened the door one-handed and he dropped halfway out of the seat and onto the ground. I dragged him by the collar the rest of the way out and, with a supreme effort, got him thirty feet away.

He was breathing, though his face was pimply with shot and his shirt flecked with blood. I put my fingers on his neck. His pulse was weak, but there. I did a quick frisk and turned up only a hunting knife. I ran back to the truck, picked up the AR-15 and was jogging for the back door, when Jay and Warren came out, wary and ready. They saw Will laid out in the grass and slowly straightened up.

I stopped. "You get both of them?"

Warren nodded. I ran a hand through my hair, shaking with adrenaline. My body was having a rough time dealing with the hours of waiting followed by the compressed and sudden violence. I took a deep breath, trying to get a grip. The day wasn't anywhere near done. "What about Mary Beth?"

Warren shrugged, shook his head.

I looked at Jay. "Was she ever here?"

He shook his head. "No. I don't know where they took her, Singer. I'm sorry."

I blew out a huge breath and sat down in the dust, beat.

CHAPTER
TWENTY-NINE

Warren, Jay, and I stood close together, watching while the ambulance crew worked on Will and zipped up the other two brothers. Jay seemed to have warily and grudgingly accepted that Warren was clean. For his part, Warren seemed to be caught somewhere between amused and irked that he'd been a suspect. What they thought of me, however, remained to be seen.

"I know sorry's not even going to cover it," I said to Jay as the paramedics lifted Will's stretcher and put it in the back of the ambulance. "But I'm sorry about the investigation."

Jay shook his head, shrugged, and looked away. "Spilt milk."

"Where did J.D. figure in all of this?"

Jay blew out a breath. "J.D. contacted our office when he got released. Offered to help. It was perfect timing. Palmer had asked us to intervene just a few months earlier and we were looking for a way to worm our way in. I was already making some progress, but Will's been keeping me on the outside."

"J.D. was a local boy, coming back after being in the big time," I said, putting it together. "It must've seemed too good to be true."

Jay made a face. "It was. That's why we staged that whole thing with the fight. Try to take the shine off him."

"Little bit of theater," Warren said, spitting to the side.

"Yep. And, let me tell you, J.D. Hope wasn't a trained stuntman. I had to get stitched up for real afterwards. Probably helped, though. They took him in after that and liked to joke about their two in-home brawlers."

"Why'd you keep Warren in the dark?"

Warren laughed. "You serious, Singer? The Brower and Warren family trees go back three hundred years. Hotshot, here, and the chief figured I *had* to be dirty."

I looked at Jay, who spread his hands. "Dirty or not, why involve him? Palmer asked for need-to-know only, and I can tell you that cops who went to kindergarten with the subjects of a DEA crackdown don't make the cut."

I went quiet, thinking things through. "What kind of deal did you have with J.D.?"

"We helped him find a place, set him up there, gave him his informant stipend."

"That's not all, though, was it."

It was Jay's turn to be quiet.

"You knew about his ALS," I said. Another statement, not a question.

Jay nodded. "We knew. We were able to set him up with an insurance plan for the treatment. Five hundred a month doesn't exactly cover the bill."

"The guy was sick as a dog," I said. A surprising jolt of anger shot through me. I'd known what it was like to be dangerously ill. I didn't like what it implied about the way he'd been used. "You were just going to ride him until he was dead?"

"His choice, Singer," Jay said, his mouth a thin, flat line. "No, his *demand.* J.D. wanted to do one good thing and this was it. He told me his life was already over. He wanted to do something real, something right. And when he found this shit was going on in his own hometown, he wanted to pitch in and do something."

I didn't say anything.

"If it makes you feel any better, I tried to talk him out of it," Jay said. "Told him to go to the hospital and take care of himself. Or hole up with his crazy mother. But he threatened to shoot the Browers on his own if we didn't let him work as a CI on the case."

"Was he getting anywhere, at least?"

Jay nodded. "Top-notch. He was ready to leapfrog me and get introduced to whoever is pulling the strings on this thing. Maybe they trusted a local boy more, maybe they just liked how he was working out. Either way, he was close to cracking the nut. Still would've meant a few weeks of work to get them on a tap and round up the evidence, but we were slapping high fives in the office when we heard J.D. was near a promotion."

"And then he was killed?"

"And then he was killed," Jay said.

"What's your theory? Did they make him? Was it all a setup?"

"We don't think so. I know Will wanted him to meet the boss, not just because it was time, but because they wanted J.D. to go back to DC and put together the buys that they couldn't. I was around enough to know they were serious about that expansion. It wasn't all a snow job to get him to relax just so they could pop him. Another month and they would've sent him to DC with a truck full of crank."

"That's a big investment," I said. "Of money. Of trust."

"Exactly. That's why we don't think the Browers or their boss took J.D. out."

I was quiet again. "You know my next question, then."

"If they didn't kill him, then who did?"

"Right," I said. "Well?"

Jay looked at me. "We have no idea."

"The kingpin," Warren said. "Find him, you find whoever offed good ol' J.D."

"And Mary Beth," I said.

We turned as a cruiser came up the drive. No siren, reds-and-blues flashing. Palmer got out of the car and started walking toward us.

"This ought to be interesting," Warren said. "Be a lot easier over a beer or two."

Palmer marched up to our little triangle and put his hands on his hips, looking at us. "Anyone want to explain this royal clusterfuck to me?"

We took turns explaining what had happened in the last twenty-four hours, or at least as much as we knew. As we stood there, we were all reminded, uncomfortably, that Palmer hadn't trusted Warren enough to bring him in on the investigation. And Palmer wasn't anyone's fool. He knew the only reason Warren probably set me on the Browers, precipitating the shoot-out, was because his detective didn't trust *him*. But they were going to have to play makeup on their own time.

"Do we have any idea where Mary Beth is?" I asked. "Jay?"

He shook his head. "She wasn't in the house or I would've known. And none of the Browers mentioned her. Tank started to say something about being on the road last night when Will told him he was going to tear his head off if he didn't shut up. That's all I heard."

"No other safe houses? Cabins? Back of a store or something?"

"If there are, they never told me," he said, running a hand through his hair. "My job was to check the labs and watch the family house. That's all they trusted me to do."

I turned to Palmer. "No leads on the brains behind all of this? The one pulling the strings on the Browers?"

He looked at me. "That's what the DEA investigation was supposed to do. We knew they were cooking meth a year ago. We didn't need to shoot them, we needed the guy running the show. That's for shit, now, thanks to you and Warren."

He was probably right, but if we started pointing fingers, we'd be here all night. "What about Will?"

"He's out and sedated. No help."

I glanced at Jay and Warren again. "So, we've got nothing?"

They both studied their feet, saying nothing. Finally, Jay said, "We can search the house, see if we find something. I never had a chance to go through their personal stuff. Might get lucky."

"What are we waiting for?" I asked. "Let's take that place apart."

"There's no *us* here, Singer," Palmer said, staring at me. "You've done enough damage. I don't want you going anywhere near that place. From now on, your involvement with this case is over."

I gritted my teeth. "That woman could be out there, right now, looking for help."

"And we'll find her," Palmer said, his face grim, emphasizing each word. "Without your assistance. If I see you near this place again or breaking into any more farmhouses or barns or homes trying to find her, I'll have you arrested. You're lucky you're not in custody now."

I glanced at the other two, but couldn't expect to get any support there. Warren raised his eyebrows and Jay gave a small shrug. It didn't make me happy, but it made sense. If Warren wanted to keep his job, he had to keep his mouth shut. And relations were probably strained enough between the local PD and the DEA, so Jay wasn't going to come to my rescue. He might be okay with me personally, but I had single-handedly stomped all over a DEA investigation that had been going moderately well before I'd pulled into Cain's Crossing.

"One last question," I said. "Who killed J.D. Hope?"

"Mr. Singer, it's time to leave," Palmer said, pointing to the cruiser like I was a bad dog. "Warren, take our guest down to the station and get a statement, then drop him off at his hotel. Singer, stick around for a few days so we can find you. But go anywhere besides your hotel or Lula's and you'll sit it out in a cell."

Warren grumbled the entire way to the station. I stayed silent, worrying about Mary Beth. I understood Palmer wanted me out of his hair, and that some procedure had to be followed, but he didn't seem to be doing anything to find her. I mentioned some possibilities to Warren, but he seemed to be done with going rogue.

"Leave it to him, Singer," he said as we pulled into the station. "Now that the case is busted wide open, he can actually trust me and the other cops on the roster to start looking for her. Not to mention he's got the DEA to help out now. I think you've started enough fires around here, bud."

We went inside where he took my statement, then we got back in the cruiser and he took me out to the auto body shop to pick up my car. "Stay out of trouble, Singer," he shouted to me as he pulled away. "It would suck to have to arrest you after all we've been through."

I cleaned off the dirt I'd put on my own car, got in, and started the engine.

And I thought.

No way was I going to just pack it in and let the chief's crew handle finding Mary Beth.

Palmer could threaten me from now until Christmas, but I wasn't ready to cash in my chips and drive north or sit in my room until I heard they'd found Mary Beth's body. It wasn't against the law to knock on doors and ask some questions. But Palmer would no doubt run me out of town once he had his ducks in a row. So, I didn't have much time. I headed back for the center of Cain's Crossing, working through my options.

I was just about out of friends. Warren was out, Jay was out. Dorothea Hope, even if she didn't blame me for leading to her daughter's kidnapping, would be of little use. Sam Bloch could help me from a distance, but once he learned that the DEA had had a live investigation on the meth angle, he would probably want to back away and let them take care of things. He might sympathize with my interest in seeing through the original goal of finding J.D.'s killer, but there was no way for a DC cop to bulldoze a federal investigation. And I wouldn't ask him to do it if he could.

That left Chick Reyes. I doubted he'd want to do anything that would jeopardize his long-term relationship with Palmer, but he wouldn't be much of a reporter if he didn't want at least a nibble about the extermination of the Brower gang. I grabbed my phone, brushed grass and dirt from the case, and thumbed through my recent calls. Chick's number was near the top. He picked up on the second ring.

"You been pretty busy," he said.

"News travels fast."

"I told you, I got eyes and ears in this town."

"You've got a police scanner is what you mean," I said.

"That, too," he admitted.

"I need a favor."

"Again? You haven't brought me much in the way of groundbreaking intelligence, man."

"Yeah, well, that's about to change," I said. "You got something to write with?"

I proceeded to tell him everything that had happened at the Browers', all the way to getting kicked off the case, if there'd ever been one, by the chief himself.

"Chick? You there?" I said. He'd gone completely silent after my five-minute narration.

"Sorry. I was just processing what you told me. There was a DEA probe going on? You're sure?"

"Yeah. But don't waste your time trying for confirmation from their office. They'll just deny it."

"Do I have the rest of this right? Hope and this guy Shero were both working undercover, trying to bust the ring from the inside, but they never found the guy who's running the show?"

"Right," I said. I was pulling into the outskirts of town, where life kept bumping along. It was an early Saturday afternoon, and people were out and about their business, despite the tremendous violence that had just occurred a few miles away.

"Jesus. But they don't think the Browers killed J.D.?"

"Nope."

"And they don't know where the lady is?"

"Negative," I said.

"They're really batting a thousand, huh?"

"Yeah, and Palmer blames me for it."

"They want you to stop sticking your nose where it doesn't belong? Or they'll cut it off?"

"You've got the gist," I said. "That's why I called you. I'm not going to get arrested over this, but I'm pretty damn interested in where Mary Beth is and I still wouldn't mind finding the guy who offed J.D. It's why I came to this stupid town in the first place."

"What do you need from me?"

"With Palmer climbing Warren's frame, I don't even have a whiff of law-enforcement help on this," I said. "You are now my only source of information in this town."

"Yeah?"

"And I could use some help running down a few things. Somebody had to know how the pseudoephedrine got into town, saw a shipment, knows something. Those eyes and ears of yours might've picked up something that helps point us in the right direction. And that might help us find Mary Beth."

"Palmer's not going to be very happy when he hears you're still hanging around. And not real happy with me for helping you, either."

"I know," I said. "So we've got to do whatever it is we're going to do quick. Think you can help me?"

He hesitated. "Right now?"

"Are you listening? I've probably got until lunchtime tomorrow before I'm screwed," I said. "Not to mention, Mary Beth's still out there somewhere, scared or hurt or dead. And I'm going to find her."

There was a pause, then, "Shit."

"C'mon, Chick. That Pulitzer isn't going to win itself."

"All right, all right. Can you handle big numbers? Let me give you my address," he said and rattled off directions to his house. "Just don't make a big noise coming here, okay? I don't mind kicking Palmer in the nuts for all the problems he's given me over the years, but I don't need to end up spending the rest of my life in a white man's jail, either. You got me?"

"I got you," I said.

CHAPTER THIRTY

Chick lived in a single-level rancher outside of town. The house perched on a treeless rise overlooking hundreds of grassy yards in every direction. The lawn's only interruption was a tall flagpole sprouting from a slate pedestal planted in the middle of the front yard like a challenge. Old Glory snapped and swayed in the breeze. A long, wet-looking driveway led straight from the road to a single-stall garage. Chick's yellow Camaro sat in front of the stall door, gleaming like a small sun.

I parked behind the Camaro and climbed out of my car slowly. The day had been long and at a level of activity I wasn't used to. As I walked to the house, the front door opened and Chick poked his head out, glancing at, around, and past me. Even after I'd entered, he took a half step outside, scanning the road and front yard leading to his house. Satisfied, he came back inside, closed the door, and looked me over.

"Holy shit, man. You look like twenty miles of bad road," he said when I came fully into the light. I glanced down at myself. I was covered in dirt, corn silk, and blood, and one of my eyes wouldn't stop weeping from where I'd taken a pine branch across the face.

"You should see the other guys," I said. "But, yeah, I didn't have time to change. Can't take me out anywhere."

"You want a drink?" he asked, moving toward what I assumed was the kitchen.

"Just water, if you got it." I glanced around the living room. I'd expected a kitschy, 1970s décor judging from the outside. Or maybe a sloppy bachelor's pad, filled with cheap furniture. But I was surprised to see a matching leather suite, a couple pieces of original art, and a large flat-screen TV mounted on the wall. Somewhere in the house, another TV blared loud enough to be distracting. "Nice place. Newspaper work must be more lucrative than I've been led to believe."

I heard the faucet in the kitchen turn on. "I'm the only game in town, my friend. Pretty much in the whole county. When you're a monopoly of one, you do pretty well. Plus what I saved in the army."

"You don't even watch TV in here, do you?" I said. I almost had to yell.

"What? Oh, that. I got a man cave in the basement. That's where I go for football. The living room is for the girls."

"Must be nice."

He returned with a tall glass of water for me and a beer for himself. Putting the beer down on an end table, he headed down a hallway to the back of the house. "Hold tight. I want to get my laptop so we can take some notes."

"Hurry up. Mary Beth's out there somewhere," I said, taking a long pull of water. I sighed as it hit my system, then paced around the room, looking at the sleek décor without actually seeing it. I was exhausted, antsy, my nerves jangling. To give my hands something to do, I pulled my phone out and checked the screen, thumbing through numbers, names, and menus. A voice mail from Sam Bloch was the only thing of note. I punched in the access number while I waited for Chick to come back.

"Marty, it's Sam," the message started. "I finally heard back from a contact in Customs over in Norfolk, trying to get some more background on Will Brower. He had a couple interesting things to say. Seems like it was well known Will got the job through some pal in the service. Apparently the door got slammed in his face because of a dishonorable discharge and this guy was there to help him."

I kept up my circuit around the living room as the message continued, idly sipping water as I stared at one of the frames on the wall. "The hiring thing made a bunch of people unhappy, because the same guy brought on a third crony from the army, bypassing standard hiring practice. Then things died down when Will and this other guy quit a few years ago. The third guy stayed on, but things have been running smoothly ever since. I know you'll want names." I heard papers being shuffled. "Will Brower, of course. The guy still at Customs is Junior Helmsley. And the last one, the one who quit, was one Ricardo Reyes. Haven't been able to find anything on him yet, but we'll get someone to pick up Junior later today or tomorrow—"

The glass of water fell from my hand as I spun in place, pawing at my gun.

I expected to see Chick drawing a bead on me with an M16, but there was nothing but empty hallway. I held my breath, listening. Sam's message continued playing from the phone in a tinny falsetto. The ice cubes in my spilled glass slipped past each other and onto the rug. From somewhere deeper in the house, the second TV drowned out all the little sounds I so desperately needed to hear: footsteps, a cough, a creaking floor.

I raised my phone again and cut the voice mail off, then dialed Warren's number, glancing at the hallway in between each press of a button. The phone rang three, four, five times, then went to voice mail. I cursed and waited for the beep.

"Warren, it's Singer," I said in a hoarse whisper. "I'm at Chick Reyes's house. It's him. He's the kingpin. Haul your ass out here."

I hung up and pocketed the phone. Still no sound from the hall or farther back in the house aside from the trumpeting of commercials from the second TV. The normally domestic swell of sound was incongruous and surreal.

I swallowed and crept down the hall, my gun raised and ready. The thought crossed my mind that I should wait for Warren to show, but I could wait all day for him to check his voice mail and by then it might be too late for Mary Beth, if she were even alive. I covered the doors with my gun, peering into spare bedrooms as I walked the length of the hall. At the midpoint, on the left, was a set of steps leading to the basement. The blare of the TV was deafening at the top of the steps. I considered. The stairwell was carpeted and drywalled, so I didn't have to worry about being seen between the treads as I went down the steps, but there was a turn in the landing, so I'd be going down blind.

I took a deep breath and descended the steps, taking each one heel to toe. The TV covered any noise I might make, but caution is a habit that's hard to break. When I got to the landing, I peered around the corner. The angle was too steep for me to see into the far corner of the basement, but the glance showed a couple of couches and an easy chair. I continued until I could see the entire basement. The décor was dark hues of brown and green, a hunting lodge style. The TV making all the noise squatted in one corner, blaring baseball scores at an empty room.

To the right of the steps was a small door. A utility closet or laundry room. The door was slightly open. I circled the room wide so that I wasn't opening the door across my body, then opened it slowly and incrementally from the far side. When there was a gap big enough for my head, I peered in. It was the laundry room, unfinished and rough. It went back about twenty feet, then turned to the right in an L shape, essentially going under the first-floor steps. I couldn't see past the angle of the turn, where a single bare bulb illuminated shelves of paint cans, brushes, and rags. I padded into the tiny room and turned the corner.

Tied to a kitchen chair was Mary Beth. Duct tape covered her mouth from ear to ear and her hands were lashed behind her so tight that she had to arch her back painfully. Her eyes were wide and white and she was breathing heavily. Standing behind her was Chick, his dark eyes boring into me. One hand pressed a large handgun to Mary Beth's temple. The other was a fist twisted in her hair, keeping her head immobile and cocked at a painful angle.

Chick grinned, his trademark teeth flashing. "So, amigo. I guess you came into some information recently. Like, in the last five minutes."

"I did," I said, watching his eyes. "Not the information I was hoping for, though. Guess I should've figured it out earlier."

"I really had you going, eh?"

"You did. Helpful small-town reporter, in touch with everything that's going on. A walking, talking *Who's Who of Cain's Crossing*."

He rolled one of those mints around his mouth and it made a clacking sound against his teeth. "I thought I'd started to lose my edge, you know, dealing with rednecks all the time. I wasn't sure if I could pull one over on a big-city cop. I came pretty close, huh?"

"Real close," I said, nodding slowly. Whatever it took to keep him talking. "The link to Customs was what did you in."

"Ah, shit," he said, almost jokingly. "You put it all together, then?"

"You and Will Brower were in the army together. You hit it off and he tells you how his hometown is so far away from everything that it would make a great place to grow weed or start a meth lab. But you don't know where to get the pseudoephedrine and without it, you're like every other tweaker out there, making meth one plastic bag at a time. No money in that."

Chick's grin never wavered, but it was brittle and his eyes were too bright. I went on, keeping my tone conversational and steady, trying not to look at Mary Beth. The TV droned on inanely in the other room.

"You figure the problem isn't making the deal to get the suzie, it's getting it into the country. But Will knows this guy Junior Helmsley, who's got a job just where you need him to be, the Customs office in Norfolk. He brings you two on, you learn the ropes, then offer Junior a cut of the profits every time he gets a shipment of bogus electronic parts through. With—what? One in ten thousand containers getting inspected?—you were almost foolproof. And if by some miracle your shipment got inspected, Junior was there to stamp it okay. With that in place, all you had to do was teach the local yokels how to cook and, *bam*, brand-new source of meth on the East Coast."

"You've really been doing your homework, Marty," Chick said. "You sure you're retired? You part of that DEA thing?"

I shook my head. "Didn't even know about it."

He laughed. "You're shitting me."

"I wish I were, Chick. I didn't even finger Jay for undercover. Must've been a hell of a surprise for you."

"I never really trusted him," Chick said. "Just like I never trusted Hope."

"That why you had him snuffed?"

"Hey, man. I can't take credit for all the crime in the county."

"Come on, Chick. You expect me to believe you didn't take J.D. out?"

Chick shrugged. "I *would've*, if I'd known. But I didn't kill him and the boys never did anything that big Will didn't tell them to do. And he didn't do anything without asking me first. Sorry, amigo, you can't lay that one on me."

I stared at him, trying to decipher what he was saying. He had no reason to lie about J.D., but I had no reason to believe him.

"So, I guess we're at an impasse," Chick continued, cheerfully. "I can't really go anywhere with you in my way. And I know you don't want to let me past you. But that's exactly what you're going to do. The three of us are going to back out of this room, close as lovers, and you're going to sit down in my man cave and watch as I head out of here with the lady."

I stared at him, frozen.

"Hey, you listening?" he asked. He grabbed Mary Beth's hair tighter in his fist and shook her head, causing her to scream through the tape. "Don't space out on me, Marty. I'll shoot her in the fucking foot, if you need a little demonstration. Is that what you want, huh?"

I was looking at Chick, at Mary Beth crying, but what I saw was J.D.'s face in the courtroom, the look of judgment, the warning he gave the last time I saw him.

"Marty, don't mess with this, okay? You, me, the lady here, we can all get out of this okay. I know you haven't told the cops yet; you didn't have a clue about me until you got here. I promise I won't hurt her if you just back the hell up—"

"You're not going to take this away from me," I said.

His grin wavered a bit, not knowing what I meant. But he thought he was in control and relaxed, though the gun never left Mary Beth's head. "Well, partner, you don't really have a choice. You're going to ask me to let the lady go. I'm going to refuse. Then you'll back away, slowly. Even if you called Warren before you came out, you're going to let me walk out of here. Either way, it doesn't look good—"

I shot him.

Placement had always been a forte of mine. My round went right above the tip of his nose and out the other side, a through-and-through meant to plow through his brain stem and stop his body from spasming, a last twitch of his trigger finger that would be fatal for Mary Beth.

The gunshot's flat clap was incredibly loud in the tiny space. Mary Beth screamed through the tape and jerked her head from side to side, trying to untangle Chick's hand from her hair as his body folded like a lawn chair and hit the cement floor with a slapping sound, the grin still on his face. The handgun fell from his fingers and clattered next to him.

I jumped forward and kicked it away, then cut Mary Beth free. I held her while she sobbed and we backed out of the laundry room and into the basement as one. I kept my arms wrapped around her while the TV blared on. And that's how Warren found us when he came down the stairs, shotgun in hand, a look of disbelief on his face.

CHAPTER
THIRTY-ONE

It wasn't what I'd wanted. We could've learned a lot from Chick if I'd talked him down. And violence is the last option in a hostage situation. But he was right. We'd been stuck and it wouldn't have gotten any rosier when Warren came on the scene. Chick had cornered himself and was smart enough to know that there were very few ways to win once you'd played that card. I couldn't see him choosing to go down solo. There would've been more than one casualty if the situation had been allowed to play out.

The circus began soon after Warren showed. Palmer, Jay, and then a host of agents descended on the place throughout the afternoon and into the evening, asking us questions, retracing the steps, second-guessing my decisions. I answered as best I could. Eventually, the interrogation ran out of steam, though Warren gave me a look that I knew well enough. This had been the preamble. Palmer and the DEA squad would require follow-ups and interviews until every last scrap of the case was examined, reexamined, and logged. I'd be booking a few more nights at the Mosby.

But that was the future. Bone-weary, I pressed them to let us go. Palmer looked unhappy, but he and I both knew there wasn't anything more to do. Finally, near midnight, they gave us grudging permission to leave. Mary Beth refused to go to the hospital, telling the medics she'd been scared, not hurt, then asked me to drive her home.

I held her hand the whole way, feeling her quiver from time to time. She was quiet and I asked if she wanted to talk. She shook her head, but never let go of my hand.

The silence of the drive back to town gave me the room to think. The night had cooled off and I had the windows down for the first time in weeks. It felt good and an odd calm settled over my thoughts. At first, it was pleasant to have a mind empty and devoid of thought.

But eventually—despite the clear, cool breeze flowing over me like water and the serenity of the night putting me at ease—my mind began toying with the layers of conversation I'd had and heard, splicing what I knew with what I could guess.

Maybe I was on the edge of a true exhaustion that had bestowed a clarity of vision. Maybe it was Chick's confession. Maybe it was just time for me to put the pieces together. Whatever the reason, with sudden crystalline clarity, all the answers I'd been looking for since I'd stopped at the billboard along the highway came together in a perfect lattice of cause and effect. Facts meshed with guesswork, dates merged with places, and people slotted into their places just so. The truth spread out in front of me like a map, with landmarks and points of interest along the way.

My deductions made me think of the extent of J.D.'s life, the good and bad that he had done, juxtaposed against my own past. I'd like to think that I'd done more good than harm in my time, but I wondered how you measured it. Was it enough to do a little good? Some of what was required, some of what you were capable of? Maybe it was all worthless if you didn't follow through all the way. Had J.D. redeemed himself simply by trying? Or would he have thought of himself as a failure for not having actually accomplished his one right thing before he died? Did any of us deserve grace if we only tried, but didn't succeed?

I turned the car onto Beal. The crickets were out again and the night was very still now that we were in town. The moon, full and luminous, worked to break free of the treetops. Driving slowly, testing my new insights, I came to a decision by the time I parked in front of the old home. I turned the car off and started to get out.

Mary Beth turned to me. Her face was as white as milk. "You don't have to come in. I'm fine."

"I think I have to," I said. "Your mother deserves to hear the whole story."

She looked at me quizzically, but got out and led the way up the walk and into the house. Inside, all was dark save for a single light in the side parlor.

Dorothea's voice, quavering, called, "Who is that?"

"It's me, Mother," Mary Beth said and hurried into the next room. I stayed in the foyer as, through her tears, Mary Beth explained what had happened. I heard the rise and fall of her voice as she described the entire ordeal, Dorothea's voice wobbling as she asked questions, her own emotions barely under control. After a moment, their voices subsided.

"Mr. Singer?" I heard Dorothea call. I walked to the parlor. The two were sitting on a divan, holding hands. The elder woman looked wan and thin, like parchment worn almost all the way through. A phone and a glass of water were on an end table next to the divan. A book lay on the couch beside her, its pages marked with a newspaper clipping.

"Mrs. Hope," I said, nodding.

"Mr. Singer," she said, nodding. "It looks like I have you to thank for rescuing my daughter."

"It had to be done, Mrs. Hope," I said.

"And I thank you again," she said primly, then looked at me expectantly. "Is that all?"

I cleared my throat. "I know this has been an incredibly trying time for both of you, but there's one thing that still hasn't been resolved."

"My God, Mr. Singer. Surely it can wait," Dorothea said, exasperated. Mary Beth looked at me in surprise and irritation, resembling her mother more than I would've thought possible. "My daughter was kidnapped, held against her will, and almost killed. I appreciate what you've done for us, but really, this is too much."

"I understand your irritation, Mrs. Hope," I said. "But if you answer my questions, this will probably be my last visit."

"As much as I relish the thought, I really must insist you leave," she said.

"Mother, I'd be dead without Marty," Mary Beth said. "The least we could do is hear him out."

"Does it have to be now? Surely it could wait a day?"

"I don't think so, Mrs. Hope." As clear as my vision had been on the way back to town, I'd been afraid of the answer I'd discovered. I needed the truth now or I'd never ask for it.

"Good Lord, if you must," Dorothea said, shaking her head.

"Where is Ferris?"

Mary Beth blinked and Dorothea's mouth twisted at the unexpected question. "This is what you need to know so desperately, Mr. Singer?"

"Yes."

"Ferris left a few days ago to visit family in Tennessee," Dorothea said with an exaggerated sigh. "I'm not sure when he plans to come back."

"That's odd, isn't it? That you shouldn't know?"

"I don't own the man, Mr. Singer. He can come and go as he wishes."

"He's almost the only help you have around the house," I said, pressing. "It seems odd he should decide to leave your side the moment you need him the most."

"What are you getting at, Marty?" Mary Beth asked.

I looked at Dorothea square. "When did you know J.D. had ALS?"

Her gaze was withering. "I knew when my daughter told me, Mr. Singer. My son was not a good communicator, as you know. I doubt he would've told me even on his deathbed."

I matched her stare. Her eyes were flat and glasslike, dolls' eyes. "That's not really true, is it?"

"What are you insinuating, Mr. Singer?"

"I've just spent a week learning about J.D. and dissecting the lives of the crooks he spent time with here. I know that he'd returned to do something better with his life, to turn it around—even if there wasn't much of it left—and leave his home better than he'd found it."

She was silent.

"I also spent a lot of time with the men who wanted to use J.D., to help them grow a drug empire, one that would make them millions of dollars if they were able to establish a connection to large cities like Washington, DC."

"And what could that possibly have to do with us?" Dorothea asked.

"These men weren't the type to kill someone quickly. I can guarantee you, if Will Brower had even the barest suspicion that J.D. was working undercover against him, your son would be in the basement of that farmhouse, suffering right now. J.D.'s death, in reality, was merciful. And none of the criminals he was involved with could be described with that word."

The old woman said nothing, just stared back at me.

"Anyone who looked at J.D.'s murder would think it was just history catching up with him, a lifetime of bad decisions and crime and violence coming home to roost. It's the way I approached it, how the cops looked at it, what the world believed. Too bad we were all wrong. None of us guessed that he was killed for something that had nothing to do with his past."

Dorothea's lip quivered slightly. Mary Beth looked as though part of her wanted me to stop, as though she knew what was coming might be better left unsaid.

"J.D. wasn't killed by gangsters or a hit man or the Browers," I said to Dorothea softly. "It was you. You had Ferris kill him."

Mary Beth gasped.

Dorothea didn't say anything, but small tears welled up and spilled, following the path of the wrinkles and folds of her skin. Her breaths came in short gasps that pulled her lower lip in like a child's.

"Mother?" Mary Beth asked.

The old woman began nodding to herself.

"Mother," Mary Beth repeated, sharply.

"It is," the old woman whispered with painstaking care, not looking at either of us, "a terrible disease. I went to that doctor of his and he told me it was nothing but willpower and medicine that was keeping my son alive. He was in so much pain. And he was running around, killing himself to help those damn policemen put the damn Browers in jail."

"It was what he wanted," I said.

She took a deep breath that caught and shuddered in her throat. Her eyes pinned me like darts. "My son was *hurting*, Mr. Singer. He was *dying*. And after you put him in prison for something he didn't even do, he possessed the decency to come home to make amends. But those policemen kept asking him for more. To hell with them. I saw him. A week before . . . before it happened. He was so weak, so sick. All he had were the pills. They were all that was keeping him alive. That's when I knew I had to do something. I had to make a stand, as I've always done. I couldn't do it myself, but I knew Ferris could."

"Not your choice," I said, not sure with what authority I made the statement.

She glared at me. "I told you once, Mr. Singer. I've always made the hard decisions. For my home. For my family. I've never made a more difficult choice than I did that night. But I made it anyway. Ferris understood that and did what was needed. He loved my son like a brother and knew what I required of him was right."

"Oh my God," Mary Beth said and let go of Dorothea's hand. "Oh my *God.*"

"God doesn't enter into it," Dorothea said harshly. "I killed my son because I loved him. And the only thing I have God to thank for is giving me the strength to do what was right."

I said nothing, looking at the floor. Around us, the old house sighed and creaked and popped. Except for Dorothea's ragged breathing, it was the only sound for a long moment. We were caught together by the awful truth and that truth did nothing to heal or help. Eventually, I raised my eyes and met Dorothea's glare.

"Does that satisfy your *curiosity*, Mr. Singer?" she asked, her voice poisonous. Her head shook with anger or age or grief. "Has justice been *served*? Have you been *redeemed*?"

I said nothing.

Mary Beth wiped tears away. "Would you . . . would you excuse us?"

I showed myself out and retraced my steps down the walkway. The moon was out in full now. Radiant, etching everything it touched in blue and silver, giving a glow to the world. I walked to my car and got in. I sat for one weary minute, digesting what I'd seen and heard and said and done, then drove away into the darkness, never sorrier that I'd been right.

PLEASE CONTINUE READING TO
SAMPLE THE NEXT MARTY SINGER
MYSTERY, *THE SPIKE*.

CHAPTER ONE

Killing a quarter hour on a DC subway platform is like being trapped in George Orwell's head the day before he started writing *1984*.

Back in the seventies, the transit authority tried to sell the people mover as a hallmark of progress and cheer by calling it *the Metro*, but the stations are still drab, concrete vaults with low lighting not so different than that of a funeral parlor. Coffin-sized depressions meant to dampen the crushing noise of trains and passengers dimple the ceiling, the pattern reminiscent of a hive colony of killer insect-men from a B-grade horror flick—a joke I'm sure wasn't lost on the thousands of drones who used the Metro to get to their jobs every day. Terra-cotta floor tiles laid in a honeycomb pattern give a fleeting sense of emotional warmth that is immediately nullified by flickering digital billboards, while a strange smell of burnt vinyl and industrial fluid hangs in the air of most stations.

Luckily, taking the Metro was unusual for me. Thirty years as a homicide cop in the city meant I had access to my own wheels at all times—waiting seventeen minutes for transportation to arrive wasn't going to cut it when someone's been shot. So for three decades I'd grown accustomed to traveling any way I liked, any time I liked. I'd pulled my cruiser onto sidewalks, across the mouths of alleys, on lawns with one wheel hovering off the ground.

But those days were gone. A parking ticket had made me rethink my low opinion of the Metro and now I was leaning against a half-wall in the Waterfront Metro station, brooding and thinking gray, Orwellian thoughts, waiting for the north- and westbound Green line to chug from its endpoint at Branch Avenue and pick me up at Waterfront. I was on my way home after visiting my adopted daughter, Amanda, at her new job as a program manager at FirstStep, a women's shelter in Southeast DC. The journey was just six or so stops, but it would be half an hour before I saw my front door.

I sighed and squirmed. I'd forgotten to bring a book—a mistake no savvy Metro-goer would make—so, to pass the time, I started naming the kings and queens of Britain after the Conquest, moved on to listing the starting offensive line for the 1982 Super Bowl Champion Redskins, and, finally, just watched people.

A gaggle of teens ate fries and laughed about something that had happened in school. A white businesswoman—youngish in a smart-looking skirt and blazer, eyes glued to her smartphone—negotiated the escalator and took a spot on the rubber mat close to the edge of the platform without once looking up. Three guys in paint-speckled work clothes, holding hard hats and backpacks, stood and talked quietly to one side, already done with the day by early afternoon. A repairman in a neon vest and Carhartt overalls jawed with a young Metro cop. The station's elevator opened and an elderly woman exited, then moved slowly and painfully to the end of the platform. A slim black or Hispanic guy in jeans and an untucked dress shirt rode the escalator down, white earphones in his ears, head bobbing to music. He was followed by two bureaucrats with plastic ID tags on their lapels, a fat guy with a cane, and a young mother trailing two little kids, blond with blotchy red faces. After a few minutes, enough commuters had filled the platform to turn it from a collection of individuals to an indiscriminate mob of people, and I let my mind wander back to history and football.

Soft amber floor lights near the lip of the track began pulsing, a warning that the train was close. People rose from their seats to shuffle closer to the edge of the platform, trying to guess where the train doors would stop, jockeying for the best spot out of habit. I stayed where I was. Middle of the day, a handful of riders getting on, probably few people looking to exit—I could afford to lean on my wall, then walk straight onto the train.

The train, still out of view, gave an unexpected blast from its horn, a warning honk, as if we hadn't already heard it thundering down the track. Everyone winced as the sound bounced off the cement floors, walls, and ceiling. Headlights lit the curved walls of the tunnel, then became bright points of light in the darkness. There were two more earsplitting honks and then the train shot out of the tunnel to our right like a bullet out of a gun. We watched it come down the track.

Had I pushed away from the wall and gotten to my feet, my head would've been down and I would've missed what happened. If I'd glanced at my phone or scratched my nose or even blinked, I wouldn't have seen a thing. As it was, I was watching the incoming train like it was on a movie screen and couldn't have had a better view of what happened next.

With exquisite timing, a man from the crowd took three running steps and exploded into the lower back of the smartly dressed business-woman, delivering a perfect body check. The woman flew into the path of the train as though she'd jumped and, in my mind's eye, the movie froze in place in that instant. Her head was thrown back and her mouth open like she was singing an aria, while her wrists and ankles trailed from the impact as though she were an angel learning to fly. A stylish neck scarf floated behind her like a pennon. Then, with terrifying speed and violence, she was swept away by the front of the train as though she'd never existed.

Images and sounds fractured from that one instant into jag-ged, discrete chunks, like reflections on a broken mirror. The train's emergency brake slammed on, the scream of the wheels merging with the screams of the onlookers on the platform. Those who had been behind or to the left of the woman had seen everything—those to her right, watching the train approach, had only a vague idea that something horrific had happened. Some rushed after the train while others stood frozen, their eyes huge with the whites showing or their hands over their mouths in shock. The repairman had dropped his tool belt and was one of those sprinting down the platform, yelling for help, while the Metro cop stared down the track, his mouth literally hanging open. One of the bureaucrats had grabbed the shoulder of the other, the fabric of the man's suit bunched in his fist as they both stared down the track. The teens hugged each other and started to cry.

Instinct took over and, like many of the others, I took a half dozen steps toward the front of the train before another part of me—the one that had been conditioned by thirty years of police work—kicked in and I stopped myself. The woman was dead. Or she had more help than she could possibly use. Nothing I could do would matter.

But no one had gone after the man who had just killed her.

I spun on my heel and sprinted to the escalator to the right, the only way off the platform and out of the station. I had no idea who I was looking for. My attention had been on the woman and I had only a blurred memory of the man's shape, nothing of his age or race. I replayed the memory in my mind while the screams and shouts rose around me—my own heart was slamming in my chest and I was hyper-aware of the seconds slipping away. A slim form, medium height—young?—and a red baseball cap jammed low on a head. *A cap. Look for the cap.*

I took the escalator steps three at a time. Another Metro cop and the station manager jogged toward me, keys and nightstick and radio jangling as they moved, already on their way to the scene. The cop yelled "Hey!" as I ran past, but I ignored him and aimed for the turnstiles that marked the first hurdle out of the station. A few commuters, unaware of the tragedy downstairs, were moving through them in my direction. Most were engrossed in books or their phones and one unfortunate twenty-something in a suit and tennis shoes wandered unconsciously into my path. At six three, two ten, I wouldn't have come close to making the cut for that Redskins lineup I'd been daydreaming about, but I was in full stride and highly motivated and I knocked him ass over tin cups without so much as blinking. Book, glasses, and body went flying. A plaintive "What the *fuck*?" floated up from the ground and followed me as I sprinted away.

I didn't trust myself to leap the turnstiles, so I slammed through the narrow gate reserved for Metro workers and sprinted for the escalators out of the station. Luck was with me—sometimes the escalators aren't running, in which case they are just stairs and, at fifty-four, I wasn't about to run up three hundred steps without inviting heart failure. As it was, I barely made it to the top even with mechanized help. The escalator popped me out into the station's glass-covered entrance and I whipped my head around, looking for the man in the cap.

The streets were crowded with mothers and their kids, retirees shuffling to the grocery store, workers on break. Roadwork blocked the right-hand lane going north on New Jersey Avenue, causing cars to choke the street for a block or more. A bored construction worker, leaning on a manual "STOP" sign and with a walkie-talkie dangling from his hand, was holding up traffic. I jogged to him, out of breath and sweating.

"You see a slim guy in a baseball cap come out of the Metro?" I asked, knowing how stupid the description sounded even as I said it. "Running like hell?"

He gave me a look. "Get away from me."

Adrenaline kicked in. I grabbed the lapels of his flannel shirt with both hands and lifted him half off the ground, screaming into his face, *"Did you see a guy in a baseball cap?"*

His eyes popped out. "Jesus, man. No."

I let him go, swearing—but halfway down New Jersey I saw a woman sprawled on the sidewalk being helped to her feet by a couple of passersby. I left the construction crew and ran toward the woman, slowing down just long enough to shout, "Baseball cap?"

Two of them looked up and pointed in the direction I'd been running, toward K Street. I waved a thanks and took off. I still had a chance to catch him—slim, yes—but still a chance. Even with the wasted seconds on the platform and asking the construction guy for directions, I couldn't be more than a half minute behind the guy. If I could keep him in sight until I could call the police, I might manage a collar.

There. I caught a flash in between the bobbing heads of pedestrians and cars. I ran after it, wondering as I went what kind of amateur I was chasing. A simple dodge down a side street would've thrown me off his trail, but this guy had left the scene in a straight line like he'd been shot from a catapult. I shrugged. Crooks and killers aren't smart and pushing someone in front of a train wasn't exactly Machiavellian in its complexity.

And it sure would be swell if he did something else stupid, because my breath was coming in ragged gasps and my legs already felt rubbery and weak. I tried pacing myself, evening out my stride so that I could get some wind back while still keeping the baseball cap in sight. He might slow down if he thought he was far enough away, which I really wished would happen. For a second, that actually seemed to be the case as he approached K Street. But some subconscious sense of my pursuit must've spurred him on and I swore as I watched him run straight into traffic, causing car brakes to be slammed and horns to be honked.

He made it across K in one piece, but traffic was flowing by the time I got there and I watched in frustration as he sprinted away. I tried twice to jump into the break between cars, narrowly missing getting flattened each time. The light turned and I finally made it across the thruway, jogging down New Jersey Avenue with my head on a swivel. The rush was even heavier here and I stood on the corner, looking for any sign of the guy in the cap. But either he'd set a new world record for the half-mile dash or had finally used his head and turned a corner, because he was gone.

Now that I could give up, I bent over double—hands on knees, my heart slamming in my chest—and swore again, loudly, creatively, and with feeling. In between sucking great lungfuls of air, I cursed the guy's mother, his father, DC traffic, cars, stoplights, the Metro, middle age, and bad luck. A few people walking by gave me a wide berth and glanced my way, checking to see how crazy I was, then moved along when I pulled out my cell phone. Not crazy enough to rate, I guess.

Hands shaking with fatigue and frustration, I dialed 911 and waited for someone to answer.

Please visit www.matthew-iden.com to find out more about *The Spike* and the other books in the Marty Singer Mystery series.

ACKNOWLEDGMENTS

One Right Thing began with an event: my wife and I saw the billboard—and a version of the message that was on it—that starts this novel on a highway outside of Lynchburg, Virginia. None of the content is the same, of course, and the fiction is exactly that, but the story started with that simple sign. I hope the family of the man on that billboard has found its answers.

None of the words in this book would be here without the support and love of my wife, Renee. I know finding her was certainly one right thing that I've done.

Friends and family have cheered me on and done much of the heavy lifting in reading all the drafts of this book. Sally Iden, Gary Iden, Kris Iden, Frank Gallivan, Carie Rothenbacher, Jeff Ziskind, Amy and Pete Talbot, David Jacobstein, and Eleonora Ibrani were all sounding boards, unstinting supporters, and readers throughout the creation of *One Right Thing*. Karen Cantwell, Misha Crews, and Amanda Brice have all been exceptional colleagues along the road to *One Right Thing*'s publication.

Many, many thanks to Chip Cochran for sharing his law-enforcement knowledge and letting me bounce about a thousand ideas off him. Any inaccuracies in a legal or law-enforcement context are mine.

ABOUT THE AUTHOR

Photo © 2014 Sally Iden

Matthew Iden writes hard-boiled detective fiction, fantasy, science fiction, horror, thrillers, and contemporary literary fiction with a psychological twist. He is the author of the Marty Singer detective series:

A Reason to Live

Blueblood

One Right Thing

The Spike

The Wicked Flee

Visit www.matthew-iden.com for information on upcoming appearances, new releases, and to receive a free copy of *The Guardian: A Marty Singer Short Story*—not available anywhere else.

IF YOU LIKED *ONE RIGHT THING* . . .

Writers can only survive and flourish with the help of readers. If you like what you've read, please consider reviewing *One Right Thing* on Amazon.com or your favorite readers' website. Just three or four short sentences are all it takes to make a huge difference! Thank you.

STAY IN TOUCH

Please say hello via email, matt.iden@matthew-iden.com, through Facebook (www.facebook.com/matthew.iden), or Twitter (@CrimeRighter). I also enjoy connecting with readers and writers at my website, www.matthew-iden.com.

My editors Bryon Quertermous and Michael Mandarano cleaned up what I *thought* was a brilliant first draft and have been invaluable in the process of making me a better writer. Bryon and Michael, thank you. Exceptional thanks and good luck to my first editor, Alison Dasho, as she finds her future. I know she and Marty share a bond that a few thousand miles can't break.

Lastly, a heartfelt thank-you to the team at Thomas & Mercer and especially my editor, Kjersti Egerdahl, for giving me the opportunity to introduce Marty to a wider world.